D0396498

# THEO TAN AND THE FOX SPIRIT

# THEO TAN
### AND THE FOX SPIRIT
### THE

## JESSE Q. SUTANTO

FEIWEL AND FRIENDS
NEW YORK

A Feiwel and Friends Book
An imprint of Macmillan Publishing Group, LLC
120 Broadway, New York, NY 10271 • mackids.com

Our books may be purchased in bulk for promotional, educational, or
business use. Please contact your local bookseller or the Macmillan
Corporate and Premium Sales Department at (800) 221-7945 ext. 5442 or
by email at MacmillanSpecialMarkets@macmillan.com.

Library of Congress Cataloging-in-Publication Data
Names: Sutanto, Jesse Q., author.
Title: Theo Tan and the fox spirit / Jesse Q Sutanto.
Description: First edition. | New York : Feiwel and Friends, 2022. |
    Audience: Ages 8–12. | Audience: Grades 4–6. | Summary: A twelve-year-
    old Chinese American boy must learn to embrace his heritage and accept his
    beloved older brother's spirit companion—a mystical fox named Kai—to
    solve the mystery of Jamie's death.
Identifiers: LCCN 2021047563 | ISBN 9781250794284 (hardcover)
Subjects: CYAC: Spirits—Fiction. | Magic—Fiction. | Brothers—Fiction. |
    Chinese Americans—Fiction. | Supernatural—Fiction. | LCGFT: Novels. |
    Paranormal fiction.
Classification: LCC PZ7.1.S8823 Th 2022 | DDC [Fic]—dc23
LC record available at https://lccn.loc.gov/2021047563

First edition, 2022
Book design by Mallory Grigg
Feiwel and Friends logo designed by Filomena Tuosto
Printed in the United States of America by Lakeside Book Company
Harrisonburg, Virginia

ISBN 978-1-250-79428-4 (hardcover)
10   9   8   7   6   5   4   3   2   1

*To the Menagerie, without whom*
*this book would not exist.*

# THEO

# 1

Hours before my alarm is set to go off for the last day of school, my seventeen-year-old brother shakes me awake.

"Wha?" I mumble, my voice thick with sleep.

"Wake up," Jamie whispers.

"What's going on?" I say, only it comes out as "Whas gong?"

"Dress warm. We gotta go." He leaves my room before I can ask anything else, and the urgency in his voice pushes me out of bed.

I shrug on a hoodie, struggle into a pair of jeans, and creep down the stairs, careful to avoid the creaky step. Jamie's waiting at the door. I look around for Kai, his companion spirit. She's usually wrapped around his neck, or hiding somewhere to scare me when I'm least expecting it, but after a while, I realize she really isn't here, and her absence perks me up a little. It's been so long since I've had one-on-one time with Jamie.

Outside, it's still so dark that I can see people's cirth pendants glowing under their shirts. Jamie leads me quietly through the back alleys of Chinatown.

"Where are we going, Jamie?" I say, but Jamie just shushes me and walks faster. I gotta say, as far as quality time with your brother goes, this kind of stinks, and I mean that both literally and figuratively.

"We're here," he says finally.

I look up at the neon sign. It says XIE'S MEAT SHOP in English and Mandarin. "Uh. The butcher's? What's going on?" I say again.

Jamie ushers me inside and follows behind, waving to Mr. Xie. To my surprise, Mr. Xie just nods at him and waves us past the register and into the back of the shop. Okaaay. I am officially dying of curiosity. Jamie motions for me to follow him into the meat freezer, closes the door behind him, and asks me about . . .

"Gaming?" I gape at him like a goldfish, my mind struggling to catch up with what he's just said. Hey, it's only four in the morning. I'm still about 80 percent asleep.

"Yes," Jamie says, impatience tingeing his voice. "That computer game you play, *War of People* or whatever—"

"*Warfront Heroes*," I correct him with a sniff. I mean, I love my brother, but honestly, sometimes he's just hopeless.

"Right, that one. You know how you get quests and you level up—"

"*Warfront Heroes* isn't that kind of game."

"Theo, please listen." Something in Jamie's voice stops me short. Jamie's always been the sort of big brother you can count on to stay calm and solve every crisis, and in our family, there's always a crisis. But now I catch a tightness in his voice I've never heard before, and it jerks me wide awake. Out of habit, I grab hold of my cirth pendant. Despite the freezing room, the metal pendant remains warm, the cirth inside it glowing like molten emerald.

He blows out a little cloud of steamy breath in frustration.

"Let's just say that in this game, you get quests and you level up, and you get bigger and tougher quests—can you stop fidgeting?"

"I'm cold. We're literally in a freezer," I say, gesturing at the giant slabs of meat hanging from the ceiling. The room smells of salt and death. Couldn't he have asked me all this stuff about gaming at home?

"It's the only place I know where our conversation won't be heard. Maybe. For all I know, this freezer might be bugged." His gaze darts around the cramped space, and he suddenly pounces on something. "Got you!"

I look at the wriggling thing caught between Jamie's thumb and index finger. "A baby cockroach? That's gross."

"It's a bug," Jamie says, glaring at the cockroach.

Welp. This is it. All the studying has done his head in. "Um. Yeah? Roaches are generally considered to be bugs, yes."

"No, I mean, it's a listening bug."

Okay, now I'm really worried about my brother. "Why would there be a listening bug in here?"

"Because!" Jamie cries. He throws the roach down on the floor and steps on it, cringing at the crunch it makes.

"Let's go," I say. "I'm freezing to death."

"I told you to dress warm before we left." The raw frustration in his voice reminds me of Ma snapping at me to stop playing computer games, to do my homework, to hold my chopsticks right, and on and on and on. Man, I don't need to take this from him as well.

"You could've told me we'd be going inside a freezer." My

retort loses a bit of its intended bite because my teeth are chattering so much, but I don't want to have to spend any of my cirth. The least he could do is use some of his to keep us warm. "Cast Frobisher's Remedy for Frosty Nights on me, Gege." I only call him Gege—big brother—when I really need his help.

Jamie raises his hands but hesitates. "I need to save all my cirth for r—" His voice cuts off in a pained grunt, and he coughs.

"Are you okay?"

"Yeah, it's just the n—" Again, he chokes on his words and starts coughing. He curses. "I'm sorry, Theo, you'll have to cast the spell yourself. I need to save my cirth for something. Something really, really important."

Under normal circumstances, i.e., when I'm not freezing to death while surrounded by headless pigs, I would've argued. I'm a total cheapskate when it comes to using cirth. Hey, you would be, too, if you get as little as I do. One cirth is the amount of magical energy required to turn a 160-pound man into a frog, and it costs money to buy. Not a lot, but my family ain't rich, so my allowance is only enough for about thirty units of cirth a month, which is basically nothing. I can't even remember the last time I had a fully charged pendant.

But I'm too cold to argue. I focus on my pendant until the power inside it glows. A buzz flows down my half-frozen arms, and I recite Frobisher's incantation. Green light travels to my hands and bursts in a circle around me. My whole body is suddenly blanketed in a toasty glow. I can almost hear the crackle of a merry fireplace and smell the rich scent of hot chocolate. Frobisher's Remedy for Frosty Nights is an awesome spell, but I can't even really enjoy its effects, because as soon as I'm no longer dying of cold, I want to smack myself for using any of the cirth I've been saving. Well, actually, I want to smack Jamie for making me use my cirth. It's all supposed to be for ThunderCon. I check my pendant, and yep, I'm down to about thirty units. Great.

Like any other spell that relies on changing the laws of thermodynamics, warmth spells like Frobisher's Remedy for Frosty Nights cost a heck of a lot of cirth. Most kids at school buy at least a hundred units a month, and some—not gonna name names—have virtually unlimited amounts. I save like nobody's business; I even write super tiny so I don't need to buy extra notebooks, and now, thanks to Jamie, I had to spend ten units just to keep my teeth from chattering.

He doesn't seem to notice the death stare I'm giving him. "Are you warm? Okay. Good." He takes a deep breath. "Back to computer games. If I get this right, sometimes you get given a quest that's too hard, and you have to ask people for help. Right?"

Watching Jamie struggle through a conversation about computer games is equal parts funny and mortifying. He's your typical teen in that he doesn't give a whit about non-cirth-powered games. He's more into stuff like Ketzelpod, a sport for meatheads who can afford the cirth to kick around a ball inside a giant floating bubble of water.

"Ask people for help?" I say.

"Like the game masters. The people who make sure all the players are safe and catch anyone who's cheating. If you get a quest that's really hard, you wouldn't try to complete it on your own, right? Promise me you'd go to the game masters?"

"That's not what game masters do." I love Jamie to death, but he's being so weird right now. He's never been interested in any of the games I play. Why would he suddenly—

A thought strikes me.

Kai. She's got to be behind this. Jamie's spirit companion and I don't get along, which is putting it mildly. Kai spends 90 percent of her time playing elaborate pranks on me. The other 10 percent of the time she spends hissing and snarling at me.

When Jamie woke me this morning and told me we were going out for a walk, just the two of us, I'd scrambled out of bed like an eager puppy. I've had so little one-on-one time with Jamie ever since he got Kai five years ago, which is the main reason I can't stand Kai. I can't help feeling like she's stolen my brother away. And now I realize it was all just a mean prank.

"This is one of Kai's jokes, isn't it?" I spit out.

Jamie freezes. "What? No!" He takes a notebook from his backpack. "Look, take this, okay? It's got some notes you may find useful."

"Useful for what?" I crack it open, but just then, the door slides open, and Mr. Xie stands there.

"You boys still here? Jamie, when you asked me if you can take your little brother to the freezer, I told you, you get five minutes." He waves his hand and mutters Pupplenot's No Strings Attached spell. Cirth flows from his pendant and twines around one of the dead pigs. The carcass unhooks itself and zooms to Mr. Xie's outstretched hand, nearly bashing into me on the way. "Go on, get outta here. This is no place for kids."

No need to tell me twice.

"Theo, wait!"

Nope.

I stuff the notebook in my jacket pocket and hurry through the crowd haggling for this pound of belly and that cut of shoulder and only pause to breathe once I'm outside.

"Watch out!" a flying cyclist, weighed down by two boulder-sized baskets of fish, shouts in Mandarin. He's flying too low, headed straight for my head. I can't believe I just escaped freezing to death only to perish by flying cyclist.

Right before he rams into me, there's a flash of green, and the cyclist is knocked aside. He lands, arms flailing, in a huge basket of shiitake mushrooms. Fish fly out and splat across the pavement like silver rain. Next moment, he's up on his feet, shaking his fist at me.

"You're gonna have to pay for this!" he shouts.

I blink. "Excuse you?"

A hand pats my shoulder, and I turn to see Jamie. I hate to admit it, but phew. He steps between me and the cyclist. "Actually, I was the one who knocked you off your bike."

"You owe me at least five hundred bucks for all this fish!"

"Okay," Jamie says.

I'm about to be ill. Mama and Baba would have to dip into their savings for that much money.

"And injuries!" the cyclist continues. "I'm feeling dizzy, and—"

"Just as soon as I file a report with the police about the incident," Jamie says, still as calm as ever. "Would you say you were flying at a height of three feet or four?"

Oho. Okay, I take back what I said about Jamie being hopeless.

He's a freakin' genius. There are very strict flying laws throughout the country, including how fast and how high you're supposed to fly (at least ten feet off the ground if you're using flying shoes or bikes, twenty feet for flying cars and other vehicles), and the cyclist was definitely breaking them.

"I guess you were flying lower than regulation standards to save on cirth," Jamie says. "I'll just get the police—"

"Whoa, hang on. I'm sure we can work this out. My head's clearing up. There's no need to involve the cops in this, eh?"

Jamie smiles. "Come on, I'll help you gather the fish."

Seriously?

This is classic Jamie. Solver of problems, charmer of strangers. I'm still annoyed about the freezer, but at the same time, I want to give him the world's biggest fist bump because only he can defuse a situation like this. By the time we finish collecting all the fish, the cyclist has told Jamie his entire life story, and they part with the cyclist giving him an affectionate smack on his back before ruffling my hair and telling me to listen to my big brother.

"Let's go home," Jamie says, draping an arm around my shoulders.

It still feels way too early, too dark, too cold for the world to be awake, but Chinatown only takes short naps, and wakes up boisterously. Above us, gray-haired aunties fling windows open and call out to one another while they shake out damp laundry and hang it on rods so it drips down on passersby, i.e., me.

We walk down Stockton Street, where all the markets and shops are. Everything's sold here—companion almanacs, fake love potions (real ones are super-duper illegal in the state of

California), mild curses and poxes, trinkets and charms, some said to be straight from the spirit world. Anything anyone could possibly want, there's a shop here that sells it.

Companion spirits flit about, chattering and tweaking their tails, running errands and doing chores. Some cultures have companion spirits as part of their magic. The Chinese culture is one of them. I think some Eastern European cultures have them, too, as well as most of Southeast Asia. People think it's cool, but it's really only cool if you can afford better ones than most of the folks in my neighborhood can. I mean, what's the use of a beetle or a gnat as a companion spirit? I've heard of other neighborhoods, more affluent ones where people have companions like dragons and phoenixes. I try not to think too much about them, otherwise I get resentful. All around me, a cacophony of a dozen different Chinese dialects is shouted and scolded and laughed, and I can't wait to get home and burrow into my bed. I hate Stockton Street and the chaos that always accompanies it.

"About what I said back there," Jamie says. "Do you understand?"

I scratch my nose, trying to work out our conversation in the freezer. "So . . . you want to start playing *Warfront Heroes*?" Despite the weirdness of our morning, I start to feel excited. No one else I know plays *Warfront Heroes*. Sometimes, I wish I lived in pre-cirth times. Nainai often tells me stories about the pre-cirth world, and it sounds awesome. There was no such thing as Ketzelpod or Quash or all the other cirth-dependent games people are into nowadays. It was all about computers and nonflying skateboards. "I mean, I could teach you—Jamie?"

He's distracted by something in the sky. "Did you see that? It looked like an Eye—"

"Yeah, like there'd be an Eye in Chinatown," I say with a snort.

But just as I say that, I catch sight of it. Huh. How weird. I watch the little orb flying around like a bumblebee, heading toward us. There's a sudden blue flash, and the Eye tumbles to the ground. It splits into two, revealing a tiny imp inside it, and instantly a gray-haired auntie pounces on it.

"Got you!" she says in Cantonese, pocketing the struggling imp.

Oh lord. The government released Eyes all over the city a year ago as a security initiative. The imps inside can scan and memorize everything that happens on a human street, and can communicate with each other telepathically. But they gave up on surveilling Chinatown because of people like this auntie. People like her zap the Eyes and sell the imps on Stockton Street, which is mortifying. It gives us such a bad rep.

"Sooo embarrassing," I say, but the look on Jamie's face stops me short.

Jamie's staring at the broken shell of the Eye, and his face has turned fish-belly pale. My stomach twists. Jamie's never been not okay. It's his thing. He's always chill, even when Ma is driving everyone bonkers, which is all the time.

"Jamie—"

"We gotta go," he says.

I have to jog to keep up with him, and every time I try to ask about our weird conversation in the freezer, he shushes me and says, "Nothing. Forget it."

Before long, we're back at home, and in the hectic confusion of Mama and Baba and Nainai swarming around us, asking where we've been and shoving bowls of steaming congee into our hands, my questions evaporate as fast as the morning dew. I steal glances at Jamie all throughout breakfast. Was he trying to tell me something important, or was it just a prank after all? But he really did look worried when he saw the Eye. Plus, let's not forget the fact that *there was an Eye in Chinatown*. When was the last time I saw one of those in my neighborhood? What was it even doing there?

Maybe there's something going on. And from the way Jamie's acting, I have a feeling it's something bad.

Okay, I don't care if it was a prank. After school, I'll ask him to tell me everything, and this time, I'll listen hard. I finish my congee, ignoring all the ugly faces Kai's making from across the table, and then grab my schoolbag.

# KAI

# 2

I'm watching Jamie's pesky little brother, Theo, pointedly ignore me across the dining table, following his every movement with my sharp eyes. What can I say? I'm a sleek predator. I can't help but stalk prey. And Theo is sooo preylike. I mean, just look at him, all big, nervous eyes and knobbly elbows. He glances my way to grab the soy sauce, and in a flash I change my face to that of a baboon's fire-engine-red bum. I only do it for a split second before changing back to my own glorious foxy features, but it's enough to make Theo turn as red as—well, as my face had been just a moment ago. Ha! He stares at me mutinously, and I stare back with all the innocence of a newborn babe.

Maybe I shouldn't tease him so. It's a bit of an unfair fight, I suppose, him being a slovenly human and me being practically a goddess. I'm about to call for a truce when he lifts his chopsticks and flicks a sliver of century egg at me. Both of my tails sprig up instinctively, protecting my face, and the black, gelatinous century egg splatters against them.

I hiss at him and turn one of my paws into a chain saw.[1]

"Tch, I said NO WEAPONS AT DINING TABLE!" Mrs. Tan snaps.

---

1 A small chain saw. I'm not one for overreaction.

Argh. Now that annoying kid has gotten me in trouble with the matriarch of the family. This means revenge! But later, when no one's looking.

I sheepishly turn the chain saw back into a paw and lick it as innocently as I can, fully expecting a rebuke from Jamie. He usually hates it when his brother and I clash. But to my surprise, Jamie hasn't even noticed a thing. He's staring off into space with a terrible frown etched onto his face.

"Frowning like that will give you wrinkles at a very young age, you know," I say, helpful as always.

Jamie blinks and glances down at me as though seeing me for the first time. The corners of his mouth lift into a smile, but it doesn't reach his eyes. His expression looks sad, and my heart twists with pain. Ever since he fully accepted me as his companion spirit, I can feel every strong emotion he's experiencing. And right now, my master is awash with awful emotions—anxiety, sadness, fear.

I leap into Jamie's lap and nuzzle his chin. "What's wrong?"

Again, that forced smile appears. I'm about to press when Mrs. Tan heaps more food onto Jamie's plate, urging him to hurry up and eat before he's late for his internship. Jamie does as she says; he's as good a kid as they come. I'll have to wait for him to finish his food before I can interrogate him in private, but when he's done with the meal, he takes an extra-long time saying bye to his family, even going so far as to hug and kiss them before he leaves. I frown as I watch him hug his father tightly. Even they look surprised. They're not really the hugging type.

When we're finally, *finally* out of the house, I shape-shift into a parrot so I can fly right in front of his face.

"Do you mind?" he says, walking around me.

"Uh, excuse you!" I zip through the air and hover in his face again. "Tell me what's going on. You've been acting weird all morning." Come to think of it, he's been acting weird a lot longer than that, but I've always been too polite to ask.

He stops walking and turns his eyes to me, and my breath catches. They look so haunted. I reach out with my vibrant green wings and squeeze his face. "Jamie, tell me what's wrong. Whatever it is, I can help. I'm your companion. I'd die for you, you know that."

Another sad smile lines his face. "I know," he says, gently peeling my wings from his cheeks. "That's the problem." He takes a deep breath. "Kai, I need you to stay home today, okay? Don't come in to work with me."

"What? Why?"

"I just—I've got a lot of work to do and . . ." He hesitates for a moment before saying, "You'll get in the way."

My feathers bristle, and I feel my sharp fox teeth growing inside my beak. "Moi? Get in the way?" Have I ever felt more offended? "I don't think you fully accept what an asset I am."

He sighs. "Trust me, Kai, I know. I just . . . it might be dangerous, and—"

"Dangerous?" I screech.

"No!" he says hurriedly. "Not dangerous, just tricky. That's all. Look, don't worry, okay? Stay home, and I'll explain everything later."

"Oh, pooh to that. I am not staying home with your snotty-nosed brother while you go to work."

"I don't have time to argue with you, Kai. I'm sorry to have to do this, but . . ." He stands up straight and takes a deep breath. "Kai, as your master, I order you to stay home and await further instructions."

"No, wait—" But the words are barely out of my beak before the order grabs me like an iron fist and flings me through the air. I zip past the front yard and whizz through an open window before finally thumping into the living room wall and falling onto the floor with a loud splat.

Jamie's grandmother looks up at me, momentarily distracted from the Chinese drama she's watching. "Oh, Kai. Fancy having you back so soon. Is Jamie back already? Did he decide not to go to work?" she says in Mandarin.

I peel myself off the floor slowly and revert back to my fox shape, rubbing my bruised snout. No use staying a parrot now that I've been ordered to stay home. Of course, as luck would have it, Theo comes striding down the stairs just then. He sees me and puts two and two together.

"Did Jamie decide you were too much of a hindrance at work?" he says with a smirk.

I scoff. "Of course not. He uh—he said I've been so helpful that I should take a personal day."

"A personal day," Theo says, arching an eyebrow.

"You know, go to a spa, do a deep conditioning treatment for my fur. It takes a lot of work to look this good." I swish my tails for emphasis.

"Uh-huh, whatever." Theo slings his schoolbag onto his shoulder and heads for the front door. "Sucks to be you."

I shift my lips into monkey lips so I can blow him an extra loud raspberry, but he's already out the door, leaving me with nothing to do but fret and worry about what my master is up to.

As expected, the rest of the morning passes by suuuper slowly. Like treacle. Except not like treacle because treacle is delicious. More like tar. Yes, exactly like tar. Slow and stinky and horrible.

True to my lovely nature, I help Jamie's parents with their chores, pouring dishwashing liquid on my tails and washing the dishes. But instead of thanking me, Mrs. Tan tells me to stop rubbing my butt all over the dishes, so I go around and try to dust, using my tails as well, but Mr. Tan tells me to stop rubbing my butt over the furniture. I scamper up the stairs and go to Jamie's bedroom in a bit of a huff. These people just don't appreciate good, honest, hard w—

The pain strikes like a silver spear plunged straight into my heart. Everything inside me feels like it's just shattered. My muscles seize. I would've shrieked with the excruciating pain, but no sound comes out of me. My fox form stretches, then squeezes into a quivering ball, then stretches again. I feel as though I'm being ripped apart like tissue.

Jamie—oh gods, I feel him being wrenched away from my soul, our bond tearing apart—please gods, don't let it happen. "Jamie—" I manage to say, and then the last shred of our bond rips, and I am whipped back, screaming soundlessly, to the spirit world.

# THEO
# 3

Know what's the best sound in the world? Nope, not the singing of sirens, or heavenly harp music. Hands down, the bestest sound in the world is the final school bell that says, *Freedommm!*

I grab my bag and join the flood of students streaming out of the classrooms. Summer vacation is here! ThunderCon, here I come! I practically run all the way to my locker. ThunderCon's fan base is small, because most people are into cirth-powered games, but we're dedicated, and I can't wait to meet the rest of the fandom in person. My costume for ThunderCon is in my locker, because the only time and place where I have privacy to work on it is at school, during lunchtime, which I realize is extremely pathetic. I've been working my butt off for months, and it. Is. Awesome. I've sewn all the feathers and leaves on, and I've been using half units of cirth to catch lances of sunlight and weave them into the leaves. I don't want to brag, but there's no way I can lose the cosplay competition.

I stop in front of my locker and mutter my password. The catch unlocks with a snick, but before I can pull the door open, it snaps shut again. Weird. I whisper the command to open it—a combination of Milton Keye's Unblock a Lock spell and my password, Warfront Heroes. You know how annoying it is to have to use cirth, even if it's just a fraction of a unit, to unlock my locker?

Again, the door unlocks, and again, it clicks shut and locks before I can pull it open. I swing round and find Skinner Bannion and his lackeys, Jordan Howard and Brittany Olson, standing behind me, snickering. Great.

"Did you forget your password again, Theo?" Brittany calls out in a voice dripping with mock pity.

"Channel your—what do you people call your mana?" Jordan says.

"I think they call it qì?" Brittany says.

Despite myself, part of me itches to tell her it's pronounced "chee," not "key."

"What Chinese spells do they teach you?" Jordan says. "Ooh, can you conjure up a plate of kung pao chicken?"

What's really annoying—aside from everything about them—is that they know I have no idea how to cast ancient Chinese spells. I'm just as American as these jerks; I'm 100 percent dependent on cirth, and therefore limited to American spells. No one really bothers trying to harness their qì anymore, not since the invention of cirth. Jamie's learning, but Jamie's always been weird like that.

"Guys, it's okay. Theo doesn't have to do that. *I'll* channel my inner qì," Skinner says. He strikes a ridiculous pose, his legs spread as wide as they'll go, hands wielding an imaginary sword. He flicks one hand and lets loose a glowing, green cirth-powered fart that propels him all the way to the other end of the hallway.

Jordan and Brittany double over, laughing as Skinner farts his way back to us, cirth flowing from his pendant and shimmering around his butt in bright green plumes.

Which is more annoying: the sight of Skinner, or seeing cirth get wasted like that? Not that it matters. Skinner has access to a buttload of cirth. He keeps his two toadies loyal by keeping their pendants permanently filled. I do the math in my head.

A pendant contains fifty units of cirth, which means Skinner and his buddies have enough energy to magically slam my locker shut about, oh, fifty million times. Maybe Jamie's right; maybe I should learn how to harness my qì—then maybe I could zap their butts to kingdom come without relying on my cirth pendant. Except I couldn't, anyway, since aggressive magic is illegal. Well, maybe I could zap them with extreme itchiness. Or intense pungentness. Not that they can't manage that one on their own.

"Don't you losers have anything better to do?" I say, trying to keep my voice calm even though my insides feel as though they're made of insects crawling and fluttering everywhere. I wish Jamie were here. I'm not sure what he'd do, but whatever it was, it'd no doubt convey to Skinner and Co. that they're being ignorant and hateful.

"Oooh, careful, he's about to do some serious damage!" Skinner says.

The headmaster's voice booms from seemingly all around us. "Are you kids causing trouble again?"

We all freeze. You do not mess with Mr. Gold. Rumor has it that he once cast Libba Ryan's Make Life Easier on Librarians spell on a seventh grader for an entire year. That's a whole year the poor kid had to spend talking in a whisper. Weirdly enough, his parents didn't complain about it.

Skinner's face morphs into a picture of deference as he looks around for Mr. Gold.

"Why are you all loitering around? Do you want to be given detention?" the voice booms again.

"Er—no," Skinner says. "Have a good summer, sir!" He cocks his head at his goons, and the three of them hurry away. At the door, they pause to activate their shoes, which have charms of weightlessness, of course. "Later, Theo!" With a whoosh, they glide into the air, hooting and laughing.

I look around hesitantly. "Um."

"Go on, get outta here, kid," the voice says. Whatever spell he's using, it's working. I'm so creeped out I can't get out of there fast enough.

I grab all my stuff from my locker and go into the bright sunlight. Students zip past on flying shoes and bikes. A couple of kids float past on vintage broomsticks. As far as transportation goes, broomsticks aren't popular (one word: *wedgies*), but there are always a handful of diehards zooming around on them.

I catch the bus just in time, beaming as it rattles and burps its way out of the school compound. I brace against the front seat as the bus lurches forward and springs into the air.

Below me, San Francisco spreads out like the world's craziest quilt—a mishmash of pastel buildings squeezed together. I love my city. I love how you can walk for fifteen minutes and pass by four different neighborhoods, some quirky and creative, others ancient and dignified, like stooping old men. I even love the way the fog covers all of SF like a blanket at times so that only the very tippy-tops of the Golden Gate Bridge are visible.

The one thing I do not love about San Francisco is my house.

My stomach twists as the bus barrels and hops through the

tunnel. Because on the other side is—I scowl, as I always do—the gateway to Chinatown.

I hate that I'm a Chinese American kid who lives in Chinatown. There are other Chinese American students in my class, but none of them has to go to Chinese classes in addition to regular school, and none of them turns up at the cafeteria with stewed chicken feet in their lunch box, so Skinner and Co. treat them like actual humans.

The bus grumbles to a stop. I trudge the rest of the way home, dodging the flying monkeys and various other scruffy spirit companions along the way.

The little bell at the top of the front door rings as I push it open, and Nainai says, "Didi huí jiāle," without looking away from her Chinese drama. *Baby brother is home.* Nainai's companion, a three-legged crow, is snoozing in her lap.

"Hi, Nainai." I plant a kiss on her wizened cheek.

"Hi, Didi!" Baba calls out from the kitchen. He waves his cleaver at me with a smile. Every time I see Baba prepping food manually instead of using cirth, it makes me wince. It's one of the many reasons why I can't bring home any friends from school. I would lose so much cred if people knew my family's too poor to afford the cirth needed to magically prep our food. Not that I have much street cred to begin with. Or friends, for that matter. "How was last day of school?"

"It was okay." Not. But my dad doesn't need to know what a loser I am at school. I drop my backpack on a chair and saunter over to the kitchen.

"Aiya, xiǎozéi! Don't touch!" Baba shouts as I pop a piece of fried chicken in my mouth. My family's incapable of talking at a normal volume.

I hear Mama's footsteps flip-flopping down the stairs from our apartment.

"Ah, Didi, nǐ huí jiāle." She pauses, her sharp eyes catching something next to me. Before I can react, she strides over and seizes my left ear between her thumb and forefinger.

"Aaaa! What?" I cry.

"What this?" Mama grabs something from my bag. Something olive green.

Oh no.

"It's nothing," I babble, "just a new jacket I'm making—" Mama twists my ear, and I wail, "Aaaa okay, okay!" She lets go and I rub my ear gingerly, glaring at her.

"Well?"

"It's—it's just—"

"Don't make me use No Lying spell on you." Mama points a finger in my face.

"It's called Bagbott's Tongue Loosener!" Why is it that even after so many years living in America, Mama still can't speak English like a normal person?

"I don't know what this Loser Tongue thing is. In China, we just call it No Lying spell. And who care if some baggy bottom came up with it? In China, there is no such thing. Any spell a weaver come up with belong to the people, no need to keep saying, oh this spell was woven by Mr. Baggy Bottom."

"It's not Baggy Bottom, it's Bagbott—never mind." I sigh. She's never going to let up. "It's my costume for ThunderCon."

"ThunderCon shì shénme?" Nainai says. Her eyes are still glued to the TV.

I want to squirm right out of my skin. Telling my family about gaming feels wrong. It's the one space I have where I don't have to be myself. Nobody in the gaming world cares that I'm a Chinese kid living in Chinatown. On *Warfront Heroes*, I can be just another all-American kid who speaks unaccented English and eats nothing but burgers and pizza.

"Okay, one No Lying spell is coming," Mama says, and points a finger in my face. Ma is really frugal with cirth, too, unless it comes to spending it on me. Then she's willing to spend all the cirth in the world, just to make my life difficult. Vines flow out from her pendant, swirl down her arm, and collect on her fingertip.

"It's just a small gaming convention for people who like old-school games," I blurt out. My voice trails away when I see how unimpressed Mama looks. "There are cash prizes," I add in a small voice. This is precisely why my plan was to let Mama and Baba know that I was going to ThunderCon only after I got to San Diego. Don't ask me how I was planning on stealing out of the house without them knowing.

"Why you wasting your time on this? It's summer! You supposed to spend it outside, not staying indoors playing your"— Mama makes air quotes, something she has picked up from me and Jamie—"'computer games.'"

"Ma, I've told you to stop using air quotes. You're not doing them right."

"Tch, don't interrupt," she barks. "You prepare for Companion

Ceremony already? You memorize all the words yet? I have to remind you how dangerous it is? You say one wrong thing and you summon a yāoguài that can swallow you whole."

"Yes, yes, I know. I've been practicing." I wish she wouldn't keep bringing up the Companion Ceremony. Mama and Baba don't have spirit companions; their families couldn't afford any when they were little. Summoning a companion spirit is expensive, because not only do you have to hire a summoner, but you also need to pay the summoner to capture a spirit from the spirit world. Most families save money by passing down companions; that way, you only need to pay for a summoner to help bring back the companion, not to summon a whole new spirit. That's all my family can afford, so I'm stuck with inheriting my late grandfather's tired goldfish, who grants small wishes if you feed it enough crickets. No fancy new companion for me.

Jamie, on the other hand, worked part-time for two years just to save up for a new companion. We all assumed he'd go for a small, affordable water dragon, since water dragons have healing powers. It would've been the perfect companion for a wannabe pre-med student. Instead, he chose Kai. Don't ask me why anyone would choose a fox spirit. They straddle the line between spirit and demon, and usually, they happen to unsuspecting victims.

The goldfish isn't so bad, but here's a secret: I'd rather not have any companion. Spirit companions aren't part of normal American culture. I don't need another reason for Skinner and his cronies to make fun of my "ying-yangy thing."

"Look at him, so ungrateful," Mama says to Nainai. "You know, Didi, when I was your age—"

The words "When I was your age" are basically a switch. Once I hear them, my mind automatically turns off. If you were to believe Mama, when she was my age, she was a: 1) national Chinese chess champion, 2) national Ketzelpod player, 3) national badminton player, 4) internationally renowned violin prodigy. Oh, and she also cooked five-course dinners for her family every night. I once asked Baba if any of this was true, and he smiled and said, "Mama is unbeatable at Ketzelpod." Which doesn't necessarily mean she's amazing at it; it just means Baba isn't very good.

Mama moves on to her second favorite lecture: an episode of Why Are You Not More Like Jamie?

"Look at Gege," she says. "He spending all his free time at that . . . program thing."

The "program thing" is a cultural outreach program at Reapling Corp., the country's biggest cirth corporation. Jamie's spent the last few months commuting to Mountain View for his internship.

"He learn so much about traditional Chinese magic," Mama says.

Yawn. Why spend time learning about old Asian magic when we've got modern Western magic? Even Mama and Baba don't use traditional Chinese magic. Over the years, they've forgotten how to harness their qì and become just as dependent on cirth and American magic as everyone else in the world. But I have enough sense of self-preservation not to say that to Mama.

Luckily, Mama's lecture is cut short by the tinkle of the bell as the front door swings open.

"Sorry, restaurant closed," Mama calls out. "We be open in one hour—"

Her voice falters, and that's when I look up. At the door are two police officers, and something about the way they're looking at us, like they'd rather be anyplace else, gives me this curdling sensation in my stomach.

"Mrs. Tan?" one of the police officers says.

"Yes?" For the first time since I can remember, Mama's voice comes out small.

"Ma'am, I'm Officer Hernandez, and this is Officer Chen. Can we come inside?"

Mama nods wordlessly.

Baba comes out of the kitchen as the cops walk inside, and they introduce themselves to him and ask us to take a seat. The sympathy in the cops' faces makes the curdling in my stomach tighten into an ugly pain.

Officer Hernandez says, "I'm so sorry. I have some very bad news for you." He looks at Mama and Baba. "Your son Jamie was in a car accident . . ."

Mama instinctively reaches for my hand.

And I know, then, that nothing is okay. Nothing will ever be okay again.

# KAI

## 4

I'm floating along the endless river in the spirit world, watching the azure sky flicker with the deepest shades of cerulean and startling fuchsia. Imps and other minor yāoguài[2] flit about in a hundred forms, bounding through yùlán magnolia trees and fighting over the fruit.

Not long ago, I would've been the loudest and fiercest of the lot, but now all I want to do is lie still and let the river take me away so I can forget, so my whole being can stop yearning for Jamie, my master, my bonded human.

Fifteen days, seven hours, and twenty-three minutes since he died, and the wound is still fresh. When I close my eyes, I hear his voice, I catch his scent, and I feel that terrible, ripping pain as his body dies and our bond shreds. Without Jamie to tether me to the human world, I was snatched back through the rift, screaming, clawing, trying to stay by his side even as my soul threatened to explode. I've never fought to stay in the human world. But I wanted—I don't know what I wanted, maybe to curl

2 Yāoguài: 妖怪. Generally means "demon," mostly made up of animal spirits or fallen celestial beings. The biggest and baddest of these creatures are found in Diyu (hell). Some might argue that fox spirits are a type of yāoguài, but those people are just jealous. You don't believe them, do you? Good. Carry on.

up at his feet one more time. To push my wet nose up against his cheek, the way I used to every morning. *Wake up, Jamie. Please.*

A small yāoguài in the form of a water bug comes close, and I watch it out of the corner of my eye. It fails to sense me; yāoguài aren't known for their intelligence, unlike yours truly. With a quick flick, I catch it and stuff the squeaking, wriggling thing into my mouth. I crunch down without any joy. Even its red taste fails to fill the hole inside me.

The sky continues to shift and twinkle with a multitude of be-seeching calls from the human world to the spirit world I inhabit.

"Shén,[3] please make everyone in my class fail the algebra test tomorrow."

"O great shén of the spirit world, please give my enemy indigestion!"

"Shén, tell my parents to buy me the biggest Benz. In black, please. The silver one they got me looked so uncool."

I submerge my head, drowning everything out. It's silent underwater, peaceful, aside from the other shén and yāoguài swimming about, occasionally brushing against me. I bump into something hard—probably a rock—and stay there, my limp form curled around it as the water flows past.

"Ahem," someone says.

I crack open one eye. The rock turns out to be a massive bull-frog. It's Chao, a fierce shén who's had it in for me for the last

---

3 Shén: 神. Can refer to "god," "deity," or "spirit." I know, we're very into specificity. That's me, by the way, in case the "spirit" in "fox spirit" didn't clue you in. If you want to get all technical, I suppose I am better known as a shénguài, which means "gods and monsters," but if it's okay with you, I personally much prefer to be referred to as a shén due to my goddesslike awesomeness.

century or so, ever since I tricked him into stealing one of Nuwa's pearls. The goddess gave him such a fierce kick that there's still a silk-sandal-shaped depression on his ample bottom.

And I've landed right in the middle of his thick lips. I should run away, but I'm so despondent I can't even be bothered to save my own life. I close my eyes and tip my head back. "Do it. Make it fast."

When death by bullfrog fails to happen, I open my eyes. "I say, what's the holdup here, frogface?"

Chao fishes me out of the water by my scruff and eyes me with distaste, which is rather insulting given he's the one with warts on his lips. "What a grumpy little húlíjīng you are."

I can't even summon the energy to get annoyed. "Look, are you going to eat me or not? I happen to have a very full day planned." A full day of crying over Jamie and beating myself up for not being powerful enough to save him. Maybe if I'd been a more powerful shén—perhaps a dragon or a hawk—he'd have let me come with him, and then I'd have been able to save him.

Chao narrows his eyes. "You wouldn't mind if I ate you? Why's that?"

A dragonfly shén lands on Chao's shoulder and squeaks, "Kai's heartbroken over her old master. She's been moping about because of him—haven't you noticed? Our Kai is a special fox spirit. While others of her kind are devious little creatures hell-bent on duping humans, Kai has a soft spot for them. Isn't that the most precious thing?"

I swipe at the dragonfly, but it flies away with a giggle and buzzes around my head while Chao studies me, head cocked.

"My word, the dragonfly's right." His thick lips stretch into a slow grin. "Who would've thought that a húlíjīng would be able to feel such loyalty to a human? It's a pity your aura's oozing with so much sorrow and anger. You'll give me indigestion."

I'm coming up with a retort when a voice from the sky captures my attention. It rises above the others, luminous among the usual sea of prayers and calls.

*"I miss him. I don't want this. I don't want anything. I want HIM."*

I get a sudden flash of Jamie, so strong I can feel his finger flicking my ear. Every muscle in my body turns rigid. I scramble up Chao's face, my paws scrabbling over his lips.

"Hey!" Chao cries.

"Shut up." I perch on his head, my whiskers quivering, unable to ignore this voice. Whoever's speaking, he and I want—no, need—the same thing. Our sorrow has the same taste. I must get to him.

"You know, Kai," Chao says, "I've been exceptionally patient with your shenanigans over the years. Everyone says I should've eaten you a long time ago, but no, I say, she can't help being what she is—a silly little húlíjīng." His voice is muffled due to my hind paw resting on his lower lip, but his next words are unmistakable. "But maybe it's time you're taught a final lesson."

I leap into the water as the bullfrog's jaws snap shut. Fish and water bugs zip away as he splashes in after me, his mouth stretched in a grin that reveals two rows of needle-pointed teeth.[4] I swim as fast as I can, but the dog paddle—or rather, the fox

---

4 Typical. I myself prefer biting wit to actual biting.

paddle—is no match for a bullfrog's webbed feet. I can't die now, not when I've just heard that voice.

I close my eyes, focus my qì, and change into a small parrotbill. I flap away into the boiling sky, fear and a sudden desperate need to live driving my little wings into a whir. Down in the river, the bullfrog roars, then changes into a falcon. He blasts up at me, fast as lightning. He retains his needle teeth. They should look absurd, crammed into a beak, but instead it is, frankly, rather terrifying.

I barrel past various shén and almost crash headlong into an iridescent goldfish that's poking around the clouds. It's looking for a rip in the membrane of our world that a summoning would open up. I catch sight of the rip, light shimmering and warping through the other side, and make a mad dash for it. The goldfish shakes an angry fin at me—then its eyes widen in shock-horror as Chao charges. The razor-sharp beak snaps shut and the goldfish disappears, leaving a scrap of translucent fin floating gently to the ground.

The falcon speeds in with claws stretched. I twist away in the nick of time and go through the rip, chasing the echo of the voice. Behind me, the falcon shrieks, the sound rending the air.

I cling to the voice with every cell, every atom, while my essence hurtles through time and space. This isn't a summoning. Or rather, it is, but it isn't meant for me. I fight the bindings that keep the human world safe from us, the denizens of the spirit world. My teeth shiver; my bones creak; my skin rattles. I'm going to be ripped apart. I open my mouth and—

BANG.

# KAI
# 5

An acrid smell fills my nose. I try to get up, but my journey has shaken me like a wet towel and wrung me dry. Every bone's broken, I know it. Such woe! Searing pain seizes my tails, and I would cry out if my throat didn't feel like it's been torn to shreds.

Water splashes over me, and the pain in my tails recedes. Gradually voices float into my consciousness.

"—is that?" someone says in Mandarin.

"A yāoguài!" someone else cries.

*Excuse you, it's most definitely not a yāoguài*, I want to say, but I'm too out of breath.

"What went wrong? Where's my goldfish?" someone says in English.

My ears perk up. The last speaker—I recognize his voice. It's the one that called to me while I was in the spirit world. I open my eyes.

Oh no. NO. Not him. I nearly died getting to the human world for *him*? Buddha wept.

Jamie's little brother—it takes a while to recall his name; I've always secretly thought of him as that chòu xiǎozi (little brat)—is about as different from Jamie as any human can get. Jamie is—was—made of gentle patience and ferocious hugs. Theo has no

hugs to give, not that anyone would want a hug from this horrible thing anyway.

"I performed the ritual as usual . . . I don't understand," a
man says in Mandarin, scratching his forehead. He's garbed in
the usual wū-summoning getup—garish crimson-and-blue silk
robe, black satin hat, the works. He clutches a ritual scroll to his
chest like a shield.

I sit up slowly. Theo doesn't seem to recognize me, which is
strange, but then again, humans have such weak, blobby minds.
The room is small and dotted with summoning paraphernalia—
pots of incense alongside clementine and chrysanthemum
offerings, mandala, a phurpa, and other knickknacks of celestial
bureaucracy that humans have convinced themselves are neces-
sities for such rituals.

"Should I eliminate the yāoguài?" a boy says. He's wearing an
equally gaudy robe that threatens to slide off his narrow shoulders. I'm momentarily distracted from the robe as the boy nocks
a peach-wood arrow into a bow and aims it straight at my head.

"Point that thing somewhere else!" I cry. "I'm not a yāoguài.
I'm a shén."

The disciple looks unconvinced. "You don't look like a shén."

"I'm very clearly a shén." I try to get up, and the arrow follows my
movements. It takes an effort for me not to bite his face.[5] "Look,
there must've been a mistake. I thought I was being summoned, but
I was wrong. I'll just go back to the spirit world, eh? No harm done."

"Why would you think you were summoned?" The shaman

---

5 I know I said I prefer biting wit to actual biting, but humans are so bitable. Especially this one.

runs his finger down the ritual scroll. "See, we called for one that is called Yangwei. Usually found in the form of a carp."

"A goldfish," Theo says.

"Right, a goldfish. Which you are not," the shaman adds.

"Oh, well done for being able to tell the difference between an intelligent, exquisite fox and a fish," I mutter.

Five pairs of eyes stare at me. Then the shaman pulls a pocket mirror from his robe and holds it out to me.

"I don't see why it's so difficult for you to see that I'm not a—" I catch a glimpse of my reflection. Ah, this would explain why Theo hasn't recognized me. My unplanned journey to the human world has left me somewhat worse for wear. If one were kind, one might say I'm not looking my best. If one weren't, one might point out that I'm a terrible, monstrous mishmash of all the forms I've learned over the years. Fish scales, a forked lizard tongue, a murky goat eye, a human belly button—let's just say I would've given Chao a run for his money.

I focus my qì and summon the last of my energy. There's a flash, and the fish-goat thing is replaced by an elegant orange fox with two bushy tails.

Theo's mouth drops open. His hand twitches like he's about to grab the peach-wood bow from the disciple to shoot me.

Mrs. Tan lets out a little gasp. "Kai?" She used to be cheerfully loud and naggy, but now her voice comes out thin. There are gray streaks in her hair, and her face is deeply lined. Before I can answer, she captures me in a tight hug. She hugs the way Jamie did—a bone-crushing hold that makes your heart feel like it has come home.

"Oh, my dear, why are you here?" she says in Mandarin.

I shake my head, unable to speak for the giant lump in my throat.

"Ruowen," Mrs. Tan says, calling Theo by his Chinese name, "it's Kai."

"I know who it is," Theo growls.

Mrs. Tan wipes away a tear. "How wonderful to have her back in the family."

"What?" Theo shouts. "Are you serious?" He turns to the shaman, and his rage is practically physical. "How could you summon my brother's companion? What sort of sick joke is this?"

"Er—I didn't summon—okay, tell you what," the shaman says, "I'll dismiss this húlíjīng back to the spirit world and perform another summoning at a discount. Ten percent off!"

Mr. Tan's face falls. "We can't afford another summoning."

"Fifteen percent off? I would do it for free if I could, but summonings drain me of so much qì . . ." The shaman rubs his chin meaningfully.

Mrs. Tan places a hand on Theo's head, which should tell you something about Mrs. Tan's survival instinct. Theo looks like an angry Jack Russell terrier who can barely hold itself back from attacking. Any moment now, he'll start frothing at the mouth.

If I were to be honest, his anger is partly my fault. When Jamie was alive, Theo and I saw each other as competition for Jamie's time and attention. He thought he had dibs on Jamie just because they were brothers or whatever, when clearly I—as Jamie's companion spirit—was destined to be his number one priority. For my part, I didn't relish having to share my master's affections. Jamie was tiresomely devoted to his little brother, and the sight of him is making me want to snarl.

"Sorry, Di—bǎobèi," Mrs. Tan says, then switches to English, "but no choice. You must be with Kai. Until we save enough money for more summoning, okay?"

"I'd rather have no companion!" Theo points at the shaman. "Dismiss the húlíjīng."

"Dismissals cost nine hundred and ninety-nine dollars—" the shaman says.

Theo gives a cry of frustration.

"—and ninety-five cents," the shaman adds helpfully. "But just for you, I'll bring it down to an even nine hundred and ninety-nine. Very good bargain!"

Theo snarls at him, but Mr. Tan jumps in front of him and says in rapid Mandarin, "Thank you for your services, Master Huang. We'll consider it."

"Of course." The shaman bows to Mr. and Mrs. Tan as his disciple collects their paraphernalia. "Don't take too long. This is a limited-time offer!"

All too soon, everything's packed up, down to the last incense stick. Mr. and Mrs. Tan usher the shaman and his underling out, leaving me alone with Theo. I still can't look directly at him. There's so much grief in both of us, an entire world of it. I focus on willing all of my sadness into a heavy box, and then I think about locking the box and throwing away the key. For the moment, I feel somewhat less like I'm about to break into a thousand pieces.

"Well, it's been a pleasure." I inch close to the window. I have enough qì to change into a gnat, or maybe a mosquito. "Can't stay long. Have your people call me when you've got enough money for a dismissal."

"Wait!" Theo cries. "Don't go. Tell me what happened! Why're you here?"

Ha! Like I'm about to admit to him that I sought out his voice from the spirit world. I turn to leave, and he points a finger at me, his expression desperate. "I'll—uh, I'll blow you to pieces!" Already, his cirth pendant[6] is glowing, green light twisting down his arm.

Oy.

"May I remind you that civilians wielding aggressive magic is illegal in your country?" I say.

Theo huffs. "They're much more lenient when it's directed at volatile entities like fox *demons*."

"Bite your tongue, little boy. I'm a fox spirit," I snarl.

He hesitates before saying, "You're a húlíjīng. The jīng literally translates to demon."

"Actually, it translates to essence. The essence of the fox. That's what I am."

Theo doesn't look convinced. "Just tell me why you're here. Is Master Huang lying? Did he make a mistake?"

"Er, not quite . . ."

"Well, what happened? Where's my goldfish?"

I scratch my snout with a graceful paw, belatedly recalling the unfortunate goldfish who was gibbering along in the clouds. That

---

6 The cirth pendant is yet another example of humans' inferiority. Every living creature has magical energy, whether you call it mana, qì, prana, etc. As with all things, it takes effort and practice to access this energy naturally. But humans, lazy creatures that they are, have managed to extract magical energy from the environment and bottle it up in pendants. So, so unnatural. I'm shuddering at the very thought of it.

wretched fish must have been the shén they were trying to summon, except I barged through and, well . . . bit unfortunate, that.

"Um, Yangwei is . . . busy." Being slowly digested in the belly of a yāoguài.

"Busy? It's a *fish*! You must've done something. You húlíjīng are always up to no good. What is it? What did you do?"

My hackles rise. I'm in no mood to be falsely accused of mischief, even if the accusation isn't technically false. "It's not me. It's *you*. *You* ruined the summoning. I heard your voice in the spirit world, clear as day." I change my vocal cords and speak in his voice: *"I miss him. I don't want this. I don't want anything. I want HIM."*

"Stop that. Don't you dare use my voice!"

"Is that not what you were thinking throughout the entire ceremony?" I goad. "That's why Yangwei had such a tough time getting through to your world. It's your fault he got eaten."

Theo's eyes widen, and I stop talking abruptly.

"Yangwei got eaten?"

Oops.

"But—I—I was going to feed him all these crickets and ask him to let me speak to Jamie one more time . . ." His voice trembles, and his jaw loses its stubborn tightness. "I really caused Yangwei's death?"

If I knew of any shén who could let me speak with Jamie one more time, I would've been first in line to beg for it. I clear my throat and make sure my voice comes out easy breezy. "Don't feel too bad, it's the great Circle of Reincarnation. Yangwei's soul will be reborn. If he was good in this lifetime, he might be upgraded to a panda or something."[7] It hits me then that the same thing will happen to Jamie's soul within forty-nine days of his death, and instead of finishing my sentence with a glib smile, I deflate.

"That still doesn't explain why you're here." And suddenly he looks tired. When he lifts his face, he looks about a thousand years old. "I hate to do this, but you're my companion now. As your new master, I demand you tell me the truth."

There it is. My first task. And, because the summoning ritual has bound me to this dreadful boy, I have to do his bidding. Defying a master's order would literally tear my soul apart. I try to resist anyway, but it's like trying to hold back a waterfall. I don't want him to know why, I don't—

"Because I miss your brother!" I cry. "Ever since Jamie died, I don't know what to do with myself. When I heard your voice, all I could think of was him, and now . . . here I am."

For the next few moments, the only sounds in the room are our ragged breaths. Then, with a defeated sigh, Theo slouches to his room. I slink in behind him. I should stop comparing, but I can't help myself. Jamie's room looked like it came straight from an extreme-organization catalog. Everything was brightly colored and arranged neatly.

Theo's room is . . . different. The first thing my eyes are attracted to is an ancient computer that looks like something Dr. Frankenstein would've built, if Dr. Frankenstein had been into computers.

---

7 This is called reincarnation. The body dies, but the soul remains and moves to a different body. Humans like to think that to be reincarnated in a human body is a reward for being good in your past life. This is wrong. Being reincarnated in a human body is a punishment. You people are so bloated, and that whole bipedal business is very inefficient. If you're truly good, you'd be reincarnated as a . . . well, I don't want to brag, but I am preening a little bit.

There's a processing tower almost as tall as Theo himself with various appendages connected to it. Little fans spin around the machine, whirring madly. There are tubes filled with neon-colored liquids. There's even a box of ants plugged into it.

"I built it myself," Theo says when he notices me sniffing the monstrous thing. "The ants have been programmed to help sort out the data. Some people use hamsters, but I can't stand the smell of hamster pee."

"Not that it smells much better in here," I mutter. "Why do you even have a computer?"

Theo's mouth squeezes into a thin line. "I can't afford the cirth needed for most games and sports, so old-school computer games are the only things I can play."

I walk around the small space, wrinkling my snout at the mess. Clothes strewn across the floor in rumpled puddles, bed full of books and papers. How putrid. And I'm supposed to live in this dump?

I hop onto his bed and try to clear out a space for myself. I'm in the midst of gathering the mess into one big pile when Theo suddenly cries out and shoves me away.

"Hey, watch it! I'm priceless, you know!"

But instead of a snarky retort, Theo ignores me. He's holding a slim notebook that smells of Jamie, his chest rising and falling rapidly. "This—this notebook," he gasps. "Jamie gave it to me the day he—the day I lost him."

# THEO
# 6

Everything around me fades into the background. The only thing that matters is the tattered notebook in my hands. The last thing Jamie gave me on the day life came to a crunching halt for all of us and everything ceased to make sense. The morning he gave it to me, I tossed it on my bed, and it got swallowed up by the massive pile of books and magazines, and later on, I was so wrapped up in grief and shock that I didn't think about the notebook at all. But now Jamie's words come rushing back.

*Take this . . . It's got some notes you might find useful.*

He must've been talking about school. He knew I was having trouble with Skinner and his cronies. Maybe the book's filled with advice on how to deal with bullies. Tears fill my eyes, and I take a deep breath before flipping it open.

Dear Didi,

I'm off to college in the fall, so I thought I'd write to you. I'm kind of dreading sharing a room with a stranger . . . ugh. They say privacy and security are always huge issues in college. I love that Mama and Baba always respected our privacy, so we never had to worry about them reading our diaries . . .

I frown.

"Why does your face look even uglier than usual?" Kai says.

I don't have the energy to snap at her. When I finally manage to speak, the words come out choked with tears. "This notebook—it's wrong. It's all wrong."

"What do you mean it's all wrong?"

And suddenly I'm crying. Not a single-tear-trailing-down-one-cheek sort of deal, but an all-out, snotty bawl. Because for a moment when Kai unearthed the notebook, I hoped that I had gotten a little piece of Jamie back. But no. If anything, this notebook feels like a betrayal. "Jamie didn't remember anything about our past. He knew nothing about me!"

"Oh, that's rubbish and you know it," Kai says. "He was always talking on and on about you and how much he cared about you." Her voice wobbles, as though she's trying not to cry, too. "Let me see that." She grabs the notebook from my hands and starts reading the first paragraph out loud. "What's so wrong about this? He's just talking about college."

I swipe an arm across my eyes. "Where do I begin?" I say, my voice dripping with bitterness. "Mama and Baba always go through our stuff. We had so many fights with them about it, and then finally, Jamie learned a minor invisibility spell that you could cast on small objects, so he used it on our journals." I recall the moment when Jamie cast the spell. I was filled with such a sense of wonder and admiration for my older brother. "I guess he forgot about all that," I say in a hushed voice. I worshipped everything he did, but apparently it was so meaningless to him that he forgot it all. Tears rush to my eyes again, and I turn away and take a few deep breaths.

"Is that the only thing that's wrong?" Kai says. "I suppose it might have slipped his mind . . ."

"He was also really excited about finally meeting his roommate. They connected months ago on the college's forum. His roommate's also in the pre-med program, and they were geeking out about the science lab and library." I shake my head. "Or maybe he was just lying about being excited? I don't know. Why would he tell me one thing and write down something completely different?"

"Who knows why you humans do anything?" Kai mutters, but even I can tell she's also reeling with confusion. She lowers her head and continues reading out loud. "'Remember the games we used to play when we were kids? Remember Hubert?'"

I freeze. Time stops moving. Kai continues reading, but I flap my hands at her and sputter, "Stop! Wait, did you say Hubert? Give me that." I snatch the book from her paws without waiting for a response. My heart is thumping so hard I can feel it in my head. I read through the next paragraph, and it's as though a heavy weight is lifting from my chest. He didn't forget everything after all. I glance up at Kai with tear-filled eyes. "Kai . . . I think this whole notebook is written in code."

# THEO

# 7

The next few hours whiz by as I try to unscramble Jamie's code. Each page is brimming with hidden meanings that I can only guess at. Who knew Jamie could be so cryptic?

"When I was five, I decided I had to have a pet, but Mama and Baba wouldn't let me have one. I cried for days—"

"Sounds like you were a delightful child," Kai says.

I ignore her. "Then Jamie told me he'd bought me a gryphon. He turned one of my soft toys invisible and made it pat my leg. He said it was my gryphon, snuggling up to me." I smile at the memory. "I named him Hubert."

"You named a gryphon, one of the most majestic creatures in the world, Hubert."

"I was five, okay? The point is, Hubert became our code word. Whenever we needed to make up a story to get out of trouble, we'd say Hubert." We'd come up with all sorts of excuses, each one more far-fetched than the last. It was a blast.

Gods, I miss him. I shake my head, trying to clear it, and go back to the first page. Something catches my eye. Jamie wrote in the notebook using a range of brightly colored pens, but only two words are in purple: "Mandarin teacher."

Interesting. He'd hated purple, ever since he messed up some spell in school and accidentally turned his skin violet for a month. And now he's writing to me in purple? Weird.

I flip to the second page.

*Remember Hubert? Remember how Hubert got lost at the Museum of Magical Energy? You cried the entire way back. I turned the roots of your hair rainbow colored to distract you. I was so scared you'd get me in trouble that I cast a spell on you so you wouldn't be able to tell Mama.*

None of that happened. Jamie would've never, ever played such a mean prank or cast such an awful spell on me, even if it was just pretend. But the words "Hubert got lost," "Magical Energy," "roots," and "wouldn't be able to tell" are written in purple.

Wouldn't be able to tell . . .

I get a flash of Jamie in the meat freezer, garbling nonsensical stuff about quests and game masters. What if what he wanted to tell me wasn't about gaming at all?

Hubert got lost . . .

"Maybe," I mumble, "Jamie wants me to look for something? And he wasn't able to tell me why, because . . ." I scratch my forehead.

Wouldn't be able to tell . . . maybe that has to do with a spell?

I draw on my pendant and cast Pupplenot's No Strings Attached spell. The mountain of clutter on my floor shifts and tumbles, and my school-issued notebook flies out from the bottom and into my hand. Two weeks ago, I would've rather gnawed off my own foot than waste cirth on something as small as fetching a notebook. But ever since Jamie died, everything I used to long for—ThunderCon, winning the cosplay competition—seems pointless. Who cares about saving cirth?

Every kid in California is issued a magical notebook that acts as an encyclopedia. Ma says it makes us lazy. "In China got no such thing. You want to learn something you go to library. American kids too spoiled," she says, whenever she sees me using my notebook. I cast another spell to fetch a pen, open the notebook, and write *Look up spells that make you unable to tell.*

The words wobble around on the page as the book digests the question, and then they fade away. The answer slowly appears, written by an invisible hand.

*MNDA—Magical Non-Disclosure Agreement, also known as Magical Confidentiality Agreement (MCA), is a binding spell that physically restricts the castee from sharing certain information with a third party. MNDAs are widely used in large companies, especially within the magical industry, such as cirth production companies or spell weaving companies. Spells to neutralize MNDAs are rare; typically only the government body has access to such counters.*

Hmmm. I wave my hands at my bed, casting Shufflebottom's Surefire Assortments Sorter. The mess of papers flies up and hovers in the air among a light green haze as I sift through it, swiping left and right until I find what I'm looking for. "Got it."

It's a pamphlet. On the cover, a familiar logo is emblazoned underneath the words REAPLING CORP. Below, in a bold, brightly colored font, is written INTRODUCING . . . KNOW YOUR ROOTS! A bunch of manically grinning kids point at the words.

"Know Your Roots. Roots!" I exclaim.

Jamie was obsessed with the program he was helping to design and plan at Reapling Corp. He mentioned it to me before, and I laughed at the cheesy program title. Know Your Roots. Now the memory of it stings me. Why couldn't I have been nicer about it? It was obviously something Jamie loved. I swallow the guilt and force myself to focus on figuring out the notebook's code.

"The only place that might have used an MNDA on Jamie is Reapling Corp. Jamie wanted to tell me something, but he had to write it in really vague terms to get around the MNDA, which means what he wanted to tell me must have something to do with Reapling." I pause and mentally pick at what I've just said. Did any of that make sense? Yes. Yes! "I'm sure of it!"

Kai's wearing a very strange expression that makes her look constipated.

"What is it?" I say.

Now it's her turn to look anguished. "He never told me about any of this. I was his companion spirit, and I have no idea why he would've left you a notebook in code. I failed him as a companion."

It feels weird to sympathize with Kai instead of seeing her as the enemy. "That sucks," I mumble. "But I'm sure he had his reasons?" That sounded so flimsy. "Anyway, what can you tell me about Reapling Corp.?"

Kai opens her mouth, but no words come out. Her eyes bug out and her fur bristles, her two tails standing up straight. After a few seconds of this, she slumps over, panting.

"Okay, you're being weird again. It's not the time for jokes, Kai. We really need to figure this out."

"I am—not joking—" she pants. "It's the—urk!" Again, she seizes up like some invisible thing has gripped her by the throat.

Oh no. Horrible understanding dawns. "Is it the MNDA?"

She looks at me with tortured eyes. It seems she's unable to even confirm or deny it. Moments later, she slumps over, breathing hard. Despite myself, I feel bad for her. I had no idea how MNDAs take effect, but what I've seen so far looks brutal. "Okay, don't try to break the MNDA again," I tell her. She sighs with relief.

I pace about the room for a bit, then I pick up my notebook and scribble *Tell me about Reapling Corp's Know Your Roots program.*

The words wobble and disappear, but no answer appears. Come on! I write down my question again, this time pressing really hard in frustration. *Tell me about—*

The notebook wrenches itself out of my hands, expands into the size of a blanket, and, before I can do anything, flies at me. I yelp out loud, and next thing I know, I'm in perfect darkness.

"Hello? What's going on? Help!"

A voice says, "Don't be afraid. We're just checking for your cultural heritage."

"My what?"

"Okay, scan complete! Theodore Tan, first-generation Chinese American."

The darkness lifts, and I gasp out loud. I'm hovering above the Forbidden City in Beijing. The magnificent buildings look like toy figurines from where I'm standing. I can't help but whimper at the height, but to my relief, I float gently down, stopping a couple of inches above the ground. I gaze around me.

Okay. I'm trying to remain cool, but it's hard when faced with the Forbidden friggin' City. I mean. Geez. The ginormous red pavilions, the steep arches of the roofs, flanked every which way with carved dragons, and the perfect symmetry of every building are mind blowing. Now I know why Jamie was always trying to get Mama and Baba to take us on a visit to China. The thought of it makes my chest tighten. There's so much guilt inside me, because whenever Jamie brought up the possibility of visiting China, I'd say, "Ew, why China? Let's go to someplace cool, like Hungary! Or Greece!" He would've loved this.

A woman wearing a figure-hugging qípáo smiles and waves as she walks down the steps of the main pavilion.

"Hello, Theo," she says. "I am Xiuling, and it's my pleasure to walk you through Know Your Roots today. Don't worry, this is just an illusion." She laughs when my mouth drops open even wider.

"I don't—I—an illusion?" Illusions are spells that, well, create a visual and sometimes auditory mirage, but they're usually pretty minor. The only illusions I've come across are things like what my algebra teacher Mr. Wilkins uses to hide his bald spot. I've heard of illusions that make up entire scenes, like this, but they cost so much cirth I never thought I'd be able to experience one myself. "But I was just—my notebook—"

"We have spells that trigger the illusion whenever anyone age appropriate does a search for the Know Your Roots program," Xiuling says. "Your notebook acted as a gateway to the spell."

"A gateway?" I feel dazed, like a piano was just dropped on my head. "Does my school know that my notebook can do that?"

"Let's treat it as our little secret," Xiuling says, with a wink. "Follow me." She begins strolling toward a red gate with impressive towers looming behind it. I hesitate for a second before running after her. It's super weird, running in an illusion. My feet aren't touching the ground, but somehow I'm moving forward. When I try to think about the physics of it, I get a pounding headache.

"The aim of our program is to connect first-, second-, and third-generation children of immigrants to their cultural heritage. This is the launch year of Know Your Roots, and our focus will be on China and India. Next year we will be branching out to children of Polish ancestry." A small phoenix, barely visible under its coat of flame, flies round and round Xiuling before swooping across the sky like a shooting star.

Connecting children of immigrants to their cultural heritage. That's definitely Jamie's thing. Or rather, it *was* Jamie's thing. My heart clenches painfully again. No wonder he adored this program.

From underneath the sadness, a small voice at the back of my mind pipes up: *Why would a company like Reapling be interested in such a program?*

Reapling dabbles a bit in spell weaving, but its bread-and-butter product is cirth. Argh, why didn't I ask Jamie about the program before the accident? Honestly, I could just kick myself in the throat when I think of how self-absorbed I was.

"You will learn about ancient rituals and mythical creatures—oh, hi, little guy!" A grinning golden monkey clambers up and perches on her shoulder. Together, Xiuling and the monkey walk through the massive gate. I hasten to keep up with them.

As soon as I go through the gate, I find myself stepping out onto the Great Wall of China. "Wow." Jamie must've lost it completely at the sight. The wall is amazing. It stretches on as far as the eye can see, like a giant serpent sleeping across the mountains. I reach out to touch the stones, but my hand goes right through them. For a second, the stones around where my hand was disappear, before reappearing slowly. Right, I've forgotten that this is just an illusion. Illusion spells are limited to visual and auditory effects, not physical. In school, Mr. Wilkins would never let anyone come close to him, for fear we'd touch his head and break the spell. I guess the same rule applies here.

The golden monkey hops off Xiuling's shoulder and lands on the back of a lion with deer antlers.

"Can you tell me what this is?" Xiuling says.

Jamie's voice echoes in my memories.

*It's so cool, Didi! It has like, the power to distinguish between good and evil, and it'll call out anyone who's in the wrong, even if the wrongdoer is the emperor. Isn't that amazing?*

I pinch my thigh to stop the tears from falling. "It's a xièzhì."

"Oh, wonderful!" Xiuling looks pleasantly surprised. "By the end of our program, you will have learned about many Chinese mythological beasts just like the xièzhì. As a reward for finishing the program, twenty children will be sent to our spell weaving site in Muir Woods."

Jamie had been so excited about being invited to Muir Woods to further his studies. Maybe what he wanted me to look for is there. My heartbeat quickens, and I have to stop myself from seeming too eager. "I can't wait to see the weaving site."

Xiuling seems satisfied. "It's an amazing place. Most people can't even begin to imagine the wondrous spells that are woven at Reapling. Which is why you must perform well in your tasks to be chosen. Right! That's the end of our tour. I will see you at the entrance test."

"Entrance test?"

"Yes. You're a twelve-year-old Chinese American boy. Based on your age and your cultural ancestry, you qualify for our Know Your Roots summer program. I assume you're interested in the program?"

Am I? Just as quickly as I think that, I realize that of course I am. This was the last thing Jamie was working on before he died. I would give up a limb to know this part of him. "Yes, I am."

"Wonderful! You've done the tour just in time for our entrance test tomorrow. We have over six hundred applicants and only fifty spots, so put your best foot forward. I'll send you the address and some forms for your parent or guardian to sign." Xiuling's smile widens. "And here's a little hint for tomorrow's test: It will involve another illusion. I know you'll do just fine, Theo."

"Wait, I—" Everything goes dark, and there's a sudden weird sensation, like my guts are being tugged out my back. I blink, stumbling a little, and when I open my eyes, I'm back in my own room.

My notebook lies open on the floor, its pages blank.

"Back from the illusion?" Kai says. She's draped across my floor like some luxurious rug, her tails swishing idly.

"You know about the illusion?" I flop down on my bed, feeling dizzy, like I've just gone on a roller coaster. "I've never experienced an illusion like that."

"Reapling's weavers have come up with a bunch of spells that they haven't released to the public."

"Is that legal?"

She shrugs. "Who knows? Since when do these big corporations play by the rules?"

I'm quiet for a while. There are too many thoughts and emotions swirling inside me. I feel as though I've just been given a glimpse at Jamie's past, and I don't know how to process it. What he was involved in was so huge, so much vaster than I had thought, and I feel regret and remorse so deeply within me for not being more interested. If I could only turn back time, I'd apologize to him for being so ignorant and selfish, and I'd listen to him talk for hours about Know Your Roots, if that's what he wanted. If only.

"So what did you find out about the program?" Kai says.

I drag my thoughts away from Jamie and the endless "if onlys" I've been torturing myself with ever since he died. It takes a moment to focus on Kai's question, and when I do, my stomach sinks horribly. "There's an entrance test," I say in a heavy voice.

There is no way I could possibly pass an entrance test, especially one that's about reconnecting with your cultural heritage. The other kids would probably be as interested in their cultures as Jamie was. They would've spent months, if not years, looking it up and learning the language. I'm filled with so much dread at the thought of the test. My chances of passing it are basically nil. Should I even try?

I squeeze my eyes shut. I have to. I must. I can't fail Jamie yet again, not without trying my very best. I open my eyes and look at Kai. "I need to pass that test at all costs."

Kai grins, showing me all her teeth. "Sounds like you've got your work cut out for you."

# KAI
# 8

"Are you sure about this, Di—bǎobèi?" Mr. Tan glances at Theo in the rearview mirror as he merges onto the 101 and heads toward Silicon Valley.

Theo winces. "Yep." I can't blame him for wincing; I too noticed the awkward switch from Didi to bǎobèi. It's nothing bad, it means "precious treasure," but it's yet another reminder that Jamie is no longer with us. Theo is no longer a didi—a little brother—because he's nobody's little brother now. True to my sensitive and caring nature, I reach out and pat him sympathetically, but he just shrugs off my paw. Okay, then.

"But this so strange—" Mr. Tan pauses to switch lanes. "You never interested in learning Chinese culture, and this program very tough."

"I told you, I want to know what Gege was doing there. I—" Theo's voice cracks. "I want to see what he was so into."

Mr. and Mrs. Tan exchange a sorrowful look. We spend the rest of the drive in gloomy silence. Ever since Jamie died, it's like we're all carrying our emotions in really thin, bulging plastic bags, and we're afraid to talk because it might scratch the bag and then it would burst and our tears would pour and pour and pour until there's nothing left of us but empty husks.

This close to Mountain View, the roads are nearly deserted.

Everyone else is zooming above us on some sort of flying contraption. I never really thought about it before, but now the sight makes my insides curl. Because if I'd been a better companion spirit, if I'd had more power, I could've flown Jamie to and from work like a companion dragon would. Then maybe Jamie wouldn't have had to drive a car. Maybe he wouldn't have fallen asleep at the wheel and crashed into the side barrier of the 101. Maybe he'd be here right now, sitting right next to me.

I gnaw on my paws, everything inside me writhing with grief. Theo nudges me, and I snarl at him. "What?"

"We're almost there."

"Ah." I try to shake off the blanket of sadness and look out the window. Sure enough, Mr. Tan is taking the Mountain View exit. I focus and transform myself into a goldfish that looks a lot like Yangwei. Better play it safe, in case someone here recognizes me as Jamie's companion spirit. A goldfish is much less likely to attract any unwanted attention. Then I hold my breath and slither into Theo's shirt pocket. Which, I quickly find out, is a mistake. "Ugh, when was the last time you washed this shirt?"

"What are you talking about? It's a fresh shirt."

"Is it just your natural scent, then?" I gag, my eyes bulging out dramatically.[8] Theo ignores me.

We drive down a road lined with uniform cypress trees until we get to a large pair of bronze gates. A bored-looking security guard aims his wand at our car and sweeps a blue beam over us

---

8 Nobody does bulgy eyes better than a goldfish, I must say.

from hood to trunk. He nods, and the gates yawn wide. Theo's mouth drops open. Much like the gate, but less nice looking.

I can't tease him for being impressed, because when I first came to this place, I myself was quite blown away. I suppose it has to do with knowing that humans are such unimpressive creatures. I mean, I could've sworn it was just yesterday that you all were living in caves and wiping your bums with leaves, whereas we celestial beings have always been elevated and refined. For a human-built place, Reapling Corp. is truly amazing.

The entire estate is made of beautiful sandstone buildings surrounding a magnificent clock tower. Little islands float above us, with waterfalls running down the sides, creating myriad rainbows. Dozens of people glide through the air, some wearing the usual flying shoes, others in what look like giant soap bubbles. There's a giant bubble pool that is as high as a skyscraper. People spiral through the water and burst out the sides before splashing back in.

The sight cracks my heart like a chisel. In every attraction, I see Jamie. He's stretched out on the thick grass with a book. He's swimming in the bubble pool and bursting out of the surface to take a huge gulp of air before diving back in. He's whizzing around on a broomstick, his mouth stretched in a half-terrified grin.

He was always scared of heights, but that never stopped him from trying out the broomsticks. I used to shift into a canary and fly after him as he zipped through the sky. The ghost of him is everywhere. He should be here to show us around. He would've loved to show his little brother this place.

Mr. Tan drives to a small parking structure. The parking attendant gestures for us to get out of the car. Once we're all out, the attendant utters an incantation and flicks a bit of bright purple powder at the car. There's a zap, and the car disappears.

"Hey! What you do to my car?" Mr. Tan says.

"No worries, sir. It's the latest Reapling spell." The attendant stoops and picks up a piece of paper.

Theo and his parents look about ready to fall over themselves. I nudge Theo. "If you open your mouth any wider, I'll be able to see your brains."

His mouth claps shut, then opens again. "B-but. Our car. It's a piece of paper." He gapes as the attendant rolls up the paper-car and secures it with a rubber band before placing it in a tiny compartment by the valet stand. He hands Mr. Tan a ticket.

"All it needs to restore it is a few drops of warm water. Next!" The guard waves the flying car behind us forward.

"How do they even do that?" Theo rambles as we walk off. "Is it a transmutation spell? It must be, right? The only transmutation spell we've been taught is Hickinnutter's Melody of Elongation, and that only works on rulers and lasts about twenty minutes. Definitely not as powerful as changing an entire car into paper. I mean, wow! That spell must've cost at least forty cirth. Maybe more? Oh my gods, how can they afford that?"

I roll my eyes. "If you bothered to learn how to cast magic using your qì instead of cirth, you wouldn't be impressed by these parlor tricks."

Not far from the parking structure is a map of the grounds.

"Hmm, where are we now?" Mr. Tan muses, squinting at the map.

A slit suddenly appears at the top of the map and opens into a mouth. "Good morning, Theo!"

Theo and his parents jump back with a yelp.

"Haven't you ever seen a talking map before?" the map says.

"Uh. No?" Theo says. "And how do you know who I am?"

"Get used to it," I mutter from inside his pocket. "They put a lot of effort into impressing newcomers."[9]

The mouth stretches into a grin. "I know everyone who comes to Reapling Corp., and where they are, of course." It puckers into a large O—if you've never seen a faceless mouth pucker, count yourself lucky—and blows out a bubble, which grows into a sphere huge enough to swallow Theo and his parents. "Step inside. It will take you to the testing facility."

The three of them walk inside gingerly, as though expecting the bubble to pop at any time. Once we're in, the bubble floats up gently. I sense Theo's heart rate increasing at the sight of the ground falling away beneath his feet.

I can't help but have a bit of fun with this. "You're rising about a hundred feet into the air, with nothing separating you from falling but a thin layer of magical bubble. What's so scary about that?" He gulps audibly, and I giggle to myself.

The ride gives us an eagle's-eye view of the compound. We fly over the giant statue of the company's founder, Hassan Taslim. I've never been able to figure out the point of statues. It's such a human thing to do—create likenesses of themselves,

---

9 Unlike yours truly, who is effortlessly impressive.

as though they want everyone to know what narcissists they are.

This one is particularly obnoxious. It's made of marble, but it moves about its podium, waving to passersby. It doesn't look like him at all; in real life, Hassan Taslim was a balding guy with a potbelly and terrible posture, but the statue has a full head of hair and bulging muscles.[10] The only recognizable feature is the pair of iconic iridescent glasses he used to wear everywhere.

"Wow, that must cost sooo much cirth, making the statue move like that," Theo says. "You know, I went to the science museum last year and they had statues that made these small, jerky movements and we were told that the spell for that alone cost hundreds of cirth. Hundreds!"

"Such shame, Mr. Taslim," Mrs. Tan says. "Great man. Before him, there was no cir—"

"Cirth. Yes, Mama, I know. We learned all about him in school."

Fifty years ago, when Hassan Taslim discovered how to create cirth, it was a revolution, and it still is, not just in how it changed the world, but because nobody knows how he did it.[11]

Everyone knew magic existed, of course. Qì and mana and other forms of magical energy have been around from the beginning of time, but the only people who could tap into those sources were highly trained individuals. And even then, the

---

10 This is very typical of humans. For some reason, they think they look a lot better than they really do. It's honestly quite baffling, because humans are missing the key ingredients for beauty: good, thick fur and a long, bushy tail.

11 Again, this is very typical human behavior. Instead of sharing knowledge for the good of the entire race, they hoard it for profit. In the spirit world, every bit of knowledge and wisdom gets passed on to everyone, which is why we are all so much more enlightened.

spells they could cast were very limited, nothing like the powerful ones that can be cast with cirth. Back then, humans were more into technological advances—silly things like computers and electronics. They were far more accessible than magic.

Once Hassan Taslim figured out how to harvest cirth and bottle it in pendants to sell to the masses, it spread across the world like the plague, obliterating the need to learn any other forms of magic.

Now, kids argue they need pendants as soon as they're old enough to figure out how to use them, and all schools teach basic spell-casting. In school, computers have been abandoned in favor of magical notebooks, and electric cars have given way to cirth-powered ones.

"You know, it took twenty years after he discover cirth before they allowed to be sold in China. Our government convinced cirth pendants not good for us, block our qì," Mrs. Tan says.

"They weren't wrong," I say.

Theo rolls his eyes. But before I can make a snarky comeback, the bubble lands in front of a huge domed building.

"We have arrived at the testing facility," says the automated voice. "The very best luck to you on your test!"

Oh boy. From what I know about Theo's grasp of the Chinese language and culture, we're going to need every bit of luck available to pass the test.

# THEO

# 9

"Bǎobèi, you have everything?" Mama says as we walk toward the testing facility. "You know what test is going to be?"

I wish. I spent last night reading through my Mandarin text-books with Kai. They were so unused, the spines were still unbroken. I understand Mandarin just fine, since Nainai speaks it to me, but I've only ever let myself reply to her in English.

See, when I was five, I made the mistake of speaking Mandarin to Mama at school using the proper tones, and my classmates—who apparently were cave people—screamed with laughter. The rest of the year, kids would make fun of me in this really nasal, singsong voice. Was that how I sounded—like a complete caricature? Anyway, just to be safe, I never ever spoke Mandarin in front of them again, and when I do speak it at home, I don't go fully tonal, to make it clear that I'm American, not Chinese.

By the time we get inside the building, my mouth is a desert. What am I doing here? Over six hundred applicants and only fifty spots! There's no chance I'm going to make it. I won't be able to figure out Jamie's coded message. It doesn't help that the lobby is so imposing, with towering sculptures of ancient sorcerers that can't seem to stand still; they strike pose after pose and wink at passersby. The marble floor is so shiny that I'm super aware of my grubby sneakers. Hundreds of kids are here—some look calm and confident, others look like they're about to pee their pants. An Indian woman wearing a blazer and bright yellow pants approaches.

"Hi, Theo!"

"Um, hi." I wonder if I'll ever get used to everybody knowing my name while I know nothing about them.

"I'm Saanvi. Hi, Mr. and Mrs. Tan!"

My parents nod and smile nervously.

"It's great to meet you. If you'd please follow me to the parents' waiting area. Theo, go on and join the others. Someone will be out shortly with instructions."

I'm almost overcome with the urge to cling to Mama's waist like a little kid.

"Good luck with test, Ruowen," Baba says. He and Mama give me a tight hug; then they follow Saanvi into a side room, leaving me alone with Kai. Well, and six hundred other contenders.

To make things even worse, as if they're not dire enough already, many of the kids are speaking to each other in fluent Mandarin, Cantonese, Hindi, and what I guess is probably Tamil. What gives?

Also, some of the Chinese kids have the craziest companions. There's a small sky dragon, a snub-nosed monkey, even a gold serpent. Definitely an upgrade from the benign goldfish I was going to inherit, before Kai happened. Their companions must have cost a ton. How can they possibly afford them? Maybe it's not that good companions are too expensive, it's just that they're too expensive for the likes of me and my family. I won't lie—I feel jealous of them. Of everyone here.

The Indian kids look just as wealthy, but they don't have companions. I recall learning in school that those who master Indian magic can summon hundreds and thousands of different spirits and beings temporarily, among other things. The thought makes me even more jealous. Imagine not being chained to a permanent companion and being able to choose what to summon when and as it's needed.

Saanvi and another woman walk up to the podium. With a start, I realize the woman next to Saanvi is Xiuling. She clears her throat, silencing the buzz in the room, and gives a big smile. Green light flows from her pendant and weaves around her neck, and when she speaks, her voice is magnified so it fills the room.

"Hi, folks, my name is Xiuling, and I'm the Chinese group supervisor. This is Saanvi, supervisor for the Indian group. Welcome to Know Your Roots! Before we begin, I'd like those of you with companions to please dismiss them. They're not allowed during the test."

What? No! I can't do this without Kai's help. Last night, while frantically studying, I realized how woefully little I know about anything that has to do with China. Dread seeps from my stomach to the rest of my body, making me break out into a sweat. As annoying as Kai is, I need her. My heart thunders so hard that my hands actually start to tremble.

Around me, there are murmured incantations and puffs of light as companions are dismissed. I inch my way to the edge of the group, then slip into the nearest bathroom and take Kai out of my pocket.

Unbelievable.

She's actually honest-to-gods sleeping. I can hear little snores as her fat goldfish body slumps like a blob of Jell-O on my palm. I poke her belly.

"Ow!" She squirms awake and glares at me. "What?"

"We're in trouble," I whisper. "I'm not allowed to take you into the testing room. But you have to help me pass the test."

"Bit tricky, that. You see, cheating is rather bad for one's karma. You do know that there are different levels of shén, yes? Yes? No? Oh dear. This is going to take some time. But basically, there is a hierarchy of spirits, me being at the top, obviously. Whenever we do something bad, like helping a daft human child cheat through his test, it kicks us down a notch on the hierarchy, and the lower we go, the closer we are to turning demonic. Which is very bad, by the way. It'll affect your karma and all that."

As Kai prattles on about karma and how it affects our yin and yang, I'm suddenly hit by a memory. Months ago, I stole a plate of pepper-fried beef from the restaurant and was about to share it with Jamie, but as I crept toward his room, I overheard someone crying. I peeped through the half-closed door, and there was Jamie gently stroking Kai's head as she wailed into a pillow. The only reason I recognized Kai was by the two bright orange tails sticking out of a tube. Half of her was in the form of a stethoscope, and I stifled my laughter at seeing this weird stethoscope-fox aberration sobbing with all the melodrama of a TV soap actor.

"I'll never do it," she said. "I can't master this ridiculous form. Changing into inanimate objects takes up so much more qì than changing to living ones. I'm not powerful enough."

"You are," Jamie said. "Remember how you mastered the scalpel form last week? If you can do that, you can definitely do this."

"The scalpel form had a blunt blade. You might as well banish me and get yourself a new companion. I'm broken." With that, she flopped back onto the bed and continued sobbing.

"Stop being so dramatic. Look, I got something for you." Jamie brandished a box of giant incense sticks, each one as thick as his thumb and as long as his forearm.

The small disc-shaped resonator lifted from the bed and stared. "They're—"

"Golden Lotus brand, yep. Cost me a heck of a lot of money, but you deserve it."

A change happened in Kai then. I could almost see golden light pouring down the top of her head—well, the disc-shaped resonator—all the way to her two tails, and where the light touched her, her fur turned black and transformed into tubes, and by the time I blinked, the fox tails were almost nearly gone, replaced by two earpieces, though two little tail tips were still poking out of them.

Jamie lifted Kai gently and placed the earpieces in his ears (ew!), then placed the resonator on his chest. "Hmm. I can hear your heartbeat as well as mine, but I suppose that can't be helped. You did it, Kai!"

Kai was so happy that the resonator popped back to become a fox's head, and she twisted and flopped everywhere while Jamie laughed and lit the incense sticks, filling his entire room with smoke.

I can hear their laughter in my head now and taste the peppery beef I stuffed into my mouth while trying to ignore the burning jealousy at the bond Kai had with my brother.

"If you help me pass, I promise to burn you one of those giant incense sticks," I say to Kai now.

Kai perks up, her already huge goldfish eyes widening.

"I bet you can practically smell the smoke already. Mmm, pungent."

"Jamie used to get me those. He'd save up so he could get me the biggest ones."

"I know."

We are both quiet for a while, our sadness pooling around us. Then Kai gives the tiniest of nods.

"Thank you," I say. "Now, can you think of a way to stay with me during the test? Fast."

"What are all the other kids doing? Anyone fighting the no-companion rule?"

"They've all dismissed their companions."

Kai snorts. "Bunch of sheep. Any other fox spirits around?"

"No, why would anyone want a fox spirit for a companion?"

"Because I'm the only creature that can help you pass this silly test? Everyone always wants dragons or phoenixes as companions, but none of them can shape-shift. Or, well, there are those who have the ability to shape-shift, but they tend to gain an unsavory reputation, like the skeleton demon, Baigujing. You know what that means?"

"That . . . you're closer to a demon than a spirit?" I say.

Kai hisses at me. Or tries to, anyway. It comes out as a squeak. "It means Reapling won't be looking out for a shape-shifter!

They'll be busy scanning for your typical companions—those silly golden monkeys and tiresome dragons, not someone with such powerful, yet subtle, gifts like myself." She stands on her tail and raises her front fins. "Behold! One of the many unusual forms I've mastered—" The words are impressive, but the effect is somewhat ruined by her high-pitched goldfish voice.

With a pop, the fish is gone, leaving a fat louse on my palm.

It scuttles up my arm, raising gooseflesh along the way, slides up my neck, and nestles on my scalp.

"Ta-da!" Kai says.

"Ewwww! No, this is a terrible disguise. Change back!"

"Look at all the privileged kids here. No one's going to suspect any of them as having hair lice as a companion. And you strike me as the type to get lice. In fact, they'd probably be more suspicious if you didn't have them."

"I've never had head lice in my life!"

I resist the urge to try shaking her off. I stare into the mirror. I hate to admit it, but Kai's disguise is perfect. I can't tell she's there, aside from the hair-raising ick factor I feel. "I guess this works . . ."

"You're welcome."

My reflection in the mirror looks terrified. But then I recall why we're here. This isn't just some pointless test; it's an obstacle to finding out what Jamie was trying to tell me. I straighten up and take a deep breath.

"Let's do this."

# THEO
# 10

"Okay!" Xiuling says. "Walk through any one of these doors"—
she gestures to the five behind her, which open on cue—"and
you will be sorted into your exam rooms."

I walk awkwardly toward a door. All of my limbs feel stiff, like
they've forgotten how to move. Oh gods, are they going to sense
Kai on my head?

"This may not be the best time to ask," Kai says, "but could
you turn off your sweat glands for a bit? I'm drowning here."

"That's not something I can control," I mutter.

"Really? Dear me, how do you people survive? You're terribly
unhygienic creatures."

I don't answer, because right then, I walk through the door.
The air instantly cools. All noise is silenced, and the corridor
turns dark. I can no longer see the other kids around me. Thin
slivers of green light travel up and down my body. At the edge
of my hearing, I catch a soft drone of incantation. It sounds like
they're creating a really elaborate illusion. I can barely breathe,
I'm so scared. At any moment now, they're going to detect Kai.
Alarms will shriek, and guards will rush out and catch me, and—

A door opens wide. Light spills out, almost blinding after the
darkness of the corridor.

We've passed the scanners. Somehow we managed to trick

them. Maybe Kai's form is so tiny it's hard to detect? That must be it. They're used to kids with more impressive companions, and like Kai said, shape-shifters are rare. My breath comes out in a relieved sigh. Who would've thought I'd be grateful for Kai's sly nature?

"Here goes nothing," I whisper, and step outside.

The light is so brilliant I have to close my eyes, and when I open them again, we're in a rural farming area, flanked by paddy fields. In the distance, there's a cluster of humble wooden houses. Weather-beaten men, women, and children trudge around carrying pails of water, tending to the rice fields, and feeding livestock. The air is searing hot and thick with the smell of ox dung.

I look down at my arms and torso and jump back in surprise. My outfit has been completely transformed. Instead of my shirt and jeans, I'm dressed in long pants and an ankle-length tunic. My Converse sneakers have changed into soft cloth boots, and my hair—

"What the heck is this?" I hiss, grabbing at the top of my head. Gone is my short, spiky hair. In its place is a bun. A hair bun. This is bizarre.

"Hey, careful where you grab," Kai squeaks from somewhere at the top of my head. "And that would be a topknot. Well, in your case, a boy bun. In ancient Han China, short hair symbolized barbarism and unfilial tendencies. Which describes you perfectly, come to think of it."

I ignore Kai. A horrifying thought has struck me. What if they expect us to use our qì to pass the test? What if they've taken our cirth pendants away? I paw frantically around my collar and relax only when I locate the familiar pendant. I clutch it tight and breathe out, forcing myself to relax. I scratch at my chest. "This shirt itches. What is it made of?"

"It's hemp. It's a type of cloth made from plant stalks. China didn't grow cotton until the Mongols invaded in 1200 A.D., so obviously we've been sent to pre-Mongol-invasion China, probably the Song Dynasty. Why do you not know this? What do they teach you in school?"

"Excuse you—"

A little rock dislodges itself from the side of the road and flies up, interrupting me.

One side of the rock flaps open, revealing a small imp like the ones that spy from inside Eyes. It waves at me. "Welcome, Theodore, to our test! All you have to do is complete one of our quests. But beware! If any of the world's inhabitants detects that you're not part of the illusion, or if you get a major injury, the illusion spell will break and you will fail the test. Be creative, and the very best of luck to you!" The rock flies back to the ground and settles there.

I blink. A "major injury"? What? No way. "You mean things here can actually hurt me? But I thought this was just an illusion—"

The imp peers out from under the rock. "It's the most advanced illusion in the world! Of course things here can hurt you. We've worked very hard to break the physical boundaries of the spell in order to achieve maximum realism." The rock lowers again and stays still.

Okay. Not reassured by the way the imp has so casually said that "of course things here can hurt you," but I suppose I don't have a choice.

Kai clears her throat. "You should probably start moving now. And don't talk to me, or the imps are going to think you're some weird kid talking to himself. Not that they'd be wrong about the weird bit, mind you."

I ignore her. Despite my nervousness, as I walk, I start getting into the illusion. It's an incredible one. "I've never heard of an illusion spell this huge," I tell Kai. "The most elaborate illusion spell we've been taught is Morigan's More and More Morsels, which makes you think there's more food on your plate than there really is. This is on a whole different scale. How did they break all the boundaries of the standard illusion spell? I can touch things here. I mean, is this shirt real? It feels real. How's that even possible?"

Kai snorts. "Humans. You should be focused on perfecting your qì energy and trying to break your reliance on cirth, but instead, you spend your time coming up with useless spells like this."

Soon, we reach the village, although calling it a village is generous. It's a small gathering of little boxy huts with thatch roofs. All the people are thin, with slender muscles beneath leathery, sun-browned skin. A bored-looking boy tending a small flock of goats looks up as we approach.

"Are you here to perform the death rites?" he says in rapid Mandarin.

"Hmph," Kai mutters. "Technically, people here should be speaking an ancient dialect, but I suppose they decided to skip that bit of reality to make it easier on you kids."

I don't tell Kai that modern Mandarin is still a huge challenge for me. I stare at the goatherd helplessly until Kai scratches my scalp, making me jump. Okay, I just have to go for it. "Death rites?" I say. Even I know the words didn't come out right. Yet another reason I hate Mandarin. It's a tonal language. For every syllable, there are four different tones, and each tone turns the same syllable into a different word. I must've mangled the pronunciation, because the boy raises his eyebrows in confusion.

"The death rites for Mr. Huang. Are you here to perform them?"

"No—"

"Don't just say no!" Kai whispers. "You're supposed to complete a quest, remember? What if this is the quest?"

"But I don't know how to perform death rites," I whisper back behind clenched teeth.

"Are you from Banpo village? Are you here to trade more soybeans for rice?" the boy says.

I struggle to think of the right words. "Um, no. I'm from a . . . foreign country. You'd have to cross oceans to get to where I came from."

"A country of bandits!" the boy cries, taking a step away from me.

What? I work out the words in my head. Argh, I've somehow mangled the word for "foreign" to sound like "thief." "No, no! A *foreign* country."

"A deaf country? I am so sorry to hear that."

I'm this close to giving up when Kai says, "Let me take over."

Oh, thank gods. I very nearly start weeping with relief. But then I realize that I have to trust Kai, to let her "take over." When I sought out her help, I wasn't expecting to hand over the reins to her completely, but here I am. Left without a choice but to trust a wily fox spirit. I take a deep breath and whisper, "Okay."

"There should be a handkerchief in your pocket," Kai says. "Everyone in ancient China had one. Good for wiping sweat off your forehead, poop off the baby's bottom, crumbs off the dining table—got it? Tie it around your face so he can't see your lips. Right, then." Kai clears her throat and then shouts in a voice that's so identical to mine it's creepy, "Heed my words, human—"

"Boy," I interject.

"Heed my words, boy! I am the apprentice of Grand Master Liaotai, who himself was a direct apprentice of Grand Master Xianfeng, who himself was the apprentice of Baosheng Dadi, the god of medicine. I may seem strange in manner, and extremely unsightly in appearance—"

"Unsightly?" I mutter.

"—but that's because I've mastered so many unearthly lessons that I am no longer bound by insipid human things such as manners or looks. Do not presume to question anything I say or do, or I will call forth the will of the gods, turn you into a fat piglet, roast you until you're crisp, and eat you with warm, steamed mántou."

Silence. I hold my breath. She did it. She actually saved the—

The boy turns on his heel and runs into the village, screaming, "A sorcerer is here and he will kill us all!"

"Er," Kai says. "Maybe I was a tad too effective."

I could strangle her. I should've known better than to trust her. But there's no time for anger or regret. "Now what?"

"Well, I would say this is a most opportune time to abscond."

"What?"

"By which I mean, RUN!"

# KAI

# 11

I peer back as Theo stumbles along the squelchy, muddy dirt road. A dozen villagers are chasing after us.

"Might want to go faster," I say helpfully.

"This—is—all—your—fault," Theo gasps.

"How are you out of breath already? You should exercise instead of playing computer games all day."

"Shut—up."

"There's a small path up ahead, to your left. Take it."

For once, he doesn't argue. The path leads us into a forest. Once we're in the shade of the trees, I focus my qì on the small path and cast a spell of illusion. As a fox spirit, illusion and shape-shifting are the rice and tofu of my magic. I'm not able to roast people to a crisp like fire dragons can, but that's so seventeenth century. My ways are more cunning and subtle.

As the villagers charge past us, Theo breathes a sigh of relief. "Why aren't they following us?"

"I made the path invisible for a short while."

He pauses. "That's actually pretty useful."

I preen a little. Somewhat challenging as a louse, but I manage.

"Of course, you were the one who created this whole mess to begin with." Theo can never quit while he's ahead. "I can't believe you said all those things to the goatherd. You're way too brash!"

"I was saving you from detection. You were about to tell that boy you're from America."

I can tell Theo is angry—he's breathing rapidly and his head is very warm, but at my retort, he gives a frustrated sigh before fiddling self-consciously with his cirth pendant. "You're right. It wasn't my best moment."

"Thank you. And perhaps I did go a little bit overboard with my threats." The two of us are quiet for a while; then Theo straightens up.

"Okay, we're going to find another quest, and this time, please don't threaten to turn anyone into a pig."

"Where's the fun in that?" I grumble. I rest my non-chin on my non-hands and wonder what sort of trouble we'll wander into next as Theo looks around the forest.

After some deliberation,[12] we decide to follow the path deeper into the forest to avoid the overzealous villagers.

"I'm telling you, we won't find anyone in here," I say. "I highly doubt they'd—" I pause, my senses pricking. "Do you hear that?"

"Hear what?"

"Go to the left."

Theo wades through the underbrush, swatting away at curtains of vines.

"Keep going," I say. "There!"

A few paces away, half-hidden by foliage, is a thin girl who looks around Theo's age. She's sitting at the base of a tree, weeping softly.

---

12 Deliberation: (*noun*) A thoughtful conversation or debate in the form of "We're going this way." "No, *this* way." "No, THIS way." "Your way is wrong." "Your FACE is wrong."

Theo approaches carefully and says a hesitant, "Hello."

The girl looks up and quickly brushes an arm across her tearstained cheeks. "I don't recognize you," she says, rather peevishly. "You're not from any of the villages around here."

"Um . . . right. I am from a very faraway land," Theo says, pronouncing every word very, very slowly in bad Mandarin.

The girl sniffs. "You have a strange accent." Her belly rumbles loudly, and she clutches it and groans. "I'm starving. Do you have any food?"

"I can conjure up some." Theo mutters a quick incantation, drawing power from his silly little pendant, and a peanut butter sandwich appears in his hand.

His pendant flashes red, and Theo's face turns pale. "I'm running out of cirth," he whispers, as he hands the sandwich to the girl.

"Your qì is incredibly powerful!" she gasps.

"Um, not really. And now I'm almost out of ci—"

I give a vicious tug on Theo's hair. "They don't know what cirth is, remember? Conjuring food used to be something only the most well-trained magician could do."[13]

"Um, I had this in my pocket," Theo says without much conviction. "I slipped it out of my pocket when you weren't looking."

The girl eyes the sandwich with all the glee one reserves for a sack of raccoon droppings. "What is it?"

---

13 Spells that require the creation of something tangible out of nothing are the most difficult to master, and therefore the most expensive in terms of energy usage. There is a reason why most schools in the States only teach their students to conjure up the most basic of food items. It's just not worth wasting all that cirth to conjure up food when you can nip to the supermarket and buy yourself a sandwich. As it is, Theo's sandwich is looking a bit sorry. I'm pretty sure the bread's stale, and that peanut butter looks a little bit too neon for my liking. Still, I can't fault him too much. You'd be hard pressed to find another kid who can rustle up a better-looking PB sandwich. Conjuration, it's hard.

"It's a peanut butter sandwich." Theo thrusts it at the girl, who shies away.

"What are those things? You're trying to poison me!" she shouts.

Sighing, I cast a spell of illusion on the sandwich, making it appear as a freshly steamed pork bun. Her eyes go wide with need, and without another word, she grabs the bun from Theo's hands and eats the entire thing in three bites.

And once again, the great and wondrous fox spirit saves the day.

"Why were you crying?" Theo says.

The girl glares at him. "I wasn't."

This is going to take a while. "Let me handle this," I whisper. I switch my vocal chords to Theo's again and bellow, "Heed my words, puny hum—girl! I am the apprentice of a grand master. He heard you crying up in Tai Shan and sent me to help with your mundane problems. I command you to tell me why you were sobbing like a trapped rabbit!"

The girl's mouth drops open. If this one runs away, too, Theo's not going to be well pleased. But just as I think that, the girl narrows her eyes and says, "Who's your master?"

"Grand Master Liaotai," I say.

"Haven't heard of him before. What's he grand master at?"

"Um . . . medicine?"

The girl jumps to her feet. "Are you a healer? Please save my father. I was on my way to Banpo village to fetch the healer, but I lost my money pouch along the way, and—"

"Your father isn't Mr. Huang, is he?" Theo says.

"How did you know?" the girl says with obvious wonderment.

"Um . . . well, I am all-knowing, obviously," I say.

"You're a true celestial being!" She kneels and bows her head until it touches the forest floor. "Please forgive my insolence. I beg you, help my father. Someone has used gǔ on him—"

"What's gǔ?" Theo asks.

The girl's eyes narrow. "You don't know what gǔ is?"

"I'm just testing you," I bark. "Gǔ is magic created by sealing poisonous creatures such as snakes, scorpions, and centipedes in a container so they kill one another. The surviving creature absorbs the toxins of the others and is used to create the strongest poison."

"You're wise indeed, O heavenly one!"

"Call me Ruowen," Theo says. "What's your name?"

"I am Tu."

"As in 'mud'?" Theo says.

The girl shrugs. "My parents meant to write shì for 'scholar,' but they're not the best writers."[14]

As Tu leads the way back to the village, Theo questions her about her father.

"Tell me his symptoms," he says.

"They are the most terrible! He has profuse diarrhea and has been vomiting for the past few days."

"Sounds like um . . . what's Mandarin for 'dysentery' or 'cholera'?" Theo mumbles.

"Who are you talking to, O wondrous being?"

---

14 For reference: the character which Tu's parents should've written was 士 for "scholar," but they ended up with 土, which means "dirt" or "mud" instead. Unfortunate, but it happens.

"I communicate with celestial spirits who have chosen to remain on earth," I say quickly before whispering to Theo the Mandarin words for "dysentery" and "cholera."

The girl gasps when Theo says the words out loud. "Oh my, they sound like the worst gǔ magic."

"Yes, you're very fortunate to have come across me," I say, then tell Theo, "Not that I know how to cure either of those things."

Theo doesn't say anything, but I can practically sense the gears of his mind whirring. By the time we reach the village, the goatherd's back. He gives a shout when he spots Theo, and others come running with their farming tools. One of the more intrepid villagers arrives with a large cleaver.

"The sorcerer has returned to eat us all!" the boy yells.

"What are you talking about, Yirong?" Tu says.

Yirong gestures wildly at Theo. "He's a sorcerer!"

"He's a celestial being." Tu looks at Theo with a world of hope in her eyes. "He will cure my father of the gǔ that has poisoned him."

"I hope whatever illusion spell they're using doesn't let you feel pain," I mutter, "because that cleaver looks sharp."

# THEO

# 12

My mind is churning as I follow Tu into one of the wooden huts. I shouldn't be here. Kai's right, I'm not Jamie. I'm not into medicine and all that stuff. But still, a part of me is convinced that this would have been the quest that Jamie chose, and because of that, I must see it through. Maybe this is even a quest that Jamie himself designed. Tears flood my vision at the thought. I must complete this quest.

Mr. Huang lies on a pallet on the floor. He's deathly pale, and his breath comes in little rapid gasps. His skin hangs loose like ill-fitting clothes, his bones jutting out sharply. And the stench is so strong, it's a physical blow. I breathe through my mouth as I crouch down to inspect him.

"Baba, I've brought a healer to cure you," Tu says softly.

Mr. Huang's crusted eyes crack open, but he can't seem to muster the strength to speak.

"There's no hope for him," Kai whispers. "You don't have enough cirth to perform anything complicated enough to cure dysentery or whatever this is, and I can't do any healing spells. If he dies on your watch, the villagers will turn on you. We must leave."

I try to shut out her words and focus on my memories of Jamie. What would he have done? He was always telling me about different diseases and how to deal with them. I have to believe in him, believe that what he told me in the past would work now.

I stand and say, "Tu, boil some sleep—no, I've pronounced that wrong, haven't I—boil some . . . water—and um, bring me salt and a knife. And please give me some privacy."

Tu and the villagers hurry out, and for the moment, Kai and I are left alone with Mr. Huang.

"Brilliant," Kai says. "You got rid of them so we can escape—"

"Nope." I take a deep breath, steeling myself. "This is where you come in, my dear shape-shifting fox."

"I'm sorry, what?"

Now or never. I've bet everything on this. "You need to shape-shift into an IV infusion set," I say.

"I—what?"

"Mr. Huang needs to be rehydrated, and the fastest way of administering the liquids is through his veins. Plus, like you pointed out, I don't have enough cirth to conjure up anything."

"I've got news for you: an IV infusion set's not one of the forms I've ever thought to master," Kai snaps.

My stomach plummets. Oh no, I've grossly miscalculated Kai's abilities. She's always boasting about how powerful she is, but I should've known that was all bluster. But I can't give up now. I desperately search for any ideas and grasp at one. "What about a needle and syringe?"

Kai doesn't answer.

"I know you know how to shape-shift into that. I know Jamie taught you to shape-shift into all sorts of medical tools."

There's an irritated huff from somewhere on my scalp. "Do you know how much qì is required for me to change into an inanimate object? It's not like shape-shifting into a different animal. Turning into an object, one without muscle and blood and a nervous system—it's very complicated. It is exhausting, boy. Takes a lot out of you. I don't—"

I swallow the lump in my throat. "Kai? Don't forget, we're doing this for Jamie."

Kai's quiet. Then she says, in a voice heavy with sorrow, "You're right. For Jamie." She scuttles down from my head to my hand, raising goose bumps on my skin as she goes. For a moment, she's perfectly still, then there's a flash of light and on my palm is a hypodermic needle and syringe, with Kai's hind legs and two tails sticking out the back.

My breath releases in a whoosh. "Thank you." I hide Kai in my pocket just as Tu comes back into the room. I wait for Tu to set everything down on the floor and leave, before slipping Kai out of my pocket.

I put her down on a piece of cloth while I mix the salt and the water. Then, taking another deep, shaky breath, I pick up the knife that Tu brought and prick my own arm.

The syringe develops a mouth, and Kai says, "That seems terribly unhygienic."

I ignore her and mutter a couple of spells while letting a few drops of blood plop into the pot of water. Cirth flows out of my pendant and down my arm. The strands of light intertwine, each made of a hundred different shades of green that blink and flicker endlessly.

"What are you doing?" Kai says as the gossamer light touches the water and creates little sparkling waves.

"Turning the salt water into the right mix of electrolytes."

"How do you know what's the right mix of electrolytes?"

"I don't. I'm using Samwell's Same Same but Different spell so the water mimics the electrolytes in my blood. And I'm adding Spraggwistle's Stroke of Serendipity for a bit of luck."

The syringe tuts. "Oh dear."

"Look, I'm twelve, okay? The only healing spell they've taught us is Scrabbleson's Grow Scab on Skinned Knees, and I don't have enough cirth to do even that. At least mimicry and luck spells are cheap. Okay, the mixture's done. Ready?" I say to Kai. I don't tell her that I myself am very definitely not ready.

"Always," Kai says.

I pick her up and fill her with the makeshift electrolyte mix.

"Um, you'll have to help me find a vein once you're in there. I don't have the cirth to do any sort of locate spell, and um, I have no idea how to do this." My hands tremble as I hold the needle against Mr. Huang's pallid arm. Now that I'm about to pierce his skin, this feels like a terrible, awful, horrible idea. But there's no going back.

"What could possibly go wrong?" Kai says, and with that, I plunge the needle into Mr. Huang's arm.

# THEO
# 13

Mr. Huang grimaces as I jab Kai into his arm. If he wasn't so ill and weak, he'd probably thrash around, especially as Kai wiggles inside his flesh, looking for a vein. I keep one hand on the syringe and raise the other, about to do a spell to take away some of the pain, when I realize I don't have the cirth to do that. I wasted it on stupid stuff like sorting through the mess in my room. I grit my teeth as Mr. Huang twitches in pain and make myself a promise to never, ever waste cirth again.

"Kai, have you found it yet?" I whisper.

Her voice comes out muffled. "It's really difficult for me to move as an inanimate object. Hang on, I need to use more qì to move—" I startle as the needle jerks a little in my hand, moving back and forth. The little paws at the back of the syringe wiggle a bit, adjusting its angle. "Okay. Ugh, his veins are all shrunken and shriveled thanks to dehydration, and it's so dark in here—oh, I think I found one. Right. I'm in."

I push the plunger slowly, watching as the fluid flows into Mr. Huang's arm. This is crazy. I have absolutely no idea what I'm doing. How much fluid should I pump into him? Is the fluid even filled with the correct electrolytes? What if I kill him? A not-so-small part of my mind is screaming, *Aaaaaaaaa!*

But even as panic gnaws at me, Mr. Huang's scrunched-up face brightens. The gray pallor of his skin is replaced with a golden light, leaving behind a rosy hue. His sunken cheeks fill out, and though he remains shockingly thin, he no longer looks like he's about to break into a thousand pieces.

"What's happening?" I say in wonderment.

"Incredibly, your plan seems to be working. His veins are fattening up."

Mr. Huang is now wearing an expression as serene as that of Guan Yin, the goddess of mercy. For a moment, I let myself relax, and that's when his eyes snap open.

Brilliant light spills out of him, blinding me. Even with my eyes closed, I can sense the dazzling light burning through my eyelids. I cry out and raise an arm to shield myself.

Gradually, voices pour in from all around me.

"—so cool!"

"What was your illusion?"

"Which quest did you choose?"

I lower my arm and open my eyes. I'm back at the facility, except there's nowhere near the original number of kids. Now, it's closer to fifty.

I pat around in my pockets—thank goodness my normal clothes are back—becoming increasingly panicked when I can't find Kai. What if she somehow got left in the illusion—

"Stop groping yourself—it's very unbecoming."

"Kai? Is that you?" I whisper. "Where are you?" I pat my head to check if she's there.

"Careful! I'm back in louse form."

"We did it, Kai!" Gratitude flows through my entire being. I almost wish I could grab Kai and hug her right now. Which is very definitely weird, because it's Kai we're talking about.

"Shh, you're getting all loud and flappy. Go make some friends. All those changes and spells have drained me. Gods, I hate changing into inanimate objects. Half my muscles still think they're a syringe. Oh, I feel awful, if only I had more qì . . ."

A short while later, I hear the faint sound of snoring from the top of my head. Great. I skulk around the fringes of the group for a bit, unsure what to do or say.

All around me, kids chatter excitedly about their successful quests. I inch toward them hesitantly. I'm trying to appear innocent, but the more I tell myself not to think of Jamie's message, the more it fills my mind. It's like trying not to think of a pink elephant. In this state, I might very well end up blurting, *Hi, I'm Theo, and I'm here to solve the mystery of my brother's dying message.*

Two boys, one Indian, the other Chinese, notice me approaching and pause their conversation.

"Hi, I'm Rishi."

I smile at him. "Theo."

The other boy looks me over. "I'm Danny."

"What was your illusion?" Rishi asks me.

"A farming village in ancient China. What was yours?"

"Mine was in Magadha."

"That's *so* cool," Danny says. "It's one of the sixteen great kingdoms of ancient India. I wish I could see it." He turns to me and adds, so very casually, "My illusion was on the Great Wall, right before Genghis Khan attacked."

Wow. Their illusions sound ten million times more impressive than mine. How come the spell plopped me in the middle of some sleepy nowhere-village?

A door opens, and Xiuling, Saanvi, and a white man I don't recognize walk into the room. The chatter inside immediately stops, and we watch intently as the three of them cast some spell of levitation so they hover over us.

"Congratulations!" Saanvi says with a huge grin. "You are the first fifty kids to pass the test! Everyone else who passes after this point will be sent home."

We erupt into cheers, and it sinks in that I've passed. I'm in. I'll be able to do the task Jamie has sent me here to do.

"After refreshments, you can go back home to pack your things. Come back here tomorrow, and you will be shown to your living quarters. Now, time for lunch!" She waves, and huge platters of food appear.

The feast is amazing—there's food from both of the countries represented here, plus others I don't recognize. There are at least six different curries, platters piled high with pork dumplings, and buns so fresh they're still steaming, and then there's dessert. Rainbow-colored rice cakes, fried golden dough balls dripping with syrup, and caramel-colored coconut candies.

As everyone rushes forward, the man standing next to Saanvi says, "I need to speak with one of you." His voice sounds hushed, and yet it slices over the noise in the room, impossible to ignore. He must be using some sort of voice magnifying spell, but I can't spot any of cirth's telltale green light.

The voice isn't the only thing that's weird about him, though. There's just something really off about him, like he's both young and old at the same time. His skin is so smooth, Ma would totally want to know what anti-aging cream he uses if she were here, but his hair is streaked with gray. And then there are the eyes, which are so light they're almost colorless, making his pupils stand out like pinpricks. I'm just saying, I do not envy the kid he wants to have a one-on-one chat with.

"Theodore Tan." His expression is cold iron. "Come outside and see me. Now."

Welp.

Somewhere in the crowd, some boy says, "Oooh, he's in truh-bullllll."

My feet move, seemingly of their own accord, to the door. I can feel the weight of eyes on me, piercing my skin like a thousand insects. Danny whispers something to Rishi, and they both watch as I leave the room.

The door closes behind me and seals tight, shutting out all the noise. I'm left alone with the tall man, and in the silence, I can hear my heart going *thwackthwackthwack* rapidly. Can he hear it, too?

"Follow me." He walks away with wide, efficient strides, his movements as graceful as those of a cat.

I've never thought about what a "clipped voice" sounds like, but now I know. The words coming out of his mouth sound like they've been snipped by a pair of very sharp scissors. I hurry after him, rushing through all my options. Above us, Eyes float here and there and stare unblinkingly at me. Burly guards stride down the corridors, pausing to salute the man as they pass.

The man leads me to a large office. The plaque outside the door says CREIGHTON WARD, INTERIM DIRECTOR.

His office is spacious and bright, everything pristine white. And I mean everything, including the stationery and every book in the floor-to-ceiling shelves.

"Sit," he says, settling into a chair behind a huge white desk. Then he suddenly grins, and it reminds me of Kai baring her sharp teeth at me. The resemblance is so close that for a second, it startles me.

I perch on the chair opposite him, which turns out to be the most uncomfortable chair in the world. The slightest move I make causes it to creak and groan, the sounds unbearably loud in the silent office. The man watches as I fidget and try to find a position I can tolerate.

"I am Creighton Ward, director of the Reapling Corporation."

"Don't you mean 'interim director'?" I blurt out. Oh man, why did I have to say that? "Sorry, I just—I didn't mean to be rude. I'm very sorry to hear about Mr. Taslim—he was a great man."

When he passed away last year, everybody was convinced we'd plunge into a cirth crisis. Rival companies that had sort of figured out how to produce cirth by studying the pendants and reverse engineering them scrambled to try to get a share of the market, but none of them came close to producing the amount of cirth that Reapling Corp. did. Taslim's method is still a secret, and by far the most effective there is.

"He was, wasn't he?" Creighton says with a dramatic sigh. His nose twitches, and it reminds me so much of Kai that I almost give a nervous laugh. "A true revolutionary. None of this would've been possible without his ingenuity." He waves a hand vaguely at the building we're in, all the people milling around and working there, and the test area. "But we're not here to discuss that." He reaches into his breast pocket with slender fingers and removes a small sphere, which he places in the middle of the table. "Play Theo Tan's entrance test."

The sphere cracks open, and an imp the size of my thumb hops out. Its skin is a deep shade of violet, and its little face is so wrinkly I can barely see its features. It stretches its arms, cracks its tiny fingers, and squeaks, "Opening file 001635276-G."

I've never seen an imp in action. I'm expecting it to read out the events that happened during my entrance test. Instead, it opens its mouth wide, and bright green light spills out, blinding us. I squeeze my eyes shut against the light. When I open them, I find myself back at the rural farming village. I can even feel the sunlight and hear the incessant buzzing of insects in the background. "What the—"

"We're inside the imp's memory," Director Ward says, bending over from behind me so his face is right next to mine, making me jump. "There you are." He points at a figure in the distance.

It's me. Wow.

Despite all the worry and anxiety plaguing me, I can't help but notice stuff like how weird my chin looks, and is that really how I walk? Are my shoulders always so slouched? No wonder Mama's always nagging me to stand up straight. And then virtual me opens his mouth and speaks, and even from this distance, his voice sounds so nasal and annoying I want to punch him in the face.

"Zoom in," Director Ward says.

The imp's memory zooms us closer to virtual me, stopping a few paces away.

"—thing itches," virtual me says, scratching at his hemp tunic.

My face burns and I swallow, waiting for Kai's response. This would be where she tells me I'm wearing hemp.

There's no answer.

"What's that?" virtual me says, frowning down at his cloth boots.

Again, there's no discernible answer, but virtual me looks offended and says, "Excuse you—" before being interrupted by the illusion telling me what I'm supposed to do.

"Pause," Director Ward says, and everything around us, including the leaves and grass swaying in the breeze, freezes. He straightens up and cocks his head at me before quirking his mouth into a playful smile. "Who were you talking to?"

Oh man. What do I say? I gape at him while a hundred years pass. With a sigh, Director Ward snaps his long, pale fingers, and we're suddenly back in his office. The imp flops on his desk, its little chest moving up and down rapidly.

"Um, is he okay?" I say.

"Never mind the imp. Such lesser shén are not worth our time. Back in the spirit world, they would be nothing but servants for the more worthy shén."

"Back in the spirit world?"

Director Ward frowns. "I'm the one asking the questions here. Theo, we scanned all of you for cheating-related spells or charms, but there will always be spells that are able to bypass standard security measures. I heard recently, for example, of a precocious little German girl who wove a new spell that makes her not only invisible, but completely undetectable physically. She's locked up in Germany's highest security prison for now, thank goodness.

"I wouldn't have pegged you as a rogue weaver, but I suppose you lot come in all sorts. Tell me what spell you used to cheat through the test, and maybe I won't report you to the Department of Magical Safety."

"I—I didn't. I've never tried weaving—I wouldn't dare! They're always accidentally blowing themselves up!" I cry, my insides twisting like snakes.

Director Ward's breath releases in a cold hiss. Before I can reply, he waves his hand at me and mutters the incantation for Bagbott's Tongue Loosener. I'm about to shout—he has no right!—but the spell seizes me, and I'm frozen to the chair. Bagbott's spell grants the caster one question, to be answered honestly before the person it's used on can be released from the bindings of the spell. The State of California allows parents and legal guardians the use of the spell on their kids, but no one else, not even teachers, is allowed to use it on minors. Even cops have to get warrants to use it on suspects.

As I watch, unable to move my lips, Director Ward leans close. I can see each white-blond eyelash lining his strange eyes. I realize then that I have never known true fear until this moment. I'm this close to peeing myself.

He opens his mouth and asks slowly, forming each word with care, "What hideous spell did you use to cheat your way through the entrance test?"

Phew. I just got very, very lucky. "I did not use any spell to cheat through the test," I say, holding his eye. The bonds of the spell break, and I slump in my seat, breathing hard. "That was illegal!"

Director Ward gives another one of his non-smiles. "You—or rather, your parents—signed a waiver that gives Reapling Corp. the right to use such spells on you if we have cause for suspicion."

What? Last night, when Xiuling sent me the forms and waivers to sign, I didn't bother to read through any of them before asking Mama and Baba to sign. If Reapling Corp. has the audacity to put in stuff about Bagbott's Tongue Loosener, what other rights have I signed away?

"Unfortunately, we were only granted the right to perform Bagbott's spell once on each candidate, but I'm sure I can rustle up some other way to find out how you cheated—"

I can't bear another moment in this man's presence. "I was talking to my brother," I blurt out.

"Your brother?" He turns to the imp, which seems to have recovered from the spell of illusion. "Scan for family match."

"Hang on—" I say. The imp jumps up and plucks a strand of hair from my head. "Ow!" I reach out to try to catch it, but it crams the strand into its mouth. Ew.

"Connecting to imp number 1279A," the imp says, as it chews. "Please search for family match." Its eyes unfocus for a few seconds as it does a mind link with some other imp. "Match found.

Jamie Tan, seventeen-year-old male, intern at Know Your Roots. Status: deceased."

Tears scratch their way down the back of my throat at the clinical way the imp said "Deceased."

"You were talking to your deceased brother . . . that's the most heartbreaking thing I've ever heard, Theo," Director Ward says, his voice completely devoid of pity.

It's hard to talk. I can't believe I'm using Jamie like this. "I started doing that after his accident."

"I'm very sorry." Director Ward links his fingers into a steepled arch and puts them under his chin. "Well, Theo, I must apologize to you most sincerely."

"It's okay." I just want to get out of here.

"Doesn't the memory of your brother make it painful for you to be here?"

What would Jamie have thought of Creighton Ward? As soon as I think that, I see him in my mind's eye, laughing and saying, *I'd like to see Creighton Ward have a face-off with Ma. She'd come at him with the feather duster, and that would be it.*

I want to have that conversation with Jamie so bad it hurts.

"I miss him so much," I say, and for the first time, I'm being completely honest with Director Ward. "He was so into this program. Being here makes me feel closer to him." The last few words come out in a whisper.

"Interesting." Director Ward's nose twitches again, and the movement is familiar in an odd way. "Well, needless to say, you're admitted to the program. See you here bright and early tomorrow," Director Ward says.

I practically run out of his office, my muscles watery with relief. I feel as though I need a purification ritual, or a charm to ward off evil. A few paces away, I glance back, and my blood freezes.

Creighton Ward is standing behind his glass office wall, watching me with his cold, dead eyes. And he's smiling the first real smile I've seen him wear—the smile of a shark who smells blood in the water.

# KAI

# 14

"Oho, what have we here?" a voice—there's no other word for it—moos.

Before I even open my eyes, I know I'm back in the spirit world. But not the part of the spirit world I'm familiar with. No heady scent of yùlán magnolia trees here, nor the chattering of the usual shén and small, mostly harmless yāoguài. Instead, I'm surrounded by dead and dying trees, their bare branches curled like a witch's fingers and weighed down with yāoguài. Ones that would make even Chao have second thoughts.

I sit up and blink blearily. This is not right. Once a companion spirit is claimed by a human master, it's extremely difficult for someone other than the human master to summon and dismiss the spirit. Whoever summoned me to the spirit world, they must be extremely powerful to be able to overcome my bond with Theo. I must step carefully.

"Could it be—surely not—Kai the fox spirit is much too prissy for this neighborhood," the voice booms.

Fear runs through my veins, but if I let even a tiny bit slip out, all those creatures hiding behind the dry brush and the rocks, all those bloodstained claws and hungry teeth will be upon me. We are dangerously close to Diyu. I can feel the heat of the volcano that's forever raging there and hear the distant screaming of the tortured souls.

*Out of the darkness, a large, brutish figure steps. My fur bristles. "Oh, it's you," I say as flippantly as I can.*

*Niu Tou snorts, and when a demon with an ox's head snorts, it's actually quite impressive. "You'd do well to cower in my presence, húlíjīng!"*

*He's right,[15] but I'm not about to admit that I'm this close to widdling myself. "Eh. Where's Horse Face?"*

*"I told you not to call my brother that!" Niu Tou roars. The trees shake, and a few of the smaller yāoguài slink off.*

*"It's quite literally what he's called," I say.[16]*

*"Yes, but you're saying it like it's an insult!"*

*"Well, he's actually got a horse's face . . . not that yours is any better, mind you."*

*"Enough!" Niu Tou lifts his fearsome trident, his massive snout flaring. "Kai, I've waited a long time to snatch your soul to Diyu, where I shall throw you down the Mountain of Knives, and then plunge you into the Cauldron of Boiling Oil, and then—"*

*"As pleasant as all of that sounds, I don't think I'll be following you to Diyu. I haven't broken any karmic laws." As I talk, I cast about for escape routes.*

*Niu Tou grins slyly. "Why do you think we decided to summon you now? Because we sensed it, Kai. You succumbed to your inherently*

---

15 My feud with Niu Tou and his brother Ma Mian goes back centuries. Back when I was a brash young spirit fox, I may have played a few ill-conceived pranks on them, like shape-shifting into one of them to fool the other. Not one of my finest decisions, even though it was good for a laugh. They are the two guards of the underworld, with direct access to the higher demons of hell, which would explain how they managed to gather enough power to summon me to the spirit world.

16 Niu Tou's and Ma Mian's names literally translate to Ox Head and Horse Face. I cannot make this stuff up.

evil fox spirit nature, which is why you find yourself here, so close to the first circle of hell."

"I didn't—" And then it hits me. I have. I helped Theo cheat his way through a test. "But I didn't have a choice. My master ordered me to," I say, my voice coming out wobbly.

"That's a pathetic excuse." Niu Tou shakes his head at me in mock disappointment. "You should've told your master what it would do to your karma."

"I—" For the first time, I don't have a comeback. He's right. I should've explained harder, made it clearer to Theo that every wicked act I perform in the human world, such as helping a human cheat on a test, will push me closer to turning into a demon. "That's not enough to turn me into a demon. It was a minor infraction. I'm a spirit, not a demon, therefore I'm not under your authority!"

Niu Tou roars with laughter. "Silly húlíjīng! We've all seen it before. You start by breaking minor rules of morality, but soon you'll break bigger ones, and before you know it, you'll become a full-fledged demon." Niu Tou narrows his eyes and takes a huge lungful of air. "I smell the beginnings of demonic stirrings within you, little fox." He grins. "Soon. I just need a touch more demon within you, and then the next time we summon you back here, I'll be able to CATCH YOU!" He pounces, lunging with his trident.

I turn on my tails and dash into the dead trees as fast as I can, but I can't outrun Niu Tou's booming laughter.

"Soon!"

# KAI

# 15

I'm not my usual chirpy, delightful self the following morning. Understandable, considering what happened last night with Niu Tou. But no matter, nothing like that will happen again. Me helping Theo cheat through his test was a one-time occurrence, an unavoidable task I had to perform to get us into the program. But from now on, I shall be the best-behaved little goldfish that ever goldfished.

Mr. and Mrs. Tan drop us off at the entrance of Reapling, and we order a travel bubble and fly in nervous silence toward the dormitories.

The dorms are a cluster of cabins at the western edge of the facility. The whole area is filled with pines and redwoods. The air is markedly cooler, and sounds from the rest of the facility are muted, replaced by the chirpings of birds. I can't help but be impressed by the area. Fox spirits like woods; that's where we come from. In the deepest and darkest corners of the forest, my ancestors were born and learned to survive through cunning alone. The woods were where they led their victims, mostly humans, to feed on their qì without being interrupted. I am past all that, of course, no qì-eating from yours truly.[17]

The bubble drops us off in front of a beautiful cabin that

_____
17 What's that stuck between my teeth, you say? Nothing. Just a bit of qì-ken. Heh-heh. No, really, it's just chicken.

looks like something straight out of a fairy tale—huge and rambling, with uneven walls and gently sloping roofs, curtains of ivy creeping all around it, flowers spilling out the windows, and a tree growing right through it. Without meaning to, Theo and I pause, staring at the sight before us. We glance at each other, and whether it's because of our surroundings or because we look so ridiculous with our mouths gaping wide, we both start laughing.

After a while, Theo says, "Hey, um. I just wanted to thank you. For like, helping me pass the test and stuff."

"Ah." I was prepared for some snarky comment from him, but the sincere gratitude is catching me off guard. "Um, you're welcome. It was a one-off favor, though. Cheating is really quite bad for one's karma."

Theo nods. "Okay. Um, also . . ." He steps closer to me and lowers his voice. "I don't know if I'm just being paranoid, and you'll probably just tell me I'm overreacting, but I was questioned by the program director yesterday."

"You were?" I say. "When?"

"Right after the test. You were on my head but you were sleeping. Very helpful, as usual. Anyway, the thing is, I think he's—I don't know, there's something off about him."

I nod. I've seen Creighton Ward around, and something about him definitely rubs me the wrong way. Every time I spot the man, my fur bristles. "Let's focus on why we're here, achieve our goal, and get the blazes out of here," I say.

Theo nods and lowers his voice even more. "The notebook's clues."

Last night, we spent hours huddled over his study desk looking through the notebook. The next part in the notebook was:

> I always felt awful about Hubert. We were
> abusive toward him. I wish that I'd released
> him, even though I know you'd never have
> forgiven me for it, and you'd probably have
> gotten me in trouble.

The words "felt awful," "abusive," "released," and "trouble" were in purple. Theo said this makes no sense, given Hubert didn't exist.

The next paragraph went on to say:

> I wish you'd read more books. Remember
> that awesome library I took you to? You were
> obsessed with this handbook you found on
> the third shelf that tells you details about
> ancient life. I told you there's buried treasure
> somewhere in the library and you went and
> ripped up a floorboard and we both got kicked
> out. Silly Didi.

Theo slumped over his desk and said he was even more confused[18] because unlike the previous paragraph, this one actually has some truth to it.

"Jamie totally loved books. His favorite saying was 'Hǎo shū—'"

_____

18 When is he not confused? That's the question we should all be asking here.

"Hǎo shū rú zhì yǒu!" I practically shouted it. "I know what his favorite saying was, too. In case you didn't know, it means: A good book is like a good friend."

"This isn't a competition, Kai. And I knew what it meant."

"Of course it isn't a competition. It would be far too cruel to pit a lowly human child against a wise, wondrous being such as myself."

Theo rolled his eyes at me. "Anyway, Jamie was always nagging me to stop reading gaming magazines and read actual books, which was a bit snotty of him, to be honest. But I never fell in love with a handbook. I mean, really now, a handbook? How uncool is that?"

"I don't know what you humans consider to be 'uncool.' For example, I would consider playing computer games to be on the high side of the 'uncool' spectrum—"

"Trust me, gaming is far cooler than a handbook," Theo said, with a tone of finality. "Also, I would never vandalize a library like that. Shooting monsters on the computer is as daring as I get."

"Well, the words 'library,' 'handbook,' 'buried treasure,' 'found,' and 'floorboards' are in purple. So maybe there's buried treasure in the library?"

"But which library?" he said.

I sighed at him. "The one at Reapling, obviously."

His eyes widened. "There's a library at Reapling?"

"Why are you so surprised by the fact that a company full of nerds would have a library?"

Now Theo tightens his grip on his backpack and says, "We gotta get to the library as soon as we—"

"Welcome back, Theo."

We both jump. My tiny goldfish heart pumps super hard as we whirl around to see who's just greeted us.

It's Xiuling, looking as perfectly put together as ever. Has she overheard us talking? But she just smiles at us and snaps her fingers. Theo's bags float up and begin to follow us back to the cabin. "Isn't this wonderful? We thought we'd go with a fairy-tale look to really whisk you away from the outside world," Xiuling says. She glances back and smiles at me. "This must be your companion!"

I wave a fin and try to look as goldfishy as I can.[19]

"Yes, her name's Yangwei. She's just a minor shén, nothing exciting about her. She's the only companion my parents could afford."

I wish I could pinch Theo so he'd stop his nervous babbling. I swim up above him,[20] plop myself down at the top of his head, and make myself a comfortable nest in his hair.

"What about you? What's your companion?" Theo says, trying to swat me off.

Xiuling's smile is a bit too ready. "I chose not to have one."

Theo and I stop fighting for a moment and stare at her.

"Why not?" Theo says.

"When I was little, there weren't many regulations in China. Many summonings went wrong—charlatans rousing yāoguài

---

19 Stare gormlessly with my mouth open. It's easy, really. Most animals do it, including humans. I bet you're doing it right this very moment.

20 Okay, I know you're probably wondering, but I'm not technically "swimming," because I'm not underwater. I'm flying, but it's weird to describe "waving my fins around" as flying, right? So let's just say I'm swimming in the air and call it a day, agreed?

instead of shén, or calling the wrong shén, or miscasting the spell in some other way. My brother's Companion Ceremony ended with him—um." Xiuling clears her throat, her eyes clouding over. "Well, it didn't end well. So I decided to forego the ceremony when I came of age."

"Good choice," Theo mutters.

I let a bit of drool drip onto his forehead, and he curses and wipes it off.

Xiuling laughs. "You and your companion make an adorable match. All right, to unlock the front door, all you have to do is stand here—yes, right here, and look into this lens. Perfect."

The security imp inside the lens squeaks, "Theodore Tan." The front door swings open, and we step inside a grand foyer that's much bigger than the outside looks. Despite myself, I'm impressed.

Interesting. The outside of the cabin made me think it was going to be all dark and poky in here, but the inside is modernized and airy. The floors are hardwood and covered in thick shag rugs, and the cabin smells of warm cedar.

"The estate is equipped with the best security system in the world. We have no fewer than five hundred Eyes, so if your things ever get lost, we'll know where to find them," Xiuling says. "We also have trained guards—"

"Whoa!" Theo says, lurching forward. Graceful, as usual.

Xiuling catches him before he face-plants. "Sorry, I forgot to warn you about the entrance rug. It automatically sticks to your shoes. It's supposed to help you take them off."

Theo steps out of his sneakers and they fly into a cabinet. Fuzzy slippers fly out of a different one and settle in front of his feet.

"We really do need to work on those entrance rugs," Xiuling mutters as she slips on a pair of slippers. "I've spent the whole morning saving kids from falling over."

"Wouldn't it be more fun to stand back and laugh as they fall on their silly faces?" I say.

When Xiuling stares at me, I quickly add, "I mean to say, yes, you really need to fix the rugs."

Xiuling flashes me a quick smile before pointing to a small stone fountain. There's no water in it. "And this is our cirth well."

Theo's mouth drops open. "You mean I can refill my pendant for free?"

"Well, usually, yes. But we've drained the well for the purposes of your program."

Theo's face falls.

"We're too reliant on our pendants," Xiuling says. "Ancient magic works much better with your natural qì than it does with cirth. And it's more important than ever to learn to access your natural qì, especially now that Mr. Taslim is gone . . ." For a moment, her face darkens, but then the smile swoops in again. "But don't worry about that! Our top weavers have come up with a dozen other ways to extract more cirth."

"Extract more cirth?" I say. "From what?"

Xiuling laughs. "Your goldfish is a hoot. Sorry, little guy, I meant to say 'create.' They've come up with many ways to create cirth."

We follow her into the living room, which is surprisingly huge. High, high, high ceilings lit with what looks to be a thousand candles. Comfortable, overstuffed couches sit in a rough circle, and a fire crackles in a stone hearth. Even though it's summer and the room should be uncomfortably hot with the fire, there's a promise of a slight chill in the air. I can't quite understand it. I don't feel cold, but I feel like I *should* be cold, and I'm grateful for the fire.

Two boys and two girls have settled into the couches. They're all showing off; various spells are being cast. One of the kids has conjured up marshmallows and is levitating them close to the fire. Another has conjured up mugs of thick hot chai, and yet another is coming up with toppings to sprinkle on the drinks, which is such a human thing to do to a perfectly fine beverage.

"Hi, everyone! Ooh, making tea?" Xiuling says.

The kids grin and say, "Yep!"

A girl with large eyes and bouncy braids at the top of her head says with obvious pride, "They're all different flavors. There's a chocolate chai, there's pumpkin spice chai—"

"They all taste vaguely of boogers, though," the other girl says, and they all laugh, not unkindly.

"This is Theo," Xiuling says.

Greetings are made all around, and another mug of hot booger chai appears and wobbles its way through the air into Theo's hands. He takes a wary sip and smiles. "It tastes great!" The chai maker grins gratefully.

I wave a fin, and they all go, "Awww! How cute!" and swarm around us to pet me. Being this delightful is a burden.

"Namita, Theo's room is right next to yours. Would you mind showing him to his room?" Xiuling says.

Namita, the girl who's conjured up all the chai, jumps up, her braids dancing as she does so. "Sure."

She chatters about some banal human stuff at Theo as we walk up to the second floor, which is sectioned off into ten rooms. A couple of the doors are open, and I catch glimpses of kids talking and laughing. Namita stops at the third door.

"Here we are."

There's a boy inside, unpacking his bag. Clothes, toiletries, and other mundane items that humans use to put themselves together are floating around the room and sliding into drawers. The boy glances up when we enter.

"Heads up, Danny! Presenting . . ." Namita drums her hands on her legs—this girl is an even bigger ham than I am, and that's saying something. "Your neeew roommaaaate!" For someone so small, she sure knows how to project her voice.

Theo gives a hesitant smile. "We've met. Hi, Danny."

Have we? I narrow my eyes at Danny but can't remember him at all.[21]

Danny just shrugs and goes back to unpacking his things.

Namita cocks her head to one side. "Oh man, did I fudge your entrance?"

"No," Theo says hurriedly. "You did great." He heads for the last bed. As we pass by Danny, I notice his companion—a fire

---

21 This is normal, of course, given that humans are so similar and forgettable. Not you, though. You're *very* memorable. What's your name, you say? I know this one. No, I know it, really. B . . . Bertha! No? Are you sure? Well, doesn't matter, I'm calling you Bertha from now on. Stop talking, please, Bertha. You're interrupting the story.

dragon—resting on his pillow. The dragon cracks one eye open and regards me as one would an inconsequential gnat, then closes its eye and resumes its gentle snoring, singeing one corner of Danny's pillow. Typical snotty dragon who thinks it's better than everyone else. I stick my tongue out at it.

"Gotta say, I'm surprised to see the cheater back in the program," Danny says.

Theo freezes.

"The what now?" Namita says, her eyes widening.

Danny lowers his voice conspiratorially, though not low enough that Theo and I can't hear it. "Yesterday, after the entrance test, Theo was the one called to Director Ward's office. We all know it's because he cheated on the test . . ." His voice trails away as he looks pointedly at Theo. Ouch.

Theo scowls. "If he called me in for cheating, do you really think I'd be here?"

"All I know is, he didn't look happy when he called you in," Danny says.

Dear me. Time to rescue my master. "Actually, Director Ward wanted to personally congratulate Theo on doing so well during his test. He mentioned that a few of the other kids"—I nod at Danny—"barely scraped by, but Theo passed with flying colors."

Danny's mouth curls into a sneer. "How curious. A goldfish shén. Couldn't afford better, I see. Does it perform a function aside from telling lies?"

"Does your face perform a function aside from looking gormless?" I say, and make a rude gesture which is somewhat lost in translation due to fish not possessing any fingers.

Danny gets the gist, though. His cheeks burn a very interesting shade of red. Behind him, the fire dragon rises slowly, languidly, growing in size until he towers over us. Smoke drifts out of his nostrils as he stares down at me.

"Little goldfish," he rumbles, and my essence vibrates with the strength of his qì, "do not presume to speak to my master in that tone, or you will find yourself burned to a crisp."

My insides turn a wee bit watery. It's hard not to when an actual fire-breathing dragon threatens you with immolation. Danny smirks.

"Ahem." Namita clears her throat. "Not to sound like a know-it-all, but I'm pretty sure burning someone to a crisp is against the program's rules. And the California health and safety code." She shrugs when the fire dragon glowers at her. "Don't look at me—I didn't make the rules."

"Stop that," Theo says, snatching me out of the air and stuffing me (not gently, mind you) into his pocket. "I'm very sorry about that," he says to Danny. "Yangwei's not the most well-behaved companion. I just got her a couple of days ago, and I still need to train her."

Danny sniffs. "There's no use putting lipstick on a pig. Teaching that one manners is a waste of time. You should dismiss her. Bad companions are worse than having no companions."

Theo sighs. "You're right. I can't afford a dismissal just yet, though, so for now, I'm stuck with her."

I won't lie; that hurt. It hurt even more because not so long ago, I was actually wanted. Jamie told me he spent weeks looking up various shén and researching their histories. And out of the millions of shén he could have had, he'd chosen me. Me, me, me.

Now here I am, peeping out of Theo's pocket, seething with shame and boiling with hurt at my new master's rejection.

And when I see Danny turn away and stroke his fire dragon's scales with a loving hand, I have to put my fins over my heart to keep it from breaking.

# THEO
# 16

As soon as I finish unpacking, I leave the room, because I can't stand being near Danny. What's his problem, anyway?

My head's still buzzing as I make my way to the commons for orientation. The commons is a beautiful clearing surrounded by cabins and pine trees, but I'm so upset I can't appreciate any of it. The whole exchange with Danny has rattled me, and I'm suddenly missing Jamie so, so much that I have to blink away my tears before I start bawling. I force myself to focus on the reason I'm here. Jamie's notebook. Right. There's a shout, and I turn around to find Namita hurrying toward me.

"Hey," I say awkwardly.

"Oh man—" She pauses to catch her breath. "I just wanted you to know that I toootally don't believe Danny about you cheating on the test."

Welp. "Um. Thank you." I pretend not to hear the small snort from Kai.

"Don't thank me. I'm just saying, it's pretty near impossible to cheat your way through a Reapling test. They've got the best security system in North America." She looks down her nose at me. Or tries to, anyway. She's a lot shorter than I am, so she has to tilt her head way back to look down her nose at me. "No offense, but I don't think you have what it takes to fool Reapling."

"None taken."

"I really hate bullies like Danny. He reminds me of a few of the kids in my school."

I stare at Namita. When I first saw her back at the cabin, I assumed that she's so outgoing she wouldn't understand what it's like to deal with people like Danny or Skinner. But I guess that's how it goes with assumptions; they're rarely ever right.

"Yeah," I say. "He reminds me of this boy from school called Skinner Bannion."

Namita makes a face. "Ew, what kind of name is that? My tormentor is called Anastasia Aurora Bella McKenny. I bet she and Danny would get along."

I have to laugh at that. "You just made her name up, didn't you?"

"No! She really is called that! I applied here to get away from the Anastasias of the world. I should've known they're everywhere. Oh gods, what if we get bullied here, too? I can't be an outcast in a program for outcasts! That's just too horrible for words!" she cries.

"You seemed like you were making friends just fine back at the cabin."

"Are you kidding? Did you not hear that girl say that my chai tastes like boogers? Anyway, whatever. It's fine. I'm glad we're here, despite the bullies. This program is so awesome. My grandparents are from Jaipur, and I've never been, but they used to tell me all these stories about their village. And would you believe it, my illusion during the test was actually in Jaipur!"

"What's Jaipur like?" I say, and listen with increasing awe as

Namita tells me about the majestic Hawa Mahal—the Palace of Winds, which apparently looks like a giant pink honeycomb.

"I can't describe it right." Namita sighs. She waves her hands nimbly and says the incantation for Seewort's See What's in My Mind, conjuring a miniature image on her palms of the most beautiful, intricately designed palace I have ever seen.

"Wow." I wonder if I could conjure up something half as impressive, but realize belatedly that I drained my pendant during the test. Dread bubbles in my stomach. How am I going to get through the program without any cirth?

"Yeah, my great-great-great-great-great-great-aunt used to deliver silks there." Namita closes her palms, and the image disappears. "Tell me about your illusion!"

"Um—" I scramble to come up with something more impressive than, *It was in a tiny farming village.*

Luckily, just then, a travel bubble flies to the center of the grass, and Xiuling and Saanvi step out. I look behind me and realize that while Namita and I were busy chatting, the rest of the kids have gathered around.

"Hi, guys!" Saanvi says. "Everyone ready to start the program?" She's met with a chorus of yeses.

"Awesomesauce! We're so excited to have all of you here. You guys blew us away with your performances during the entrance test. Some of you came up with absolutely brilliant stuff . . ."

From the corner of my eye, I notice Danny simpering, as though Saanvi has just addressed him personally. Barf. He reminds me so much of Skinner Bannion, in how much they both suck up to teachers and how much they both suck in general.

"The purpose of our program is to reconnect all of you with your ancestral culture's mythology. Now, unfortunately we don't have the time to delve into every specific regional culture because there is so much variance within each country. India alone has thousands of different cultures with distinct ethnic and religious histories. But we've chosen the most popular historical texts that most of you should have an ancestral connection to, namely the *Mahabharata* and the *Shan Hai Jing*, though I promise most of our work will be practical. All right! Ready to start?"

Another chorus of yeses greets her, although this one's less enthusiastic. I'm glad I'm not the only one here who thinks reading old texts sounds about as fun as braiding nose hair.

"Awesome! Take off your pendants."

We stare at one another in confusion. She might as well have asked us to shave our heads.

Saanvi laughs. "Trust me. Take them off."

Reluctantly, we do as she says. I lift the necklace over my head and hold the little golden oval in my hand tightly, hating how small and vulnerable I feel without it.

Xiuling raises her hands, and our pendants are yanked from our fists. They fly toward the two adults and straight into a bag that Saanvi has conjured up. My heart is beating like a war drum, and the other kids are muttering unhappily.

"Calm down, guys," Saanvi says. "They'll be given back to you at the end of the program." She has to raise her voice above our protests. "Listen, we're not taking away your pendants for kicks.

Did our ancestors have cirth back then? Heck no. They had to rely on their own innate magical energy.

"Up to this point, none of you has had to access your magical energy. Maybe most of you aren't even aware that you have this resource within you."

I shift my weight from one foot to the other, my insides squirming. I mean, in theory I know you could do magic without cirth, but heck if I know how to even begin doing that.

"The thing about magic is that doing it without any training is like trying to read with really bad eyesight. Having a ready source of cirth attached to you is a bit like wearing reading glasses. They help make the task doable, but without your reading glasses, you're helpless.

"But if you learn to unlock your inner source of magical energy, well . . ." Saanvi grins at us. "That would be like fixing your eyesight so you have 20/20 vision. You wouldn't need cirth. We all have this energy. Different cultures may call it by different names—qì, prana, numen, mana, and so on, but it's in all of us.

"It's not going to be easy. Your inner source of magical power is harder to use than cirth by about a bajillion times. But it's so much more powerful when mastered."

"Ha!" a little voice says beside me.

It's Kai, and she's wearing the most obnoxious expression there ever was on a goldfish. "Good to know they're ridding you kids of your cirth dependency," she says.

Don't get me wrong, I like the thought of not being so dependent on cirth. But let's face it—this is total mumbo jumbo. I don't buy for a second that our inner magical energy is more powerful; there's a reason why cirth became such a huge part of everybody's lives. If everyone could access ancestral magical power, why wouldn't they?

As though reading my mind, Kai adds, "It's not just your family that can't easily afford cirth, you know. There is such a lack of diversity in cirth magic, it's really affected many communities, especially ones who aren't as privileged."

My instinctive reaction is to make a face at her, but even as I do, it hits me that she has a point, and a huge part of me is ashamed that I never even thought of how that has affected the poorer communities.

At the end of her speech, Saanvi walks us through simple exercises to help us tap into our "energy source," but instead of breathing deep like she teaches us to, all I can do is worry about my confiscated pendant. Saanvi's reading glasses analogy might sound good, but I've got a better one: using our own "energy source" as opposed to using cirth pods is like choosing to rub two sticks together to make fire when you could just use a lighter. I know technically my pendant is useless now that it's drained, but I just hate knowing I'm without it.

Thankfully, everyone else seems just as disoriented and worried. Even Namita is looking significantly less chirpy, though she follows all of Saanvi's instructions with wide eyes. When Saanvi tells us to hold out our palms and "turn our attention to our core" to access our energy source, whatever that means, Namita's one of the few kids who manages to create sparks of light. The rest of us stare anxiously at our hands. I try to will something—anything—to happen, but my palms remain stubbornly spark-less.

What if I just don't have that magical energy? Will they kick me out of the program? But I'm so sure that this is where Jamie wanted me to go to figure out his message. I can't allow myself to get kicked out.

"You're doing awesome, guys!" Saanvi says, despite all evidence to the contrary.

"Don't worry if you can't produce sparks yet, we don't expect you to get it so soon. As with everything, practice makes perfect," Saanvi says.

Somehow, I doubt practice is going to make much of a difference when it comes to me.

# KAI

# 17

The next few days are challenging. On one hand, I enjoy watching Theo struggle to make do without that silly little pendant hanging from his neck. Every morning, in his half-asleep state, Theo waves at his toothbrush or his comb, and then stands there with the most vacuous expression when the objects fail to fly into his hands. I snort and say, "No pendant" in a singsong voice, and he turns red and grabs his toothbrush like he's trying to strangle it.

On the other hand, his inability to access his qì is seriously putting a damper on our quest. Because of how behind he is, Xiuling has assigned him extra lessons, taking up all of the free time he's supposed to have and thus keeping us from getting to the library.

During the regular lessons, the kids are separated into groups to work within their specific cultures. While Theo's group practices the timeless art of qìgōng, using meditation and moving through martial arts postures, Namita tells us that hers does yoga.

"Yoga?" Theo exclaims, rubbing his sore legs. "That sounds so much easier than qìgōng!"

"Well, we have to do yoga while levitating two feet off the ground. We fall when we lose focus."

"You won't even be able to get yourself an inch off the ground," I mutter to Theo. It's possible that I'm a bit snippy because I expected us to be able to nip into the library and nip right out of Reapling on day one.

"It's pretty easy, once you get the hang of it," Namita says. She is ever so sweet, this one. "It took me a while to understand the concept of it, but you'll get there in no time." And ever so foolish.

Because anyone can see that my master has no hope in Diyu of unlocking his qì. His mind is shrouded under an overdependence on cirth, and his heart is filled with disdain for anything that has to do with his own heritage.

"Look deep within yourself," Xiuling tells him gently, during lessons. "Root out that passion, that longing to reconnect to your ancestral roots."

In answer, Theo nods and pretends like he's trying really hard, which only makes him look like he's desperately trying to stop himself from passing gas.

"Tough, isn't it, when you don't actually have any longing to reconnect with your roots?" I say, and then have to duck quickly when he swats at me.

While the rest of his peers slowly get better at accessing their qì to cast spells, Theo remains about as magical as a lump of rock.

As the days fly and Theo gets no better at unlocking his qì, I can't help but notice that Xiuling is always glancing over during lessons. She checks on Theo's form (pathetic) during qìgōng, adjusts his posture (slouched), and tries in vain to nudge his train of thought (already derailed) onto the right tracks. Without fail, Xiuling always wears a smile while guiding Theo, but with each failed attempt, the smile becomes more and more strained, and a concerned frown begins to crowd it out.

Once, as the children are trying to use their qì to coax paint-brushes into doing Chinese calligraphy, I spot Creighton Ward studying them from a distance. It might be just my imagination, but I could swear that his colorless eyes are trained on Theo. I scrutinize Ward from afar judiciously.

Something about the man isn't quite right. Something is lurking under that flawless veneer of his, but I can't quite put my paw on it. He's like an elegant sonata being played in the wrong key.

I nudge Theo, and he pales when he notices Ward. Teeth gritted, Theo waves his hands at his brush, fighting to get it to stand, but all it does is shiver slightly before clattering back to the table. I look up in time to see Xiuling give Creighton Ward the tiniest shake of her head. His lips thin into a straight line, and he strides off, leaving me with a growing sense of unease deep in my fishy guts. I can't help but wonder if we're about to get kicked out of the program before we even have a chance to set foot in the library, where Jamie's next clue awaits.

# THEO

# 18

By the time we're given our first test, four days after the start of the program, the lack of progress is eating away at me. But between the extra lessons and the rigorous program, there hasn't been a minute free when I could steal away to the library.

After breakfast, instead of our usual lessons, we're told to gather in a cavernous auditorium. Once everyone arrives, Xiuling clears her throat and casts another spell to amplify her voice. "You guys have worked hard to develop and strengthen your inner magical energy," she says. "You've all done well, and we think you're more than ready for your first task."

Cheers and hoots meet her announcement. Everyone's eyes are bright. They're all smiling and leaning forward, eager to put their newly learned skills to work. I can't stop twirling my pen in a manic circle. Whatever the task is, I know I'm going to fail it.

"Awesome!" Saanvi says. "We've hidden magical creatures all over the facility. Your job is to find one and think of ways to release them from their cages. Don't release them yet, just think of ways to do it. Straightforward enough?"

Namita raises her hand.

"Yes?" Saanvi says.

"How big are these creatures? Are any of them dangerous?" Namita says.

Saanvi laughs. "No, of course not."

Next to her, Xiuling makes seesaw motions with her hand.

"Well, some are less friendly than others," Saanvi adds. "But all of them have been enchanted or caged to make sure they can't cause any harm. It's perfectly safe."

Again, Xiuling makes *ehh* faces. "Just approach them with a certain degree of caution and you'll be fine," Saanvi says. "This is your chance to use all these ancient spells we've been learning about."

My stomach lurches. As if it's not challenging enough to have to cast spells without any cirth. But none of the other kids look bothered by it. In fact, many of them look pleased. Monsters.

"What if we locate a creature that isn't from our ancestral culture?" someone else asks.

"Great question," Saanvi says. "Because the program's all about reconnecting you with your heritage, if you do come across a creature that isn't from your ancestral culture, please leave it for someone else to find and continue your search. Sound good?"

This time, there are no more questions.

"All right! Go!"

We disperse like bees looking for flowers. Some of the Chinese kids—like Danny, for example—immediately call up their fancy companions and ride away on them like actual knights. Even I have to admit that Danny looks pretty darned cool, flying off on the back of his fire dragon, which has grown to twice the size it was inside our dorm room. There are at least three other kids with some sort of dragon, and another who rides away on a phoenix. Meanwhile, many of the Indian kids have called forth demigods and spirits to aid them. All around me, yakshas and kinnaras and other spirits I don't recognize appear, their forms powerful and breathtaking.

Then there's me, left alone with my "goldfish." For a second, I feel self-conscious about having a companion who's nowhere near as flashy as the others. But a small voice reminds me that actually, Kai's proven to be a lot more resourceful than I gave her credit for. Maybe she's not as cool as a dragon or as breathtaking as a phoenix, but she did help me get into the program.

As I walk briskly away from the auditorium, it hits me that this is it. While everyone's scattered all over the campus looking for creatures, this is the perfect chance to get to the library! I run to the nearest map and locate the library on there. I'm about to call for a travel bubble when I realize that it might attract too much attention, so I decide to go on foot instead.

Kai pops her head out of my pocket as I run to the other side of campus. "Where are you off to in such a hurry?"

"The—library!" I gasp.

"Ooh, finally." She peers up at me. "Have I pointed out to you how out of shape you are?"

"Many—times."

By the time I get there, I have to pause, resting my hands on my knees to catch my breath while Kai snickers from inside my pocket.

The library looks even smaller than it did on the map. This is great. It won't take me any time at all to find whatever it is Jamie's hidden. When my breath goes from a wheeze back down to just slightly rapid breathing, I straighten up and walk toward the double doors. This is it. I'm finally about to solve the next clue to Jamie's puzzle.

Then I open the doors to the library, and my eyes go like: o_O

I'm inside the largest, most complicated-looking building ever. It's so big it's as though I've stepped into a whole new dimension. I'm in an atrium, with many, many floors visible above me, so many of them that I can't see all the way to the top, and each floor is fitted with endless shelves of books. But from outside, it's so short! I mean, wow. I wish—gods, do I ever wish it—that Jamie were here to show me around.

As I walk deeper into the lobby, I spy a counter where they loan you flying shoes. Flying shoes! I almost cry when I hold my first ever pair of flying shoes in my hands. They smell like gym socks, but who cares? Flying shoes!

I zip up so fast that my eyes well up with the force of the wind. This is amazing. For the first time in weeks, I feel as though I could almost outrun my grief, if only for a moment.

"Slow down," Kai gasps, trying to keep up with me. "They'll kick you out of the library for speeding, and good riddance to you."

Sure enough, one of the Eyes cruising around the library flies toward me and squeaks, "Theodore Tan, there is a flying speed limit of four miles an hour within the library."

"Sorry." Four miles an hour? I might as well be crawling.

"Can I help you locate a particular book? I know all five million, two hundred and forty-seven thousand titles by heart."

I'm about to say no when I look around the library and realize, with crushing certainty, that this was Jamie's favorite place in

Reapling. He would've spent all his free time here. He wouldn't have wanted to take off the flying shoes. I can just see him now, zipping—okay, maybe floating, thanks to the speed limit—around, wearing the dorkiest grin. He would've done somersaults to every section, twirled into every secret nook in here, and you just know this is the kind of place that has fifty million secret nooks. I smile at the thought. And he would've been most interested in the . . .

"Is there a section on Chinese history?"

"Of course. Please follow me. At a sensible speed."

I follow the Eye up and up and up. My legs tremble slightly when I look down and see that the ground floor is no more than a dot. The Eye stops at one of the floors. We follow along into a seemingly never-ending space with shelf after shelf of books. Just when I think the library can't get any bigger, a whole new section opens up. It's all so beautiful, too. This section is built like an ancient Chinese library—dimly lit, mysterious, with hundreds and thousands of square drawers for the books and red benches lining the walls for quiet reading. The air becomes musty, heavy with thousands of yellowing pages.

"Here we are. Can I help you locate a specific book?" the Eye says again.

"Um, no. Thanks!"

"Please press the yellow button on the wall before you if you need any assistance. Goodbye." With that, it flies away and is soon lost among the endless shelves.

There are a handful of people here, all of them reading quietly. I can practically see Jamie weaving among the dusty bookshelves, his fingertips trailing the wooden drawers. A glance at Kai tells me I'm right; she's looking around like she might burst into tears.

"Did Jamie often come up here?" I say softly.

She sniffles and turns away.

"Kai—"

"I'm not crying, YOU'RE crying!" she wails, and swims away before I can catch her. A couple of people look up, frowning at the noise.

I swallow the lump in my throat. *Focus*, I tell myself. I take Jamie's notebook out of my backpack and rifle through it, looking for the words that are in purple again. "Library," right. I'm at the library. "Floorboards." Hmm. The floorboards seem pretty firm. Maybe I could walk up and down the Chinese history section of the library and check for a loose board? But the section is vast, and I'd probably get scolded by yet another Eye for walking too loudly or something. I look through the list of words again. "Handbook."

I put the notebook back in my bag and press the nearest yellow button. An Eye floats down toward me.

"What can I assist you with, Theodore?"

"Um, are there any handbooks in the Chinese history section?" I feel silly even asking that.

"There are exactly two hundred and seventy-nine reference books, also known as handbooks, in this section of the library."

My stomach falls, but then a thought strikes me. "Are they all located on the same shelf?"

"Most of them are. Follow me."

*It'll turn out to be nothing,* I tell myself as I walk behind the Eye. And yet. All my veins are thrumming with fizzy energy. I know I'm getting close to whatever it was Jamie wanted me to find. He was here. I know it.

When the Eye leads me to a particular corner and I feel the floorboard beneath my feet creak, I want to shout with joy.

I wait until the Eye leaves. Then, making sure no one's paying attention, I kneel down, wedge my fingers in between the boards, and pull as hard as I can.

There, underneath the floorboard, just as my brother promised, is the "buried treasure."

# KAI
# 19

"Kai!"

I turn and stare, mouth agape, which I suppose is typical for a goldfish. For the first time since Jamie died, Theo's aura isn't his usual depressive gray, nor is it the blinding rage it sometimes bursts into. It's pulsing with bright, vivid colors, and he's grinning so hard his face is mostly teeth.

"I found it," he says. "Let's go." He doesn't bother with a reply before leaping off the balcony and speeding back down to the ground floor.

"What is it?" I say, once we leave the library, but he shushes me and runs all the way outside the boundaries of the facility, pushing aside underbrush as he forges his way deep into the surrounding woods.

When we're far away from the main facility and well out of range of roaming Eyes, Theo stops, breathing hard, and takes a small box from his backpack.

"Oh. OH," I gasp. "Finally!"

Theo nods. Slowly, carefully, he opens the box. There are so many emotions bubbling in my little fishy belly that I very nearly explode. *Buried treasure*, Jamie called it. Something he'd hidden so well. What could it possibly be? Maybe a likeness of me, but made in gold. Yes, yes. Definitely a likeness of—

I cock my head at the thing Theo holds in his hand.

It's a tiny cage. And behind the thin bars, there's a . . .

"A baby bird?" Theo says, his voice incredulous. "The secret is a baby bird? How's it even still alive?"

I can't quite formulate a response, because I'm thinking the exact same thing. It's the smallest baby bird I have ever seen, and certainly the most pathetic-looking, with wrinkled skin and tufts of minuscule feathers poking out here and there. But there's something about it that I can't quite put a finger on—

Just as I peer closer, the bird's swollen eyes crack open, and it snarls, *What're you looking at, little fox?* Its voice skips my ears and travels straight into my head.

I startle. This puny, half-bald bird is powerful enough to see through my goldfish disguise. Even Danny's fire dragon can't do that. Uneasiness washes through me, along with another wave of sorrow. Why didn't Jamie tell me anything about this? Why did he keep me in the dark the whole time? It must be because I'm only a minor spirit. He didn't think I could be of much help to him.

I force myself to focus on the present moment. "Um, that's not a baby bird."

"Really?" Theo lifts the cage nearer to his eyes, making me wince. "What is it, then? A shape-shifter like you?"

"I don't think so. Let's not get too close to it . . ." I push the cage away from his face while the bird screams, *Come closer, human! Release me, and you shall be acquainted with the wrath of all ten circles of hell!* "Also, it's saying really threatening things right now."

"How come I can't hear it?"

*Your eyeballs will squelch like soft-boiled eggs under my claws—*

"Trust me, you're not missing out on anything," I say. "Hey, shush."

*How dare you shush me! I am the great Peng! When I fly through the sky, my wings are mistaken for clouds, so huge they are, and when I beat them, the force turns oceans into tsunamis that have crushed entire countries!*

A shiver runs from my head to the tips of my tails. Peng is one of the greatest creatures in the history of Chinese mythology. Last I heard, he was flying around in the spirit world, carrying a mountain of Immortals on his back. You know how heavy Immortals are?[22]

"Great, so I've found a rude baby bird," Theo says. "What am I supposed to do with it?"

*Free me, as I was promised! Release me and I might choose not to crunch your bones like little toothpicks!*

I try my best to ignore Peng's mental shrieks. "Erm, I would put it back under the floorboard. It's dangerous. Believe it or not, this is Peng."

Theo looks blankly at me.

"Ye gods, your grasp of Chinese history is truly atrocious, you know that? Peng's usually compared to the Leviathan. You know the Leviathan? Sea monster, lots of teeth, likes eating entire ships whole, does that ring a bell?"

Theo gnaws on his bottom lip. He finally looks worried. Good.

---

22 Think about it: Immortals are known for looooving food and wine. But have you ever heard of an Immortal going to the toilet? Nope. These aren't waifs we're talking about.

"So let's stop annoying him, okay? Stand aside, let the master of charm reason with him." I clear my throat and swim closer to Peng, though not thaaat close. "O great and magnificent Peng, please tell me what we can do for you so you may spare us our lives."

Theo snorts and opens his mouth when I bow my head, but I shoot him the most withering look I can muster.

*Nothing can persuade me to spare you your worthless lives.*

"Um, well, you mentioned that someone had promised to release you from your bonds?"

*Yes! A human creature, much like the one that stands beside you. I was peacefully flying one day when I—I got myself trapped somehow, and oh, such pain! I shrank to a hundred-thousandth of my true size. Days later, or maybe years, a human offered to help me escape, and though he was puny and most unworthy, I accepted. I allowed him to turn me even smaller and entrap me in this cage, and now he has reneged on his promise, as humans are wont to do. I will destroy him as well, right after I annihilate the two of you! And then I shall wreak such destruction upon this place as you have never seen. It shall be turned into a gate to the first circle of hell!*

Despite the bit about destroying the whole of the Bay Area, my tiny heart threatens to swell and burst out of my chest.[23]

"Do you know his name?" I say, my voice wavering. It shouldn't

---

23 Literally. Shape-shifting is a tricky thing. Wearing any form aside from my true fox form requires a certain bit of concentration. If I lose focus, my organs forget that they're supposed to be a bee's, or a gnat's, or, in this case, a fish's, and they'd transform back to their original foxy organs. It creates a horrendous mess.

matter. I know it was Jamie. But it does. It matters. I need to know that *he* knows. I want to hear him confirm it.

*I do not bother with such trifles. The lives of humans are as short to me as the blink of an eye. There are a million names etched in my memory, and none of them belongs to a mortal human.*

I hold myself back from hissing at him. Barely. Instead, I gesture at Theo, who's still scowling at both of us. "Can you sense *his* aura?"

*It is the most unpleasant thing, all sharp and jagged and broken by sorrow.*

I purse my lips.

*Just like yours.*

"Look beyond the broken parts, at its core, its original shape. Is it the same core as the boy who promised to free you?"

*They are not exactly alike, but they have the same shape, and the same roots.*

Tears fill my eyes. "Jamie. That was his name. The boy who saved you."

"What's going on?" Theo says.

I turn to him, and it takes a second for my voice to return. "I think—no, I know—that what Jamie wants from you, from us, is to save this creature."

# THEO
# 20

"So let me get this straight," I say. "Peng got himself trapped in the human world, but he has no idea how, or why. Jamie came across him, locked him up in a cage, stuffed him under a floorboard, and left clues for me to—" My voice cracks then, and I lower my head for a moment.

Everything inside me is a mess of nausea and explosions of worlds. My mind dashes through the past few months, sifting through my memories of Jamie, trying to identify anything that might make sense of all of this.

"I don't understand," Kai says. "Why would he turn a demigod into a small bird? Why not just release it?"

Why, indeed. But the biggest question rattling in the recesses of my head is why did Jamie hide it from *me*? It's a poisonous thought, all sharp edges. We used to tell each other everything. Well, most things. And then Jamie got Kai, and we started drifting apart . . .

It takes all of my willpower not to snap at Kai. The sight of her only reminds me of how much I've lost. I place the cage on a flat rock and glare at Kai as she floats down toward Peng.

"Why did the boy turn you even smaller?" she says.

Silence.

I'm about to say something when I see that she's staring with rapt attention at Peng.

"What's he saying?"

I half expect Kai to shush me, but after a while, she says, in a slow, thoughtful voice, "'He said he'd help me.'"

"Jamie wanted to save a god," I half sob, half laugh. That is so Jamie.

Kai nods. She startles and looks sharply at Peng.

"Did he just say something?" I say.

"He says, 'His name does not matter! I have told you how inconsequential human lives are. And he lied to me. He shall be the first I kill.'"

Fire floods my chest. His name doesn't matter? "He's dead," I say. "He tried to save you, you ungrateful scrawny chicken, and now he's dead, and his name was Jamie."

"Theo—" Kai lifts her fin toward me, but I shrug it off. I can't let Kai comfort me. It still feels like a betrayal to Jamie, having her as my companion.

There's silence, and then Peng speaks, and for the first time, I hear his voice. He sounds like a thousand voices speaking at once, in harmony, and the voices have skipped my ears and gone straight to my brain.

*He . . . is dead? The boy who promised to save me?*

I meet his eye. "Yes."

I expected Peng to be contrite at the news, but instead, he roars, *Then how will I get out of this blasted cage?!*

I'm momentarily deafened by his bone-shattering howl. Which is why I am unable to detect movement until it's too late.

The bushes next to us rustle and part, and there stands a winded-looking Danny with his fire dragon. I'm not sure who's more shocked to see whom.

"What are you doing here?" Danny says.

"What are *you* doing here?" I say.

Danny narrows his eyes. "Xiaohua said she sensed a creature with a great aura in this vicinity. The aura has been greatly reduced, but my dragon is very sensitive to such things, unlike your silly little goldfish."

Kai snorts. "Xiaohua—your dragon's called Little Flower?"

"Did someone say 'fried fish'?" Xiaohua rumbles.

"Hey! Just because you're bigger and faster and more powerful and more experienced and are able to breathe fire, doesn't mean you're better than I am!" Kai cries.

"Pretty sure that's exactly what it means," Danny says. "So where is this creature with the dazzling aura, anyway?"

I almost look over at the flat rock, where Peng's cage is. I stop myself in time, but my caution means nothing, as Xiaohua says, "I can feel its aura from over there."

Danny and I pounce at the same time, but he gets his hands on it first. He scrambles away, practically crowing with triumph.

"Give it back!" I shout. I lunge at Danny, but Xiaohua flies, quick as a puff of air, and is instantly between us.

"Step back, please, small human," Xiaohua says. Smoke curls out of her nostrils.

"You don't understand!" My voice cracks with desperation. "It's not one of the creatures they meant for us to find. Please, Danny!" I scour my mind for a way to reason with him. I must be able to reach even bullies like him. "I know things haven't been great between us, but please—this is so much more than you and me. It's from my brother—"

Danny sneers at me. "You know what really irritates me about you, Theo? It's the fact that you don't want to be here. Everyone knows it. Do you know how many kids would kill to come here? Hundreds. Maybe thousands. But somehow you managed to cheat your way through the test and take one of their spots. A spot you don't deserve."

Guilt and frustration tangle in my chest. Is it really that obvious that I have no interest in all this mythological stuff? That I don't actually belong in the program?

Danny dangles the cage between a thumb and forefinger and peers inside. "Huh. It's a worthless little bird. Xiaohua, you got me to trek all the way into the woods for this? The best creatures are probably all discovered by now!"

Xiaohua sighs. "It's not a mere bird, Master."

"Then what is it?" Danny says, rattling the cage with a finger. He snorts when Peng nibbles on his fingertip.

Peng's voice rushes like a hurricane through my head.

*Stick your finger in farther, human, and I shall snap it in two!*

Danny doesn't give any indication of having heard anything.

"Master, please don't do that," Xiaohua says, and for the first time, I sense fear in her voice.

"Can she hear Peng, too?" I whisper to Kai.

She shakes her head. "He hasn't chosen to let her hear him. But she can sense his anger, I think."

"Whatever this creature is, it's extremely powerful," Xiaohua says to Danny. "The cage is imbued with spells to hide its aura, and having been shrunk has further reduced its aura, but still, my qì is bending toward its aura."

"What does that even mean?" Danny snaps.

"Have you not learned physics? Typical," Kai says. "Large masses have their own gravitational force. Earth, for example, is a large mass—rather like your head—and so it has its own gravity. That's the thing that keeps you from falling off the planet, by the way. Not that any of us would miss you."

Xiaohua turns away, but before she does, I swear I catch the glimpse of a smile.

"So the fact that our qì is being pulled into this bird's qì gives you an idea of how powerful it is," Kai says. "And it belongs to Theo, so hand it over posthaste." I can tell she's fighting to keep her voice reasonable. Her little goldfish face is crinkled, as though she's trying hard not to snarl at them, and her goldfish tail has grown a bit of orange fur. Luckily, neither Danny nor Xiaohua seems to notice the change in Kai.

"Oooh, I'm so scared." Danny cocks his head at the bird again. "Tell you what—I'm not a complete monster. I'll trade you the creature I found." He gestures at Xiaohua, who produces an ancient Chinese gourd.

"That's a wine gourd!" Kai gasps. "Do you know what under-age drinking is going to do to your brain development?"

Danny ignores her. "There's a shén inside it," he says to me. "It's probably better than your current companion. You can probably ask Xiuling to help you find an on-site summoner to help switch companions. Wouldn't that be nice?"

"Please, Danny, it's not just another creature that the program has left for us. It's from my brother, I swear!" I reach for it, but Xiaohua turns into a whirlwind of smoke and strikes at me, fast as a whip, flinging me back. I hit the ground hard, air crashing out of my lungs in a painful wheeze.

"Do that again and you'll never get back up," Danny says.

With that, he flings the gourd at me before climbing up onto Xiaohua's back. I close my eyes against the gust of wind as Xiao-hua leaps into the air and flies away with a cage containing a very angry demigod.

# THEO
# 21

I've never felt such rage, such helplessness. I stay frozen, a million panicky thoughts zooming through my mind, exploding like Pop Rocks.

*WhatdoIdowhatdoIdowhatdoI—*

"Come on," I bark at Kai. "We've gotta get Peng back."

Kai smacks her fins over her face and gives a frustrated howl. "I know, but how?"

"I don't know, ambush him in our bedroom?" Images of me holding some sort of weapon to Danny's neck flash through my head. Is that ridiculous? No! I need to get Peng back. Jamie left him for me for a reason!

"If it's just Danny on his own, then yes, I'd say we can easily take him. But his fire dragon is a problem." She rubs her eyes and groans. "Curses! Why aren't I more powerful? I can't take that obnoxious fire dragon. I'm not strong enough."

My whole face is burning hot. I share Kai's frustration. Why isn't she something more powerful that can easily take down Danny's dragon? A phoenix, for example, would give Xiaohua a run for her money. Even a golden monkey could do something—cast a spell of thievery . . . oh!

"Do your thing!" I cry.

"Eh?"

"The illusion thing! Isn't that what you fox spirits do? You fool people into thinking they're seeing something entirely different from reality!"

Kai shakes her head mournfully. "I can easily make Danny think his feet are his hands and his face is his bottom, but dragons are immune to my spells. Xiaohua will see right through it and break the enchantment."

I sink to the forest floor. Twigs and broken branches bite my legs, but I barely feel them. "I don't know what to do," I whisper. The first solid link I've found to Jamie, and it's immediately taken away. Part of me wants to cry for Mama and Baba. I miss them so much. I miss Nainai's gentle voice.

Something pats my head softly. Kai floats down, looking as broken as I feel. "I'm sorry," she says. "If I could fight his fire dragon, I would. But I'm just a useless fox spirit." Her voice wobbles.

"It's not your fault." I reach out and poke Kai gently. "I know we haven't always uh—seen eye to eye, but . . . you've been really helpful throughout this entire thing. I wouldn't even be here if not for your help."

"I know," she sighs.

Despite everything, that gets a small smile out of me. "Jamie would have known how to fix it . . . ," I say. This used to be something I did all the time. Whenever I ran into a confusing situation, I'd pause and wonder, *What would Jamie do?*

And just like that, the cogs click back into place and begin to whir. What would Jamie do? Well, that depends on what he was doing before.

I turn to Kai. "Jamie cast a Make Small spell on Peng . . . and then he put him in a cage . . . Why bother with the cage?"

"Turning Peng small doesn't diminish his aura, so the cage is necessary. Obviously, it doesn't hide all of his aura, but enough of it so it's not so easily detected," Kai says.

"If we find him, all we have to do is break him out of the cage, and he'll want to help us."

"I doubt that. He said the first thing he'd do once he's out is flatten the Bay Area to show how annoyed he is."

"What? Isn't killing living beings bad for one's karma? Wouldn't Peng be punished in some way if he did that? Like, get turned into a demon, or get sent to Diyu or something?"

"Nah, Peng's basically a god, kiddo. Just like how the ultrarich and powerful in your world play by different rules than the rest of you plebs, the gods and higher deities in our world also have special rights. If Peng goes on a rampage in your world, he won't turn into a demon or anything, but he'll have some explaining to do to the Jade Emperor—the Jade Emperor is the highest deity in the spirit world, by the way. And I daresay if Peng told the Jade Emperor that he had been kidnapped and tortured by you lowly humans, the Jade Emperor would empathize with him and let him off the hook."

I groan and massage my temples. "Great, so Peng can go around killing as many people as he wants without any repercussions."

"Pretty much. That's why you humans really shouldn't go around kidnapping gods."

"I know that! I'm not the one who kidnapped Peng." Then

a thought strikes me, and I freeze. "Danny's going to open the cage."

Kai snorts. "Serves him right."

"We need to stop him. It's going to kill him!"

"You talk like you don't want to see Danny get eaten by a bird the size of Japan."

"That's because I *don't*," I say.

"Not even a little bit? You can tell me, I'm good at keeping secrets." Kai's forehead wrinkles a little. I think she's trying to wiggle her eyebrows.

"Well—maybe a little . . ."

Kai gasps. "I knew it! You malicious thing! Ooh, the horrible things your evil little mind dreams up!"

I roll my eyes. "Very funny. What about casting a spell to keep Peng small even if Danny opens the cage?"

"Do you know how much qì that requires? To turn a creature as powerful as Peng, who's naturally the size of a country, to a baby bird?" Kai says.

"Jamie did it."

"Yeah, but Peng also said he was shrunk to a hundred-thousandth of his true size. He was about the size of an elephant by the time Jamie got to him. Not that what Jamie did is any less impressive, mind you. I certainly don't think *you'd* be able to do it. How's your qì training coming along?"

I glower at her. "Thought so," she says. "Ah, such woe! Danny's a goner, and so is everyone in the Bay Area. We need to cut our losses and get out of here. We'll go to Europe. It's lovely this time of year."

"If I could get my hands on a cirth pendant, I might be able to—"

"Nah, cirth won't work on him," Namita says, straightening up suddenly from behind a bush.

Kai and I jump about a mile. Seriously, what magic is this girl using that she can sneak up on both of us like that?

"How long have you been here?" I say.

"Long enough to know that Danny took something of yours. A creature the size of Japan? Sounds bad." She raises a hand before I can say anything. "I wasn't spying or anything, if that's what you're wondering. I have better things to do, thank you very much."

"Then what were you doing out here?" Kai says.

Namita shrugs. "Nobody let me join in their search, so when I saw Danny and his dragon heading here, looking all excited, I thought I'd see what the fuss is all about."

"That's literally the very definition of spying," I say.

"Only if you want to get all technical about it. Anyway, I don't understand why your brother would leave you a creature that's so obviously dangerous."

I hesitate only a second. There's just something about Namita that makes it so easy to open up to her. Maybe it's those silly braids of hers that bounce crazily with every move of her head. Maybe it's the way she acts like she can solve every problem. Whatever it is, I find myself telling her the truth about Jamie's notebook and the way he died. I even tell her the truth about Kai—that she was Jamie's companion spirit before I inherited her, and that she's really a fox spirit and not a goldfish.

"Wow," she says, her eyes wide. "Theo, I'm so, so sorry." And she actually looks genuinely sorry.

"Thanks." I look away for a second, unable to stomach the sadness in her eyes. "Anyway, why did you say cirth won't work on him?" I say.

Namita and Kai exchange a glance. "You do the honors," Kai says.

Namita smiles, obviously loving the chance to show off her knowledge. "Peng's what we call a 'creation creature'; he was here when the world was being created. Modern magic isn't going to do anything to him. You need old magic. The older, the better. And for powerful old magic, you need prana. Or qì, in your case."

I groan. "Then how did Jamie do it? I mean, he was smart, but he was also a teen. He wouldn't have had the energy to turn something the size of an elephant into something that fits on my palm."

"Oho!" Namita crows. "A mystery! I live for these kinds of things. Back home, they call me Sherlock, except with cuter outfits, obviously." She flicks her head, her braids flinging back.

"They do? I thought you said you were bullied back home."

Namita scowls. "Okay, so maybe they call me Sherlock in a really mean way. Anyway, you're missing the point here. You're obviously in dire straits—"

"Dire straits?" I say.

"It means you're in desperate need of help. But don't you worry. I will take your case. But on one condition: that I get to use this as my summer project. I will be taking meticulous notes as we go. Oh, my teacher back home is going to flip out when I hand in my paper! An investigative report on the mysterious case of a lost deity. Can you even imagine?"

"You really don't have to."

"Shush, I'm thinking . . ." Namita strokes an imaginary beard on her chin. "What did Jamie use to do whenever he had a difficult problem to solve?"

"That's easy," Kai says. "He'd go to the library." With that, both Kai and Namita start heading toward the library. I grab the wine gourd that Danny threw at me before jogging to catch up with them. Despite myself, I'm starting to feel glad that Namita came across us. I'm used to facing things alone, but the presence of Kai and Namita is actually bolstering my spirits. We may not have Peng with us, but by gods we will take him back, whatever it costs.

# KAI

# 22

"These are the last ten books your brother checked out of the library," the librarian says to Theo. His name tag reads NORMAN.[24]

"Thank you," Theo says, before he almost collapses from the weight of the books. I laugh, and he shoots me an affronted look.

"I'll help you with those," Norman says.

"Thanks," Theo says.

They lug the books to a nearby table, and Norman asks if they need anything else.

"No, thank you."

Norman hesitates. "I—um, I'm sorry about your brother. He was really cool."

A look of pain crosses Theo's face, and he mumbles his thanks without meeting Norman's eye. It hits me then that it's probably still hard for Theo to talk about Jamie to strangers, just as I find it nearly impossible to do so. I reach out and pat his shoulder lightly, and he gives me a small smile. How strange it is, to feel empathy toward this boy I abhorred not so long ago.

"All right!" Namita says, rubbing her hands. "Get reeeeady to ruuuumble!" Heads whip up and people shush her and she goes, "Oh, sorry." Then she whispers, "Get reeeady to ruuuumble!"

---

24 Please normalize wearing name tags so that I do not have to take up brain space trying to tell you blobby humans apart!

I like this kid.

Theo and Namita each flipped open their first book, and their eyes immediately glaze over. I peer over Theo's shoulder and see why.

There are two different forms of written Mandarin: simplified and traditional.

For example, the word for "listen," pronounced *tīng*, would be written this way:

Simplified Mandarin: 听 Traditional Mandarin: 聽

Guess which one the book is written in?

"I can't read this," Theo groans.

"You can't read it? What about me?" Namita cries, slumping over the desk.

Theo glances up at me. "Kai, can you cast the spell of illusion on the book and make it seem like it's not written in Traditional Mandarin?"

"Oooh," Namita says. "Good idea. You're smarter than you look, Theo!" She looks at me with newfound admiration. Lowering her voice, she says, "I keep forgetting you're not actually a fish spirit."

"Of course, child," I say with an indulgent smile. Fish spirits can't normally do illusions.[25]

Theo looks at his book. "*Eine Geschichte der Prinzessinnen—* Kai, this is in German!"

"It's a wonderful language, is German."

"I'm sure it is, but I don't know it," he says through gritted

---

25 Come to think of it, what CAN fish spirits do? Aside from blowing bubbles, perhaps, or looking very startled? I'm being quite ungracious, aren't I? But it's tough not to be, when one is so superior.

teeth, while I hold back my laughter. Really, it's too easy to get to him. "Change it to English, please. No, wait, I won't know the exact words for the spells if you do that. Change it to Simplified Mandarin."

"Why didn't you say so earlier?" I say innocently, waving my fin at the book again.

"Could you change mine to English, please?" Namita says.

Theo glances at his book again. "'A History of Princesses in the Qing Dynasty,'" he reads out, painfully slowly. He reads Simplified Mandarin the way small kids read picture books: one finger trailing across the page, lips moving silently. I try not to breathe down his neck with impatience, but it's tough, especially given the urgency of the situation. "'Gurun Princess Hexiao, Manchu princess (1775–1823). Tenth daughter of the Qianlong Emperor.'"

While he struggles through the book, I scan the rest of the pile, but nothing jumps out at me. Though I seem relaxed on the outside, my mind's actually going a hundred miles an hour, whizzing ahead to try to figure out what it is I'm missing.

"How's yours looking?" Namita says. "Mine's no good. It's just got all these love poems."

Theo shakes his head, and they go on to the next book, and the next, until with a huge sigh, both kids slump over the desk.

"None of these books seems right. There's got to be something else," Theo says.

I can only nod, feeling once again like a huge failure.[26] I'd been

---

26 You must be wondering how a being as stupendous as I could possibly feel this way, but ah, low self-confidence affects even the best of us sometimes.

so sure that we'd find something in the library, but nope. I was wrong. Did I really know so little of my old master? My scales burn with shame; even Jamie, the master I loved with all my heart, thought I was unworthy of his secrets.

"Let's go," Theo says. He and Namita lift the heavy tomes and stagger toward the return cart. On their way out, they wave goodbye to Norman.

"Found what you were looking for?" he says.

Theo shakes his head. I'm about to follow him when something overcomes me and I squeak, "What was Jamie's favorite book?" It burns me to have to ask a stranger a question about Jamie. I should know everything there is to know about Jamie, but well, here we are. I have to admit that my old master kept secrets from me. That I failed in my duty as a companion spirit.

As though sensing the pain it has cost me to ask the question, Theo mutters, "That's a good question, Kai."

Norman gives us an embarrassed smile. "I'm glad you brought that up, actually . . ."

"Why?" I say.

"I didn't want to mention it before, because it seems so minor and petty, but um, Jamie sort of . . . owes a library book."

Theo blinks. "Sorry?"

Norman fidgets, adjusting his glasses. "Jamie borrowed one of our books a week before he—um, the accident—and I'm guessing it's probably somewhere in your house. It was his favorite book. He must've borrowed it about seven times."

Seven times? And I never knew? Honestly, I could just self-combust out of sheer frustration right now.

"If you want, I could order a travel bubble to your house for you so you can look for the book."

"What book is it?" I say, and I have to clear my throat halfway through because the anticipation makes me choke.

*"The Farmer's Almanac, Year 1320."*

I freeze. "An . . . almanac? Is that like a—um—a handbook?" Theo and I exchange a look, and I have no doubt what's going through his head. Jamie's message: *. . . you were obsessed with this handbook . . .*

"Yeah, I guess you could call it that."

Theo and I grin at each other. "Order the travel bubble," he says. "I'll find the book."

# THEO
# 23

Jamie had so many books in his room it takes a while for Namita and me to find the almanac. I find it so incredibly painful to search through my brother's room that I decide to dive into it as quickly as I can. I just want to find the book and get the heck out of here, before the emotions of being back in Jamie's room, knowing he's permanently gone, catch up with me and turn me into a sobbing mess. When I finally find the almanac, I yank it out impatiently. As expected, it's a doorstopper of a book, the script on the spine painfully small and as tightly spaced as humanly possible, as though whoever printed it viewed empty space as a personal affront. Getting through this is going to be hell.

"This is it? Jamie's favorite book?" I say to Kai.

I was expecting her to snort and say something along the lines of "Obviously," but instead, she looks at the book silently before turning away.

"Kai? What is it?"

With a shuddery sigh, she says, "I don't know. I saw him reading it a few times and never thought much of it. I've missed a lot. Failed to notice things that a companion should. I'm afraid I wasn't as good a companion as your brother deserved."

Her vulnerability is disarming. I have no idea how to react. I reach out and pat her gingerly. "You were an awesome companion. He was always telling me how much he loved you."

"Yeah, I have to say, Kai," Namita pipes up, "if I could have a companion, I would totally steal you from Theo."

"Hey!" I say.

Kai sniffles and gives us a small, watery smile. "And I would be delighted to be your companion, Namita."

"I'm right here!" I cry, but by then we're all laughing.

Just as we're about to step back into the travel bubble, footsteps rush up the stairs and Mama and Baba burst into Jamie's room, out of breath. Mama is carrying a cleaver and Baba is brandishing a feather duster.

"Oh, Theo!" Baba says. "It's you. We heard noises up here and thought—"

"Aiya, we thought we were getting robbed!" Mama cries.

Namita is gaping at them, her eyes wide. This is terrible. This is the most embarrassing thing I have ever lived through. Might not live through it, in fact. The first ever time I bring a friend back home and my parents very nearly attack her with an actual meat cleaver.

"I told you not to climb in through the second-floor window," Kai says with a roll of her eyes. "Did I not tell you? Use the front door like a normal person, I said. But did you listen? Nooo."

"Um—" I manage to choke out.

As though Mama has only now just noticed Namita, her face melts into a surprised grin. "Hello! Hi! What your name?"

Namita brightens up. "Hi, auntie. I'm Namita. I'm Theo's friend from the summer program."

At the word "auntie," Mama lights up. Her smile widens. "Oh, you so polite. So polite! Theo, this is very good girl. I like her very much. Come, come down and have some tea and cake."

"We really should be getting back," I say.

"Nonsense!" Baba says. "Come, we will take out the special biscuit tin. The Royal Danish—"

"Royal Danish butter cookies?" Namita says.

We all stare at her, and she laughs. "That's exactly the kind my family has for special occasions, too. And my mom saves the tins to store her sewing needles and thread in."

"Oh, I do that, too!" Mama says, linking arms with Namita. "Come, you tell me everything about your mama and yourself while I make tea."

Surprisingly, having tea and cookies with Namita and my family isn't quite as excruciating as I thought it would be. Mama practically adopts Namita as the daughter she's always wished for, while Nainai watches on with a smile, and Namita seems comfortable with all the attention thrown her way. Baba asks me and Kai how the program is coming along, and I tell him it's fine and that we're only back to pick up some stuff I forgot to take with me.

Finally, we're done, and we all pile into the travel bubble. Baba and Mama and Nainai stand in Jamie's room, waving at us as we float away, and for some reason the sight of them brings tears to my eyes. I look away, sniffling, and though I'm sure that Kai and Namita both notice, neither one says anything. But they each put a hand—well, a fin in Kai's case—on my shoulder, and the small act makes me feel less alone than I've felt in the weeks since Jamie's death.

Back in the library, I get Kai to turn the book into English for the sake of expediency. She does so. I snap, "*Modern* English."

*Part I: The General Weather Report and Forecast.*

"*This* was your brother's favorite book?" Namita says, wrinkling her nose.

"There must be something more to it," I say, and read on. Apparently, the weather in 1320 was very much like the weather in 1319 and 1318, but not quite like the weather in 1317, when there had been a freak thunderstorm of very disgruntled penguins in the village of Dongbo. They didn't have a name for penguins back then, having never come across one, and called them "peevish black-and-white chickens." There's a reference for spells that the villagers used in an effort to deal with the belligerent penguins and the rains of blood.

I flip to the next page and find a piece of paper with Jamie's handwriting on it.

"Is that . . . ," Namita says.

I nod wordlessly, holding the paper as carefully as though it were a fragile baby bird.

> A Poem to Stop the Cry of the Sky—Can be used on other things? Maybe try in shower.
>
> A Serenade for an Irate Penguin—Can be used on other animals? Maybe only birds? Try with schoolyard chickens.

"Wow, that's such a great idea!" Namita says, reading over my shoulder. "Never would've thought of that."

She's right. This is why Jamie was such a brilliant student. My instinctive reaction is to dismiss the spells as nothing useful; his reaction was to try finding ways to apply them in everyday life. The thought of it makes me want to both cry and laugh. There really is no one like Jamie.

I flip through the rest of the book but find no other notes. At the very back of the book, however, there's a reference of spells most commonly used by farmers.

"A Lamentation for Chicken Ovulation?" Namita says, giggling.

"I prefer the Path of the Pig Be Big," I say.

The spell names make me think of Ma complaining about the names given to American spells. Admittedly, these spells are much easier to remember.

Under the "Animal Husbandry and Management" category there are gems like a Balm to Calm and Cool an Angry Bull.

Then there's a "Miscellaneous" category with Do Not Despair, the Wheel Will Repair.

I get Kai to turn the book into Simplified Mandarin, take out my book, and write down all the incantations, no matter how mundane the spells seem. I know without a doubt that these are the spells I will need to complete the task that Jamie's given me.

Except, of course, writing them down is a lot easier than actually casting them. But now I realize that I'm not alone. For most of my life, I've always felt like an outsider, always left out of everything. But now I have Kai and Namita.

I turn to them, my heart thundering, and say, "If we're going to free Peng, I need to know how to cast these spells. Can you help me?"

Kai and Namita look at each other and grin. "Of course!" Namita says.

"Indubitably," Kai says. Which I think means yes.

And just like that, a weight I didn't know I've been shouldering is lifted. Joy flows in a warm glow from my chest, all the way down my arms, and for the first time, I know what it's like to have friends.

# THEO
# 24

Straight after dinner, we scurry off to the floating playground, which is deserted at this hour. It's definitely one of the coolest attractions here—a floating island with towering trees holding up a maze of bridges and tree houses. We step onto a stone slab, and it floats up to the island and drops us off. It's breezy up here, a welcome respite. We sit in a circle on the grass.

"Right," Kai says, rubbing her fins together. "First of all, let's get one thing straight: Being Chinese American doesn't mean you can automatically cast Chinese spells. It doesn't work that way, kiddo. You need to have an emotional link to the culture to be able to access your qì, which is why you've been having such a hard time with your lessons."

I wince. "But that's just it. I don't have an emotional link to China. It's just the place where my parents came from, you know? And I want to be interested in it, I do, but—"

"I get it," Namita says. "You can't really force yourself to be interested in something you're not. But, dude, if you're not into this stuff, why are you here?"

For a split second, panic scrambles my mind. Namita knows that Jamie wanted me to find Peng, but she doesn't know details about Jamie, about how he died and left that giant gaping hole in my life. Should I just give her some lame reason? Maybe something about it being for school credit—

But even as I think that, I see the earnestness in Namita's face, and it hits me that she's the first friend I've made in forever. If I can't get into this stuff with her, who can I get into it with?

"Because of my brother."

"Oh, Theo. I'm so sorry." She genuinely sounds sorry.

And just like that, it's like something inside me cracks open and all the pain comes rushing out. "He was always spending his time here. He was the biggest nerd."

"He does sound dorky, but in a cool way," she says.

I laugh through my tears. "He was definitely both. He had a way with people, you know? Everyone loved him. I miss him so much." It feels good to finally say that out loud to someone other than Kai. It makes me realize just how much I've wanted to talk about Jamie, but I could never find the right time, or the right way, or maybe I've always just been too afraid. "He was so excited when he learned about qì and how it meant that he didn't need to be so reliant on cirth. He was such a cheapskate—well, so am I, honestly—"

"You guys are such Asian stereotypes," Namita laughs. "But I'm a total cheapskate, too."

I laugh again, wiping away my tears. I feel lighter than I have in weeks. Is this what having a friend you can confide in is like? Someone to share your burden with?

I'm just about to say something more when Kai yells, "I got it!"

Namita and I both jump.

Kai's swimming round and round in frantic circles. "I have an idea!" she cries, her little fins waving so fast they're an orange blur. "Jamie can be your bridge! Your connection!"

"I don't follow."

"Okay. Identity is very complicated, isn't it? Especially when you're an immigrant or a descendant of immigrants."

"Tell me about it," Namita says. "I have so many feelings about Jaipur, and I don't even understand them all, but I really, really want to go there someday. I mean, that's the whole reason I'm spending my summer here instead of hanging out with my friends back home. I've always wanted to know more about my ancestors' lives. It's like a piece that's always been missing from the giant puzzle that is the Incredible and Wondrous Life of Namita Singh."

"I've never felt that longing for China. I don't even know which part of China my ancestors are from," I mumble. I can barely look Namita in the eye. She must think I'm the world's most ignorant kid.

"Right," Kai says. "But identity isn't just about being interested in a place."

"It isn't?"

"It's not, Theo." Her voice comes out gentler this time. "It's also about being connected to those who shape it. Your family. Jamie. These are people who have made you into who you are. Not quite Chinese, not quite American, but both. So focus on the memory of Jamie. It'll build a bridge for you to connect to your ancestral roots."

I feel as though a large fist has caught hold of my chest and is starting to squeeze. What Kai said makes sense, but . . .

"I don't know," I say, and once more, I find myself fighting back tears.

"What's wrong?" Namita says.

I hate that my voice comes out so small and thin. "Thinking of Jamie's like digging into a fresh wound. Every time I think of his face or, like, his voice, it just—" The words are choked with unshed tears.

To my surprise, Kai floats down to my chest and gives me a tiny hug. "I know," she says in a soft voice, her eyes shining with tears as well. "It's the same for me."

Then Namita reaches out and takes my hand. "I'm sorry, Theo."

I look at her hand on mine, feeling slightly taken aback. Namita's definitely the most touchy-feely person I've ever come across. My family doesn't really go for touching. Until recently, the only time I got touched was when Mama yanked my ear. I used to tell myself it's fine, that touching is unnecessary, but it's actually really nice. The sense of Namita's hand on mine, along with Kai's fin on my shoulder, is like an anchor, firm and reassuring.

"I'll do it," I say. "But, um, could you . . ."

"I'll be here," Namita says.

"Me too," Kai says.

We smile at one another. Then I close my eyes, hold my palms up, and lower my head.

It's not going to work. I know it isn't. Using Jamie's memory as a conduit is far-fetched, but even as I think that, Kai's words wash over me. About Jamie being a huge part of my identity. Because it's true. He's always been there, whether as an annoying older brother or my role model. Every dinner was a chopstick fight with him over who got the last piece of char siew. Char siew that Baba cooked for hours, from a recipe handed down to him from Nainai, who got the recipe from *her* nainai.

Jamie. He was more than my brother. He was the thread that linked me to my cultural roots. Tears fill my eyes, and warmth bubbles in my hands.

"Theo!" Namita cries.

I open my eyes, and my jaw drops. The air above my palms is warping, as though all the light that's going across them is bending, breaking, turning into flashes and glimmers.

"It's working!" Kai says.

"Do a spell!" Namita says.

"Um, ah—" I wave my hands around. "I can't think of any!"

Kai swims frantically, and Namita ducks to avoid my hands, which are still spitting out sparks.

"Cast anything!" Kai says.

I think of the spells I read in the almanac and settle on the first one I can remember. Something about repairing a wheel. But I must have mangled the words, because instead of any wheel repairs, there's a sudden bolt of blinding light flashing from my palms. It shoots up into the sky and fizzles in the darkness. We gape up at the empty sky for a few moments, then Namita and Kai squeal and hug me.

"You did it!" Namita says.

"I knew you always had it in you," Kai says.

I let out a shuddery laugh, gazing down at my hands in disbelief. Then I look at Kai and Namita. "Okay, now I need to learn the right spells to be able to free Peng safely."

We're going to do it. We're going to fulfill the task that Jamie sent us here to do.

# KAI
# 25

We spend the rest of the night helping Theo practice the spells from the almanac, using the wine gourd spirit from Danny for practice. I use my powers to have a bit of a chat with the wine gourd spirit and surmise that it's a rather bad-tempered little gnat spirit. She's not too happy about being used as a guinea pig, but when I tell her it's the only way she's getting out of the wine gourd, she acquiesces. After about two hours of failed tries, Theo finally manages to cast the Balm to Calm and Cool an Angry Bull spell on the gnat spirit, and we're gratified to hear gentle snores coming out of the gourd's mouth.

"Tomorrow they'll probably ask us to free the spirits we've found," Theo says. "Danny will bring Peng to class, and I'll do the mind-link thingy with him to try and reason with him."

"Mind-link thingy? Who ever said kids nowadays aren't articulate? Anyway, Peng needs to initiate the mind link," I add helpfully.

Theo sags.

"Or you could focus on something—a memory or a person or a thing—that you know means a lot to Peng while simultaneously thinking of him. That'll forge a connection. Sort of like a cosmic phone call. Mind you, he's not likely to accept the link.

I certainly wouldn't. Very unhygienic, making mind links, especially with human children. A less odious species I have never come across."

Namita laughs and pokes me. "You love us and you know it, Kai."

I sigh ruefully. "I suppose I can just about tolerate you lot."

"Right, so." Theo swallows nervously. "I'll uh—I'll make the mind link with Peng and then um, if it doesn't work, I'll cast a Bind the Horse's Behind spell on him to keep him from wreaking havoc once Danny releases him from the cage."

"Theo, no offense, I don't think you should cast a spell on a monstrous being whose true size is as large as Japan. Do you know how big Japan is? It's one hundred fifty thousand square miles!" Namita says.

Theo stares at her. "You know the actual size of Japan?"

"Who doesn't?" Namita cries.

I purse my goldfishy lips. "I suppose if you do it before he grows back to his true size, that should work. But you'll have a few seconds at best to cast the spell. After that, he'll be way too big and powerful."

Theo nods, looking markedly pale. "I can do it. I know I can."

"Not to put undue pressure on you or anything, but the fate of the Bay Area sort of rests on your scrawny shoulders," I add. "Last chance to abscond to the Mediterranean."

Neither of them gives me a second look. "Don't worry," Namita says. "Reapling has a ton of safety measures in place. I've read up on them. If you can't control Peng, they will."

"Yes, although one would think that there's a reason why

Jamie kept Peng hidden from Reapling in the first place," I point out with infinite wisdom.

"I agree. I'm sure Jamie hid Peng for good reason, and I won't fail," Theo says, but his face is drawn.[27]

The next morning, we all gather at the auditorium. When I catch sight of Xiaohua, I make the most dreadful face I can muster[28] but am ignored. At ten o'clock sharp, a spotlight illuminates the podium, and Xiuling and Saanvi appear suddenly, like a clap of lightning. The kids gasp. What show-offs. Spells of teleportation are rare and devilishly difficult to cast.

"Good morning!" Saanvi says.

The kids chorus a greeting back to her.

"Has everyone found a creature?" she says. "Great! What we're going to work on today is how to release your creature from its confines."

Uh-oh. Danny's definitely going to release Peng from his cage. I shoot Theo a worried glance, and he returns it with an anxious frown.

"We've used traditional ancient spells from your ancestral culture to secure the containers. So to unlock these containers, you'll have to use an ancient spell." She calls up a holographic screen. "You guys have been working on the most basic spells the past two weeks, and we think you're ready to step it up. Here are a few of the more intermediate spells from ancient China and

---

27 And it's not a good drawing.

28 Hard to do when one is so gorgeous, but I manage.

India. Remember, with ancient spells, it's less about the precise measurements of cirth, but more about being precise with your words. You must speak with accuracy, which is why we had such a rigorous test to make sure your grasp of the various languages spoken in China and India is up to par. Once you are confident with the spells, you can add words to them, such as 'dian' in Mandarin, to make the spell less powerful, and so on."

We look down the list of the Chinese spells.

"A Route to Connectivity Through Affinity," Theo mutters. "What does that even do?"

"It allows casters to combine spells. For example, if a farmer doesn't have enough qì to cast a spell for rain, he could ask his neighbor to cast it with him. Their qì combined increases the spell's effects exponentially," I say.

"A Rite to Make Skin White . . . seriously? How's that supposed to help?" Theo says.

"I don't think these spells are supposed to be directly applicable to your task. That would be spoon-feeding you kids."

"Kai's probably right," Namita says. "Also, a Rite to Make Skin White is one of the most popular spells in China, just so you know. And India. And the rest of Asia."

Theo grimaces. "That's horrible."

Namita nods. "That's colonization for you."

"It's a vile spell," I pipe up, "but it's the easiest one out of the bunch, and it's temporary. The effects will fade after about a day."

Theo huffs. Then he points a finger at me and starts casting the spell.

"Stop!" I scream.

"What?"

"You've just said 'make skin into sparkling water.' Do not finish that spell. I mean it!" I add when I notice his mouth trembling into something that looks suspiciously like a smile. Next to him, Namita is shaking with silent laughter. "Don't try it on me, for gods' sake, I'm too precious. Try it on someone less important, like the president of the United States or something. Ooh, I know, try it on Danny."

We all look over at Danny and his annoying dragon, who now sports a mane of lustrous black hair and is pink in color instead of her usual flaming red.

"Figures he'd cast the spells perfectly," Theo grumbles. Then his eyes widen. "Look, there's Peng. I'll do the mind link now." Sure enough, peeking out of Danny's bag is Peng, still secured in his cage. Peng looks even grumpier than before, if that's at all possible.

Theo closes his eyes and concentrates.[29] Meanwhile, all around us, spells are being cast with non-catastrophic results as the three mentors make their way around the room, giving advice. Oh dear. Won't be long before one of the three mentors notices that Theo's just sitting still with his eyes closed.

"Er, hello?" I say. "Feel free to come back to us anytime now, O dear master of mine."

No answer.

---

29 And by this, I mean he assumes a very constipated expression. You know the one I mean. You humans only have three facial expressions: happy, sad, and constipated.

I exchange a worried glance with Namita. "Now what?"

"Oi, wake up." Namita raises a hand and smacks Theo's forehead.

Still no answer. He doesn't even seem to have felt her hitting him on the head. An ugly feeling surfaces deep in my gut. Something's wrong. And I don't know how to fix it.

# THEO
# 26

When we came up with the plan to make a mental link with Peng, I didn't foresee being yanked into Peng's mind the way a tiny boat would be in a stormy sea.

Peng's mind is a red rush of nonsensical images. I scramble fruitlessly, my limbs flailing, before realizing I have no limbs. I have no body. I open my mouth to scream, but nothing comes out, and then—

*Who's there?*

The voice reverberates all the way through me.

"I—it's me, Theo."

*I do not know who that is.*

"Um, my brother Jamie was the one who promised to save you, and I'm trying to—" Trying to what? I falter. I can't remember why I was even here to begin with, and the nonstop swirling of warped images is driving me mad.

*Ah. The little brother. You can't possibly help me, O puny human.*

"I could try. I mean, if you'd give me a chance, I could maybe—"

*You don't know what you're up against!*

Suddenly the rushing stops, and there's an expectant hush as the images stand still. Then, all at once, they leap straight at me.

Peng's memories are horrific, all broken and mixed up. There's a flash of Peng, stabbed all over with giant needles pumping all sorts of drugs into him. The needles are attached to tubes the size of my legs. Peng thrashes just in time to catch sight of scalpels being brought into the room by floating hands. A scalpel flies toward him and buries itself in—

The scene changes. Peng is soaring above the clouds, the wind brushing past his iridescent feathers, the sun so close it seems within reach. Somehow, though I barely know any Chinese mythology, I know he's close to Kunlun Mountain, which connects heaven and earth. Through Peng's eyes, I feel its pull, pure and irresistible. For the first time, I feel at peace. Far from everything, from the pain of Jamie's death and the weight of trying to survive at Reapling. Joy floods my being, and—

The scalpel is digging, digging, and the pain is excruciating. And all the while, the tubes are sucking everything out of me—

I am dying. I pray for death. I beg for it.

*Enough.*

A massive force flings me. I crash through the raging memories. Bright lights blind me, and I slam into something solid. Which turns out to be my body. Which I discover when I fall flat on my butt.

"Oh my gods!" Kai says, flapping around my face. "You're back. Are you okay? You were just sitting there all blank, and I was about to call the supervisors over—"

Namita's crouched next to me. "Did the mind link work?"

I scrabble to my feet and grab the edge of the table as the room swims. "It did," I rasp out. I barely recognize my own voice. Everything feels so unreal. "It's so much worse than we thought."

"What? How?" Namita says.

I look around, making sure no one's listening. Luckily, everyone else is so busy trying out various spells that the room is borderline chaotic. "Peng dumped a whole bunch of memories into my mind. I don't understand them—they're all broken and mixed up—I think he's confused about the timing of events, he was pumped with all sorts of drugs—there were needles, and tubes, and—and—scalpels." I have to stop then because the lump in my throat is too big to swallow. I'm overwhelmed by sorrow and fear.

Namita's mouth drops open in horror. "What?"

Kai turns green. "I thought Peng had fallen into a random trap by accident." She stops when Namita shushes us and points.

My blood turns cold. Xiuling, making her rounds and giving students help, is approaching Danny's table. The sight of her and of Saanvi nearby fills me with dread—they're Reapling employees—who knows how much they know? Are both of them in on the whole thing?

I turn to Namita and Kai, feeling white-hot panic flowing through my veins. "What if they were the ones who captured him in the first place? What if Reapling sanctioned it? We can't let Xiuling see him."

Kai spins in a tight, frantic circle. "What do we do?"

"We can't wait for Danny to figure out how to open the cage, and I definitely can't cast the spell to Bind the Horse's Behind. That'll only make Peng even more vulnerable!" An idea strikes me. "I'll cast the Path of the Pig Be Big spell on Peng. That'll break him out of his cage. Jamie wanted me to free Peng. I can't fail him now."

"Have you forgotten that he's the size of Japan?" Kai says. "If you cast that spell on him, it'll counter the spells your brother cast on him, and he'll swell back to his original size. We'll all die."

"Saanvi said we can tweak ancient spells. I'll add a 'dian' to the end of the Path of the Pig Be Big, so it becomes Pig Be *a Bit* Bigger." My voice comes out a lot more confident than I actually feel. "And then I'll uh—I'll create some diversion while you and Namita get Peng out of here."

Kai and Namita look at each other and then nod at me. "We've got this," Namita says, though she looks somewhat uncertain.

"Yes, we've got your behind," Kai says.

"Your back," Namita says. "We've got your back."

"That's what I said."

Before I can second-guess myself, I wave my hand at Peng's cage and cast the spell.

# THEO
# 27

I can't stop thinking of Jamie as I say the incantation. I see him lifting his hand just as I'm doing, opening his mouth, letting a string of Mandarin words stream out as effortlessly as a brook slipping over stones, and freeing Peng from his captivity. I feel his urgency, his fear, and above all, his grit. For the first time, I understand that his notebook isn't a fun treasure hunt; it's about saving a life.

This is what he meant for me to do: free Peng. I know it.

I don't believe in old Chinese magic, but I believe in my brother.

Before the last syllable of the spell finishes its journey out of my mouth, I feel it wrenching out, powerful, muscled, and wild. Never has a spell felt like this, a hurricane sweeping through me, drawing everything out of me. I don't fully understand it, but now I know what Saanvi meant when she talked about how using your innate magical energy is like fixing your eyesight. I've never felt so focused, so strong. This is how magic should be—

Peng starts clucking madly.

"Oh my gods, oh my gods!" Kai squeaks next to me.

Peng's still squawking, though it sounds more like cackles. And he's beginning to grow. I've done it! My chest swells with pride.

"You fool!" Kai cries. "Blithering, insane fool! You've cast it wrong!"

Wait, what? "But—I said, 'Make bird a bit bigger'—" I sift through all the syllables. Yes, I've definitely said the right words.

"You pronounced 'a bit' wrong! It's supposed to be 'diǎn.' You said 'tiān'—that means 'the sky.' Make bird as big as the sky!"

What?

The joints of the cage split open. Danny and Xiaohua, focused on their own little spells so far, finally notice what's happening, but it's too late. Peng's free.

"Make it stop!" Kai cries. "Quick, before he gets too big and powerful!"

That's right. The bigger Peng gets, the more powerful he'll become. He's only the size of a small watermelon now. I can still overpower him. I point at Peng and start to cast a makeshift Pig Be Smaller spell, but the well of power inside me has been sucked dry by the first spell. The Pig Be Smaller spell fizzles and dies before it's even halfway there.

"Danny!" I shout. "Make it small!"

Danny opens and closes his mouth, staring at Peng, who's now the size of a Labrador retriever. "Wha—I—but—" He raises his hand at Peng, who turns to face him, and his beak, which only moments ago was so tiny and harmless, now looks like the world's sharpest pair of shears. Peng grins, revealing jagged teeth, and stabs his beak at Danny's head, but Xiaohua snatches Danny and flies away with him.

By now, the other kids are scrambling from their desks. Namita makes a complicated motion with her hands and shoots a bolt of golden light straight at Peng. But with a flap of his wings, the spell warps, turning into a golden sword and ricocheting straight back at Namita. Saanvi casts a blocking spell at the last second, and the sword stabs into an invisible shield, its point less than an inch from Namita's chest. Saanvi barks at Namita to get out of the auditorium, while casting spells manically around her, shielding kids as they scramble away. And Xiuling is . . .

Xiuling is staring right at me, her mouth open in a perfect circle. My heart punches its way all the way down to my stomach. She knows it's all my fault.

"We need to get out of here." Kai tugs on my hand. "Come on."

"But I can't abandon him. I still feel him in my head, I need to protect him—"

An alarm goes off, and a dozen Eyes swarm into the auditorium. They blink, and when they reopen, there are darts in the middle of their pupils. I look closer and realize the darts are actually arrows held by the imps inside the Eyes.

"Shoot!" Xiuling barks.

The arrows fly toward Peng, their points unforgivingly sharp. Peng swipes a wing across his body—he's now about the size of a hippo—and most of them bounce off harmlessly. A couple manage to find their mark, burying into the side of his neck, where his feathers have yet to catch up with his sudden growth and his skin is wrinkled and pink. He throws his head back and screams. The windows shudder, and I wail in pain. Peng's shriek is unearthly, a physical rending of my bones. He staggers, crashing into tables and chairs, giant beak swinging this way and that. For a few seconds, he stops growing. Everyone watches expectantly. I wonder if I could get him out of here somehow—

One eye bulges out grotesquely, suddenly twice as big as the other. Peng moans. "I don't feel good." His voice comes out alien, broken, like a few people talking at once.

His top beak bulges out, suddenly as big as a rowboat, and the weight of it pulls him to the floor. He flaps his wings this way and that, but he's unable to lift his massive beak.

"The arrows are poisoned. They're making him unstable," Kai says. "We need to leave now!"

Guards fly in on winged shoes, more Eyes streaming in behind them.

"Get that kid out of here!" one of them shouts, pointing at me.

"But I—" A spell from a nearby guard hits me in the chest. Upon contact, it grows tentacles and ensnares me. I'm lifted from the floor, my hands and feet bound in an iron grip. The spells start flying before I'm even out of the room, and Peng's cries of pain pierce all my senses. I twitch and shiver and shriek.

"Break the bond with Peng," Kai says. "Break it, or it'll kill you."

I won't. I can't. He's dangerous, yes, but he's also a link to Jamie. I need to save him.

Outside the auditorium, the guard's spell releases its hold on me, and I fall in an unceremonious heap on the ground. All around me, alarms are blaring and people are screaming and running away. There's a crash from inside; apparently the guards aren't having an easy time apprehending Peng.

"I need to make another mind link with him, but I don't have enough qì—" Desperation claws at me. Am I to fail Jamie after all this time?

"Take mine," Kai says.

"What?" I stare at her. "How does that even—"

"The same way you did the mind link with Peng." She meets my eye and nods.

There isn't time for second-guessing. I close my eyes and try to connect to her in the same way I did with Peng, to tap into her sorrow, her tortured longing for Jamie. I know the shape, the smell, the sharpness of it. I know it all. And now I know the power of it.

Kai's sadness gives me a surge of burning energy, and as before, I focus on my memories of Jamie while thinking of Peng at the same time.

*Peng,* I say. *Can you hear me?*

His voice stabs through my head. *Such pain! Everything is on fire!*

*I'm sorry, I'm so sorry. Listen, please, I can help you.*

*Why should I listen to a human? Look what your brothers and sisters are doing to me!*

*I'm going to stop them.*

*I don't trust you!*

*I will. But please don't harm anyone here. Leave this place without taking a single soul.*

*Ha! I will most definitely not do that! Oh, the destruction I will wreak upon all of you—*

Without warning, he sends another wave of memories rushing through my mind. They're brutal, filled with blood and agony. But then, as the jagged memories threaten to slice my consciousness into pieces, I catch a glimpse of him. Jamie. I grab hold of it and cling on with all my strength.

He's frightened—shaking, really, his breath coming in and

out in ragged little wheezes. Around him are the bodies of five guards, unconscious. Jamie managed to incapacitate five guards? Whoa. He runs up to Peng's enclosure, raises his hands, and yells out something. I struggle to hear his voice, but I'm limited to what Peng could see and hear, and the thick glass ensures that he hears nothing.

*That's my brother.*

One by one, the tubes are yanked out of Peng's body with a horrible sucking noise. He screams in pain, and Jamie aims his hand at him and yells out something else. The pain recedes, if only a little bit. And Peng blinks his bleary eyes and sees Jamie clearly for the first time. He sees his fear, and behind it, his kindness. His strength.

*That's. My. Brother!*

I shout it with all my might at Peng. His mind turns all its attention toward me, like a massive whale that's noticed a little ship in the vast ocean. I almost quail at the weight of it, but I stand firm. *I'm here. I'm his younger brother. Please trust me.*

His rage dives into me, and I let it. There is so much, I can't possibly stomach all of it, but somehow I draw on my memory of Jamie, on his depth, and somewhere there, I sense Kai, too, pouring her energy into my mind. We take in Peng's anger, wave after wave of it, until only the core of him remains.

*I . . . thank you.*

*No time for that.*

I open my eyes. All the noise—the shouting, the explosions, the commands—come crashing back like a tidal wave. Now that Peng no longer has rage driving him, he's less powerful. Which means he's in danger of being recaptured. I point at the auditorium. Breathe in. I can do this. I have to. Then I cast the simplest Chinese spell I can think of—A Rite to Make Skin White, with a couple of tweaks.

Screams spill out of the auditorium.

"I hope I haven't killed anyone," I moan.

"Hard not to when you turn their skin into flowers," Kai says.

"I—what? No, I said, 'Make skin smooth and long.' I thought maybe they'd trip over it or something . . ."

"Nope. You said 'huā' instead of 'huá.'"

"You just said the same word twice!" I wail.

"Spoken like a true lǎowài."

"Oh gods, oh gods, oh gods . . ."

I must look like a complete mess, because Kai's expression softens and she pats my head gently with a tiny fin. Somehow I muster enough energy to move my feet. Images swirl through my mind as I walk back toward the auditorium. Broken bodies strewn across the floor, flowers everywhere, their petals drenched in blood.

Except when I get there, there's no blood. Well, actually, there might be blood, but I can't see beyond a thick wall of flowers. I push through the mound—jasmine, roses, hydrangeas, sunflowers, hyacinths—their combined scents so strong and heavy that the air feels like it's made out of sugar. But everyone's still in one piece. And alive. Albeit buried under a mountain of flowers, but at least their insides are still nicely packed under their skins. Holy cow. How?

"Curiouser and curiouser," Kai says, next to me. "Ooh, you said 'bi' instead of 'pí.' You turned the walls into flowers, not their skin. Cunning."

A few feet ahead, there's a particularly large heap of peonies. As I struggle forward, the peonies explode, and Peng rises like a Leviathan from the ocean. He shoots up, growing every second, vibrant feathers sprouting from his skin in every shimmering color—purple, blood red, gleaming gold, royal blue. With a soul-rending cry, he crashes through the remaining roof of the auditorium. Shards of glass rain on us. A steel beam crashes down toward my head. I can't move, I'm about to die—

A gigantic wing swoops in and knocks the beam aside as easily as though it were a toy.

"Wha—" I splutter. Before I can say anything else, the wing scoops me up, and I catch a glimpse of Kai swimming frantically toward me before I'm lifted so fast I'm squashed against the feathers by the momentum. Then I'm standing before the biggest eye I've ever seen. It's as big as my house. No, bigger.

*Hello, my puny savior. Your little stunt with the flowers gave me just the chance I needed to break out of there. Unfortunately, I'm still stuck in your godsforsaken world for now. I need to know what summoning rites were used on me in order to reverse them. Alternatively, I could kill the person who summoned me, thus severing the bond.*

"Um, hi," I squeak. Even though he's no longer roiling with with hate and rage, he's still terrifying. "Can you not break the summoning bond yourself? Being a higher deity and all."

Peng snorts. *Of course I can. But it would be an incomplete severance of the bond, leaving me with the stench of its remnants. I want*

*a clean break, one that would leave no traces of this cursed realm on
my being.*

"Oh. Right, okay."

*I should just destroy this whole place. It would most likely kill the
person who summoned me. Very quick, very—*

"Um, please don't! I swear to you I will find out what rites they
used, or I'll find the person who summoned you and you can
make them dismiss you."

*Are you sure it is wise to leave this place standing? You have seen
what they are doing.*

"Yes!" I say hurriedly. "Please don't destroy the facility! What
can you tell me about the kidnapping? Do you remember any
details?"

*One moment I was soaring through the skies, the sun warm on my
back, and the next moment, I was summoned. As soon as I arrived,
spells hit me from every direction—such cruel, malicious spells. I was
knocked unconscious. Then those needles—filled with drugs. They
ensured that I was never conscious enough to know anything. You saw
them for yourself.*

"I'll finish what my brother started. I'll find out who was
behind your kidnapping, as well as the particular rites they performed, so you can break the bond cleanly."

*Hmm. Take this.* His massive head lowers and he plucks a pure
white feather from his shoulder. The feather is as long as I am tall,
but once it touches my hand, it shrinks to the size of my thumb.

*Once you have found the one who took me, burn this feather, and I
will answer. When the moon is rebirthed, I will be back. If you haven't*

*found the one who kidnapped me by then, I will destroy this place. You know, of course, that as a higher deity, I am not bound by simple karmic laws? I can destroy this entire place with impunity.*

"When the moon's rebirthed. Right, yes!" I squeak, stuffing Peng's feather in my pocket.

*Do not disappoint me, little one.*

With that, Peng lets go of me, and I plummet through the sky like a rock, crashing into the middle of a huge mountain of hydrangeas. Peng flies away, each beat of his wings a thunderclap.

A familiar form swims into my vision. "Survived the encounter with Peng, then, did you?" Kai says. "All your organs still nicely encased in your body? Yes?" She laughs nervously—more a cough-sob than a laugh, really.

I can barely summon the strength to respond. Kai reaches out, and to my surprise, she puts her little fins around me. I close my eyes and hold her tight. It's weird how glad I am to see her, how comforting her tiny hug is.

It takes a while for me to maneuver myself out of the suffocating mound of hydrangeas. I'm covered by so many scratches and wounds, I'm basically one giant bruise.

When I finally manage to crawl out of the mess, I realize I should've remained hidden, because before me is Xiuling, standing with her arms crossed. She's wearing an expression very much like Ma whenever she catches me doing something bad.

# THEO
# 28

"So you have no idea how you found Peng or how you managed to release him and turn half the auditorium into flowers?" Xiuling says. One eyebrow's arched so high it's almost disappeared into her hairline.

As she talks, I can't stop the questions crowding in my head, each one an alarmed whisper tinged with fear and distrust. Jamie found Peng during his internship here. Which means he was kidnapped by someone in the company. Or maybe it was sanctioned by the company itself. The next obvious question is: Who knew about it? Was Xiuling part of the whole scheme? I have no idea how much or how little I should say, but one thing's for sure: I can't let them find out about Jamie's notebook.

"I told you," I say, trying to appear weary and not in the slightest bit guilty. "I stumbled across Peng in the woods while I was hunting for creatures. And then Danny took him from me, so why isn't *he* being interrogated?"

"Danny's being questioned as well. But there are a few things that aren't quite adding up here. First of all, I don't understand how you found Peng when none of the Eyes or guards was able to sense him, and something like Peng would've had an incredible aura—"

"To be fair, Theo was just bumbling along as usual, and I was the one who sensed Peng," Kai pipes up. "It's—er—one of my specialties as a fish spirit. Yes, see, when I get near powerful creatures, my scales curl up like so—"

Xiuling turns her laser gaze to Kai. "And you didn't think it strange that we'd have such a powerful creature just randomly caged up?"

"Lady, do you have any idea how odd I find humans in general? Who knows what's normal or abnormal for you? You use fiddly sticks to eat your food instead of your gods-given fingers, you mask your scent with soap and perfume when it's clearly the best way to detect emotions, and let's not even get into undiepanties—"

"Undiepanties," Xiuling echoes. She has the glazed look people often get when they talk to Kai.

"That thing you wear to cover your unsightly bits, not that the rest of you is any less unsightly, but the bits that are particularly hideous—"

"I get it!" Xiuling takes a deep breath. "So neither of you realized that something was awry when you found Peng. And then . . ."

"Then Danny swooped in on his silly dragon and stole Peng from us, didn't he?" Kai claps her little fins together. "Conclusion: It's all Danny's fault, well, and also his dragon, did you know the dragon's name is Xiaohua—"

"Stop talking!" Xiuling snaps. She turns to face me. "Theo, I take this program very seriously. And if you're not a hundred percent focused, you stand to put everyone around you at risk."

Dread sours my stomach. I need to make this right. "But—"

"I'm sorry. You're obviously a talented child. You must have so much qì to be able to turn the auditorium into flowers—but I'm afraid you have to leave the program. I can't have you here endangering the other kids. Please pack your things. I'll arrange for a travel bubble to your house."

With that, Xiuling walks off, leaving me with nothing but burned rubble and a sinking realization that I've just ruined my chance of finishing Jamie's work and finding Peng's kidnapper.

And it hits me then. Jamie's notebook. On the last page, he had written:

> There's so much I wish I could tell you, but I'm running out of time. I'm worried about you going to ThunderCon by yourself. There are bad people around. Please get an adult or a good companion to go with you, okay?

I recall now that the words "running out of time," "bad people around," and "get an adult" are in purple. Maybe this isn't code for anything. Maybe there literally are bad people around.

The thought sinks in quietly, like a sudden frost blanketing my bones. Maybe Jamie's death wasn't an accident. Maybe that's what he meant by "running out of time." Maybe the "bad people," whoever they are, got to him. No. That's not possible. The paramedics, the cops—everyone—they all said the same thing:

Jamie fell asleep at the wheel. There were no signs of sabotage. His brakes worked fine. He wasn't drugged or anything. It was just an accident.

And yet.

For the first time, I can't help wondering if there's something more to the accident. Something everyone else has missed.

# KAI

# 29

"Kai, you need to fix this!"

If ever there are words that define all of my relationships with my masters. *Kai, fix this! Kai, fix that!*

Except—curses!—I actually do want to fix the mess this time round. Which is a bit awkward, on account of me having no idea how to do so.

"We can't go home now. There's something really bad going on here, I know it. Something big!" Theo cries, flapping his arms frantically.

"I know." I swim back and forth, trying to sort out the jumble of thoughts in my mind. "Peng was kidnapped by someone here. You don't just kidnap a god on your own. Whoever did it had to have access to the company's resources."

"Yes, exactly," Theo says. "What if it was sanctioned by the company after all? What if they're all in on it? What if—" His voice wobbles and he chokes. "What if Jamie's accident wasn't an accident after all?"

My mouth opens and closes, but nothing comes out. Because I was just thinking the same thing.

"Do an illusion!" Theo says. "Make Xiuling think . . . um . . ."

"I can't make Xiuling think that this whole debacle never happened. It'll last for about ten seconds before someone comes up to her and goes, 'So how about that building getting destroyed, eh?' and the spell will break."

"Shape-shift!" Theo shouts. He grabs me—not gently, mind you, his eyes wide and crazed, his nostrils flaring. "Turn into Creighton Ward and convince Xiuling not to throw me out. I need to fulfill my promise to Peng and free him from the human world, like Jamie wanted me to do. I can't be sent home now."

It's an utterly mad idea. It's a brilliant idea. It might work. I can't do it. I mustn't. The first fox spirit shape-shifted into a beautiful maiden to lure some unsuspecting male[30] into the forest before she lulled him into an eternal sleep and feasted on his qì. Ever since then, her descendants have followed suit, shape-shifting into beautiful women and using more elaborate spells of illusion (there are accounts of fox spirits creating an illusion of an entire village) to lure more gormless males away from human civilization. As a result, shape-shifting into a human, especially combined with the purpose of deceiving a human, is now deemed one of the worst things a fox spirit can do. Doing it would surely turn me even more demonic and cast me closer to Ox Head's and Horse Face's clutches.

I try to say as much to Theo, but I get as far as, "I would love to do that, but—"

"Then do it!" His words hammer down with the finality of a judge's gavel.

---

30 Don't ask me why he was unsuspecting. Listen, if you're traipsing around in the woods and some ethereally beautiful woman with flawless hair and makeup wearing a silk dress and satin slippers appears from behind a tree and beckons you to come close, would you be suspicious? You'd better be nodding right now. Those of you who aren't, quick! Tell me your name, date of birth, and social security number! Why? For good luck. Don't ask so many questions, please.

There's no use arguing, not when he's made the order so clear. I can't refuse a master's order. And, to be perfectly honest, I *want* to do it. I need to fix this somehow, and tricking someone is marginally more ethical than tearing their throat out. Yes? Yes.

With my mind made up, I zip away and locate an appropriate hiding spot. Fortunately, most of the Eyes are still preoccupied around the rubble, trying to locate people buried under the avalanche of flowers. I close my eyes, conjure up an image of Creighton Ward, and . . . change!

When I open my eyes, my feet are encased in polished leather shoes and my eye level is considerably higher than it was as a goldfish (or a fox, for that matter). I wiggle my fingers, wrinkling my nose at how pale and sausage-y they look, and then it strikes me that I'm being strangled. Gasping, I clutch at my throat and realize somewhat abashedly that the thing strangling me is a silk tie. Also, it's not actually strangling me. It just feels that way because apparently, Director Ward loves to wear his ties really tight.

It's been a while since I've shape-shifted into human form. Generally, I've stuck with animals or objects, due to the aforementioned karmic consequence and also the natural inferiority of the human body, the latter of which I am reminded of as soon as I take my first step.

"Why are you lying down on the grass?" Theo hisses. I haven't even noticed him following me, that's how deaf and blind my current form is.

"Obviously I fell, didn't I?" I snap. I spring back upright and smooth down my hair. "What are you staring at?"

"You really do look like him. It's weird."

I straighten my tie. "You should expect nothing but the very best precision from a top-notch fox such as myself. Right, off I go to save the day."

I take all of two steps before Theo grabs me.

"Kai! Your tails!"

Oops. I look at him sheepishly before closing my eyes and centering my focus, envisioning a tail-less bottom. But my magnificent tails remain stubbornly there. "Well, maybe Xiuling won't notice."

"Right, she won't notice two bright orange tails sticking out of Creighton Ward's butt!"

Before I can react, he grabs my beautiful tails, ties them up with a grotty rubber band, and shoves them up my suit jacket. He brushes my jacket back into place and then pushes me forward. "Go!"

I pause, hesitation coursing through every part of me. I need to tell him about Ox Head and Horse Face and the threat they pose to my life. My very soul. How convinced Ox Head was about me turning demonic, and how dangerous my task is. How very closely it toes the line between good and evil. I open my mouth, but the sight of Theo's stricken face stops me. The thought that Jamie's accident might have been connected to whatever sinister thing is going on here is overwhelming. No matter the cost, we must find out the truth. And so, with one last tug on my tie, I go.

# KAI

# 30

It's basically impossible to travel fast as a human. After all, humans are missing two legs. By the time I get within shouting distance of Xiuling, I'm out of breath.

Xiuling looks confused when she sees me. "Where've you been? I was just on my way to your office to speak with you. I didn't see you back there—"

"Never mind that." I try my best to look imperious, which is somewhat challenging to accomplish when one is so out of breath.

"This is a mess," Xiuling says, more brusquely than I was expecting, but I guess the woman's somewhat rattled, having had a building disintegrate into flowers and everything. "I've had to contact our publicity department so they don't let the media report on this. You know how everyone's sniffing around since Taslim's death, just waiting for Reapling to slip up." She rakes her fingers through her hair. A roaming Eye flies close to us. Xiuling glances at it and straightens up. "I'm sorry about the damage, sir. The child who caused it is from my group. I was actually about to speak with you about removing him from the program."

"Oho! Looking to pawn off responsibility for the incident onto a poor, innocent child's shoulders, eh?"

"What?" Her eyes snap to mine. "No, as I told you before, we shouldn't have allowed him to enroll in the program after what happened—"

"I don't want to hear any more of your excuses!" I crow, rising to fill my role magnificently. "Theo must stay on in the program."

"What? What are you talking about? Did I mention that it was Theo?" Xiuling glances at the Eye again and speaks in a calmer voice. "I don't think that's the best idea, sir. He's too brash and unpredictable. Why should we keep him in the program?"

Why indeed. I wasn't expecting her to actually question me. I make my voice silky low. "Are you questioning my authority?"

Xiuling's forehead is so tightly knotted it resembles a coiled rope. "Are you all right? Is it the—um, do we need to perform another ritual?" she says, very softly.

"Ritual?"

Her eyes narrow, and she says in a whisper, "A purification ritual?"

What is she talking about? But never mind that, I can't afford to let this go on for much longer. I lift my chin and attempt to stare her down. "Don't be silly, I'm all right. Theo stays in the program. And I will tell you why."

Xiuling watches me expectantly.

Ummm . . . hmmm . . . any second now, a brilliant idea's going to strike . . .

I stare back, hard. "Be . . . cause . . . of reasons . . . to do with . . . uh, Peng?"

Her entire demeanor changes. The expression on her face closes up. "Sir? I don't think we should talk about it now, out in the open like this."

A poison bubble deep in my belly pops, and out pours anger. She knows. She knew. She was a part of the whole kidnapping scheme.

The realization enrages me, takes over my entire being until I'm no longer sure what I'm about to do until I do it. I reach into the depths of me and cast a spell. A spell that's so strongly forbidden I haven't dared use it in over a hundred years. A spell of obfuscation.[31] The moment it's cast, I change my mind and try to catch it back. For a split second, I grasp it tight, but then it wriggles and slips free and hits Xiuling right in the middle of the face.

Xiuling's eyes widen, and then they glaze over. "Oh!"

"No, no, no—"

"Of course, sir," she says, and although her eyes are on mine, they're no longer sharp. "Yes, that makes perfect sense. We should definitely have Theo stay in the program."

My stomach turns into a lead weight. I think I might throw up.

"Well, the mess should be cleared up by evening, and we'll have the auditorium rebuilt by morning, so no harm done, really. Thank you for your leniency." With that, Xiuling walks away.

Oh no. I've committed one of the most wicked deeds I could possibly do—obfuscated a human directly.

Even as I think that, I feel my essence start to come undone, like a jacket being unzipped. With beings that operate on a higher plane, like fox spirits, when we succumb to our base selves, the results are dire. Every immoral act serves to strengthen the base

---

31 As its name would suggest, it's a spell that is meant to confuse the target. It's a form of mind control, which defies all boundaries of consent, which makes it one of the wickedest spells around.

self, until it becomes so powerful it overcomes our entire consciousness and turns us into demons.

Somewhere in my brain, I know this is what's happening to me. I yell it at the rest of me, "Kai, you're being corrupted into a demon, FIGHT BACK!"

But I don't.

Like a drop of ink plunged into water, my base self permeates into the rest of my essence, and it feels . . . good. I was expecting pain, maybe a slight burning, but no. It's actually pleasant, like a sip of hot chocolate on a cold autumn day. One by one, my muscles relax, lengthening, hardening, and I feel so STRONG. My pupils dilate, my heart turns into a galloping stallion. I could grab Xiaohua by the mane and fling her about as though she were nothing but a small worm.

If I wanted to. And I do, I do, I do! I want to tear straight into the sky, rip through the clouds, and yank down the stars, burning, blazing, and hurl them back to earth. Maybe then they'd know what it's like to lose Jamie.

*Jamie.*

The name gives me pause. I can't quite put a paw on it, at first. It meant—means—something to me, a long time ago. But . . .

Oh. Jamie.

The fog lifts. My newfound strength leaves me so suddenly that I collapse onto the ground, breathing hard, weak as a pup.

Footsteps rush toward me. "Did you do it?" Theo says. "Did you convince her not to kick me out of the program?"

Sourness fills my gut. I blink at him through bleary eyes. "Yes. Now go away, I feel terrible."

"You can't just lie down here! There'll probably be another Eye coming by any minute." He yanks at my arm with surprising strength and pulls me, stumbling, to my feet.

I know Theo's right, but as I stagger after him, demonic bitterness rushes through me. He doesn't care a whit about my well-being. He's only helping me out of here because he doesn't want to get found out.

Once we are deep into the cover of the woods, I slump to the ground, exhausted, and change out of Creighton Ward's awful form.

"Why are you in your fox form?" Theo says. "Someone might see us. Change into your goldfish form!"

I ignore him and start licking my front leg. My entire body feels horribly sensitive, like I can feel tiny air molecules brushing past my fur. It's setting my teeth on edge. I have an almost uncontrollable urge to bite something.

"Hello, Earth to Kai."

I bound up and bare my teeth at him, growling. How soft his skin looks. How plump! How good it would be to sink my teeth into his neck—

"You know, I just realized . . . I haven't thanked you."

—I can practically feel his blood gushing into my mouth—what?

"The whole mess with Peng . . . that was all on me. You cleaned up my mess, and I haven't even thanked you. So thank you, Kai. You've been . . ." Theo takes a deep breath. "Invaluable."

A wave of emotion I don't understand wells up in me. "Excuse you, I am extremely valuable!" I say to cover it.

Theo rolls his eyes. "That's what 'invaluable' means, genius."

"Oh, really? English really is the most terrible language, and I know pretty much every human language there is." As I continue a nervous patter complaining about the shortcomings of human languages, it sinks in that I no longer feel as though I'm about to burst like an exploding star. I pause my tirade and take a tentative breath. Then a deeper one. Having Theo thank me has taken away the heat of my rage, and with it, the unsettling feeling of losing control. He's acknowledged something I did as being valuable. At the end of my exhale, I feel more like myself. The strengthening bond between Theo and me cleanses my soul, just a little. I glance at Theo, and his flesh no longer looks as bitable.

"How did you convince Xiuling not to kick me out?" he says.

My cheeks warm up. I can't tell anyone, least of all Theo, that I obfuscated Xiuling instead of using my irresistible powers of persuasion to accomplish my task. How embarrassing. "Never you mind. By the way, Xiuling said something rather curious while I was talking to her."

"What?"

"She asked me—that is, Creighton Ward—if I needed another 'purification ritual.'"

Theo looks at me blankly. "Purification rituals are performed to cleanse your soul," I say.

"I know that, but why would she ask you if you needed one? Maybe you misheard her."

Exhaustion catches up with me. Shape-shifting into one human and obfuscating another one have taken everything out of me. "It's probably not important. But please be careful. I'm quite certain that Xiuling was aware of the plan to kidnap Peng. In all likelihood she was involved."

Theo nods, his face pale. "Maybe we should go to the police?"

"You could try, but I doubt the MNDA you signed would allow you tell any outsiders sensitive information about the company. And I also doubt that the police would believe a kid going on and on about kidnapping a god. The company will have their best lawyers shut the whole thing down, before shutting you up. Best to stay quiet for now and . . ." I sigh. I am so, so tired. "Wait."

"Okay," he says quietly.

Summoning the last of my strength, I change into my goldfish form and settle inside Theo's pocket. He hasn't even gone five steps before sleep takes me over and I'm plunged into darkness.

# THEO
# 31

Once I get back to the cabin, I take a scalding shower. Namita ambushes me after that, demanding an update. I'm in the midst of telling her what I know when the bell for dinner rings, startling both of us.

"Could've sworn dinner would be cancelled after today's catastrophe," Namita says.

"Yeah."

When we finally get to the dining hall, I feel as though my insides are filled with dynamite. I could explode at any moment and take this whole place down. I wish Kai were here. She was still asleep, so I chose to leave her in the cabin. But at least I have Namita with me.

I tense up as soon as I spot Xiuling at the dining hall, but she merely smiles at us benignly and then turns to speak to Saanvi. I watch the two of them, staring so hard that I half wonder if their senses are tingling at my laser glare. Are they really part of Peng's kidnapping? Of Jamie's death? But they look so happy and relaxed, and when a couple of girls approach them, both Xiuling and Saanvi look so genuinely friendly that I feel twinges of guilt. Maybe I've made a mistake. Maybe I'm being paranoid due to grief.

"We've gone all out tonight to help everyone recover from today's mishap," Saanvi says, and she's not exaggerating.

The table's positively groaning under the weight of food. There's a huge platter of tandoori meats—lamb, chicken, fat shrimp—all of them charred to perfection and smelling spicy and salty and begging to be eaten. Namita grabs an overstuffed dumpling.

"Eat up," she tells me. "We need to keep our energy up, especially if there's something bad going on." She bites into it and her eyes widen. "Momos! My grandaunt used to make them for us. She'd use lamb meat and tons of cumin and they are so yummy. I haven't had these in years."

Namita's right. I might as well eat. I need my energy to solve whatever mystery's going on here. I reach for a dumpling and bite into it. Immediately my mouth is filled with the taste of home. Tears fill my eyes.

"Do you like it?" Namita says.

I swallow the huge lump in my throat before replying. "Yeah. But this one's filled with chives and pork." It's a jiǎozi exactly like the ones Jamie and I used to make together.

Jiǎozi is the only Chinese food I've ever allowed myself to learn to make, and only because it meant I got to sit down with Jamie and chat with him for hours as we stuffed dumplings and folded them into funny shapes.

"Mine's filled with sweet coconut and jaggery," a girl named Sarah says. "Wow, these must magically turn into your favorite dumplings!"

At that, the other kids all grab a dumpling each, and there are delighted cries of, "Ooh, black sesame paste!" and "Punjabi-style aloo!"

I put down my half-eaten jiǎozi on my plate. Even though it's as luscious as I remember Jamie's dumplings to be, or maybe because it's exactly how Jamie's dumplings used to be, I feel violated. Whoever's in charge of cooking the food for us has no right to use such invasive magic.

It doesn't seem like anyone else has the same reservations about the food; they all eat merrily, and afterward, they slump in their seats, wearing dazed smiles and patting their bellies. My own belly is only half-full and knotted tightly with anxiety. I have no idea what my next move is.

A small glass appears in front of each of us, filled with some sort of shimmering liquid. Light fizzes out of the glasses, painting the walls and ceiling in myriad colors.

"This is liquid energy," Saanvi says. "Drink up, because the night isn't over. Tonight we're having a slumber party!"

Namita and I look at our drinks warily.

"Something the matter?" Xiuling says.

"No," Namita says, sitting up straight, her face reddening.

"Then why aren't you drinking?"

We look around the table. Everyone else has downed theirs, and they look perfectly fine. Happy, even. With Xiuling and Saanvi staring at us expectantly, we're left with no choice. I take a cautious sip, and then something takes over me and I gulp the rest down.

Oh. My. Gosh.

"Liquid energy" is the perfect way of describing it. The drink sparkles its way through my system, and everywhere it goes, it shatters my fatigue and my caution and everything bad inside me and leaves behind an explosion of electricity. If they asked me to run a full marathon right this very second, I TOTALLY WOULD.

The others look just as happy; in fact, many of them have literally shot out of their chairs. I jump up as well and am somewhat taken aback when I fail to graze the ceiling with my fingertips.

"Okay, kids! Hey, listen up!" Saanvi claps a few times to catch our attention. "We're breaking you off into groups for the slumber party, okay? Please follow your group leaders."

I zip over to Xiuling and crash into Danny. I barely feel anything. I don't even feel annoyed or angry at him. Neither does he, apparently; all he does is laugh and bounce back to his feet.

"I don't like this," Xiaohua says. She's twined around his neck like a scarf. "They've given you kids an elixir that increases your ability to access your qì."

"That's great, right? Isn't that great? It sounds great!" Danny says, hopping from one foot to another.

"It definitely feels great!" I say.

I race after Xiuling as she leads our group to a separate room. There's a bunch of sleeping bags arranged in a circle on the floor, surrounded by what looks like hundreds of red candles.

"Well, that isn't a fire hazard at all," Xiaohua mutters.

"I'm sorry to have to do this, but I'm going to ask you guys to dismiss your companions," Xiuling says.

"Why? Danny, I don't—" Xiaohua says, but Danny is already reciting the dismissal incantation, and Xiaohua's yanked into the air and disappears with a small pop. All around us, the other kids are doing the same thing. Guess it's just as well that Kai's back at the cabin.

# KAI
## 32

"Look! Who do we have here?"

My insides curdle at the sound of that voice. But before I can react, another voice booms from the slithering darkness.

"Brother, it is Kai."

"Yes, I know it's Kai. I was asking for dramatic effect," the first speaker says irritably.

The darkness recedes just enough to reveal my two nemeses, Ox Head and Horse Face. Ox Head's carrying his trademark trident, while Horse Face brandishes his prized spiked club. Ox Head is noticeably larger, more solid, more real, than when I last saw him. Their stench fills my nose—that burning, sulfuric tang mixed with blood and cattle sweat. The yāoguài are no longer weighing down the dead branches of the magnolia trees. They're scuttling across the cracked ground, their nails clicking, scraping. They can't have me, not quite yet, but they're prodding at the boundary that separates me from them, hissing and grinning with their sharp teeth.

Something brushes the very tips of my tails, ever so slightly, and I jump, snarling.

"Look how she jumps, brother!" Ox Head crows. "She shall give a fine dance in the Cauldron of Boiling Oil."

Horse Face takes a deep breath, his nostrils flaring. "It's been a while since I had fox meat."

"I was following my master's orders—" My voice is so tiny, so weak. Flimsy, like my excuses.

Ox Head and Horse Face roar with laughter, the bangles hanging from their weapons jingling. "Keep telling yourself that, little fox!" Horse Face says. "You know what they say about the road to hell . . . What is it paved with again, brother?"

"Well, ours is paved with the broken skulls of evildoers," Ox Head says.

Horse Face sighs, releasing white steam. "I didn't mean it literally."

Ox Head looks at him blankly. "Um, well, the path made of skulls is also lined with gored intestines—"

"Good intentions!" Horse Face shouts. "It's paved with good intentions!"

"You don't have to be so rude about it, brother!"

They turn to face each other, both raising their weapons, and I take the chance to run away. Ox Head and Horse Face really are each other's worst enemy—

I crash into a wall and bounce off it like a Ping-Pong ball. Ox Head towers before me, grinning.

"Silly little fox. Surely you didn't think it would be so easy to escape the guardians of the underworld?"

"You don't understand," I warble, "there's something awful going on. Something dangerous. They kidnapped Peng—"

"Humans kidnapped a deity as powerful as Peng?" Horse Face says. They roar with laughter.

"Look at me, I'm a puny human! I'm going to kidnap a god!" Ox Head says in a high-pitched voice.

"No, really. You can check if you don't believe me. Peng's not in this realm!"

"Probably off on vacation," Ox Head says.

"I hear Phuket is nice this time of year," Horse Face says. They both turn and look down at me, grinning.

"Even if you weren't lying, little fox, it does not matter. Revenge is not a worthy cause. It does not cancel out the fact that you have wreaked much havoc. You obfuscated a human!" Ox Head says. "How wicked."

"How demonic."

"No, but—" I scrabble back and bump into Horse Face's thick legs. There's nowhere left to go. This is it. I'm going to get captured and sent to Diyu, my soul forced through the tortures of the ten circles of hell for eternity. I will be boiled, stabbed, peeled like an orange, and worse still, made to listen to opera and pretend to like it.

Unless I can somehow get to Theo. If I could just get back to the human world, I might be safe. Like all denizens of the spirit world, Ox Head and Horse Face can't get to the human world unless they're summoned.

Ox Head raises his forelegs, and the trident glints in the pulsing light. I try to focus every atom in my body on Theo. His face. His voice. Ox Head thrusts the trident down, aiming straight for my heart.

"Theo!" I scream.

# THEO
# 33

"Okay, guys, step into the circle and pick a sleeping bag," Xiuling says. "We're going to play a few games and sing some traditional songs."

I bounce into the circle, picking a sleeping bag. I notice belatedly that I've chosen a spot right next to Danny, but surprisingly, I don't even care. He glances at me and smiles dopily. Since my mind's basically a bunch of colorful fire sparks, I can barely follow any of the "games" Xiuling teaches us. Only flashes of the activities remain with me—some sort of little sticks thrown in a wild pattern on the floor, dark red paint that we're told to dip our fingers into—and all the while, we're asked to chant a curious, heady rhyme in Mandarin that, as usual, I struggle to pronounce properly. As I warble and try to keep time with the other kids, images of Kai flash through my mind. None of the images make any sense.

Kai's back in fox form, running hard. Fear surrounds her like a noxious cloud. What's she so scared about? She pauses, staring at something I can't see, and then she opens her mouth and screams my name, and I start screaming, too, because I'm flying at the same time as I'm rooted to the floor. I'm being torn in two, and nobody seems to be able to hear me.

I'm falling, and I can't stop it, I'm flying, falling, flying . . .

Something slams into my chest at full force, knocking me back to the ground. We both shriek, kicking and thrashing wildly.

"Theo? It's me! It's Kai!"

I blink at the form sitting on my chest. "Kai! Kai? Wait, am I imagining you again? I—"

"Why are you here?" she cries, ignoring all of my questions. "*How* are you here?"

I scramble to my feet, hugging Kai close, and look around. Whatever words I'm about to say die before leaving my mouth. I stare, and stare, and stare. Kai says something else, but I barely register her.

I'm in a land whose fabric nightmares are sewn out of. Voices whisper-scream at the very edges of my hearing. Snatches of cackles and sobs. The sky is literally boiling, the clouds churning like a vat of soup, with streaks of lightning fracturing it now and again. There are trees around me, or suggestions of trees, though I can't seem to focus on them in the non-light. They appear when the land is lit by lightning, but when the light dims, the trees disappear completely, I'm sure of it. I never thought that trees could be scary before, but these are terrifying.

The ground is cracked and covered by tangles of thick, gnarly roots that seem alive in a way that I can't explain. They look like they're waiting for the right time to uncurl and ooze along the broken ground in search of ankles to wrap around.

Worst of all, worse even than the strange sky and the strange trees and the strange roots, is that I feel . . . uncontained. Like a thousand needle-sized holes have been stabbed through my skin, and my essence, my very being, is leaking out while my noxious surroundings seep in. Fear snakes through my veins. I can't remember the last time I was this scared. Maybe when I was five and woke up from a nightmare, screaming my head off.

I hug Kai tighter. She's the only thing that seems real here, and I'm beyond relieved to have her with me. With a start, I realize that there's no one I'd rather have—aside from Jamie, of course—than Kai next to me right now. I have to resist the urge to bury my face in her familiar, soft fur and wail like I'm all of five years old again.

"Kai?" My voice comes out warped, an echo floating from afar instead of my very own mouth. "Where are we?"

"I've been trying to tell you." Kai's face is tight with fear. "We're in the Doorway."

"What Doorway?"

Kai looks at me, her teeth bared, her ears flicking this way and that, as though listening for something bad. "It's the land separating the spirit world from Diyu. Theo, we're at hell's doorstep."

# KAI
# 34

Every hair on my body is standing on end, every neuron in my brain firing at maximum speed, and one single question shouts above the chaos: Why is Theo here?

We huddle close under a grove of yùlán magnolia trees. The trees are in full bloom, their flowers deep violet with blood-red centers, and each one gives off a sickly sweet stench that makes me want to retch.[32] Still, the trees offer us a bit of cover from whatever might be following.

"Why are we here?" Theo babbles. "Kai, what's happening?"

"Calm down. Hey, hey!" I poke his forehead, and he stutters to a stop, staring at me with wild eyes. "Look at me. Just focus on me, your very winsome companion, Kai. Yes? Okay. Tell me everything you remember before you woke up here."

He jabbers on about a feast. "And then before I know it, I woke up and—"

"No, you're missing something. Go back to the meal. Did they serve you anything strange?"

"Yes!" Theo gasps. "After the meal, I was so tired, but then they gave us a drink and I felt amazing."

My ears perk up. "Tell me about the drink."

---

32 Go to the perfume department of any store where overenthusiastic salespeople prowl and you'll know what I'm talking about.

"Xiaohua didn't like it. She said it was some sort of elixir that messed with our yin and yang—"

I narrow my eyes at him. "Really? And all of you drank it without asking what it was?" I resist the urge to shake him and give him a lecture about stranger danger.

"I remember thinking I was a balloon . . ." His eyes become glazed, and his voice falters.

"Hey!" I snap. I poke his forehead again. "Look at me!" If he loses focus long enough, he'll end up lost in the Doorway forever. "Then what happened?"

"Then we went to a slumber party and Xiuling got us to play some games . . . They were really weird and not very fun at all . . ." Theo yawns. "We threw sticks on the ground and tried to get them to form a certain pattern, and then there was a rhyme." Before I can stop him, he starts singing.

Electricity shoots through my body, from snout to tails. "Stop singing it," I hiss.

Theo blinks at me. "Hmm?" He's wearing a dopey smile. "Why not? I like the song."

"It's not a song, it's a bloomin' spell to open up a portal to the spirit world. And you were pronouncing the words all wrong—oh my gods. I know why you're here!" I jump. "For some reason, they wanted to send you kids to the spirit world, but your atrocious Mandarin must've gotten you lost along the way!"

"But isn't it sooo expensive to like, travel between the human world and the spirit world?" he says.

"Very expensive, and not only that, but very difficult. It is incredibly hard, especially for a human, to traverse through the planes." The thought of how powerful a spell Reapling must have used to transport these children makes me shudder. "Reapling must have developed some sort of special elixir to unlock your qì and allow you to move between realms. I daresay such things are not FDA-approved."

"Silly FDA," Theo slurs. "I really really really enjoyed the elixir."

I'm about to shake him, but a thought strikes me and I pause. "That doesn't explain how you ran into me, though."

His head lolls forward, and I poke it extra hard.[33] "You yelled out my name . . . ," he mumbles.

I called out his name? Impossible, I . . . I . . . oh. I did. When Ox Head and Horse Face were about to capture me, I cried out. And it was for Theo.

Cripes. In my time of need, I sought him out. Not Jamie, not my own trickster instincts, but him. Theo. The boy who's currently about to fall asleep in the worst possible place. Fear grabs me in an unforgiving grip, so hard that I nearly squeal. Despite how irritating he is, it hits me in a sudden blow that I care about him. He's my master now. And I don't want to lose him.

I don't bother poking him this time. I turn my front paws into hands and grab him by the shoulders. I shake until his head flops back and forth and I can practically hear his brain rattling around in his skull (it's not a very big brain, is it?).

---

33 Am I getting the very slightest bit of satisfaction from poking Theo's face? Of course not! We're in a very dire situation and I am a professional! What? Oh. I'm still poking him? Am I? You're just imagining things, Bertha. Shush, we need to be very quiet right now.

"Ow, stop that!" Theo pushes me away, and as he does, I catch a glimpse of writing on his right arm.

"What's that?"

"What's what?" He turns around and glares into the pulsing darkness.

"No, I meant on your arm."

"What?" Theo holds out his arm and gasps.

There, written in bold, incandescent red letters, are the words *THIS IS YOUR SECOND TASK. IN ORDER TO PASS, BRING BACK A VIAL OF RIVER WATER FROM THE SPIRIT WORLD.*

"Right," I say. "So now we know what Reapling wants you to do. They must've given you something to help guide your way in case you get lost. Let's see . . ." I push up his left sleeve, and sure enough, there's something written on his left arm. This one is written in cursive.

*In case you lose your way, point your left index finger and it will guide you to the river. To get back to the human world, make a small cut.*

"What do they mean by 'make a small cut'?" Theo says.

"They mean cut your arm. The pain of a physical wound will sever your bond with this world and launch you back to the human world. I volunteer to do it when it's time for us to return." I shape-shift my front paw into a chain saw and give him an angelic smile.

Theo chooses to ignore me. The sight of the words on his arms seems to have sobered him up a bit, and he's standing straighter, which is quite a relief. "Okay, let's try this." He points with his left hand. A small beam of light immediately shines from the tip of his finger toward our right.

He turns to where the light's shining, and we begin our trek, scuttling from the cover of one tree to the next. I cast a spell of illusion around us to make it seem like Theo and I are dung beetle yāoguài rolling two small balls of poop. Thank gods there are no celestial spirits like dragons and phoenixes around, who would see through my spells in the blink of an eye.

The deeper we go into the yùlán trees, the thicker the stench of the blooms—a rotten stink so thick it clogs up my mouth like rank honey. I can't help but notice the yāoguài that have begun to gather above us. They wear the shape of míhóu—macaque— except these macaques are in shades of black and silver and have teeth straight out of nightmares. I keep an eye on them as we scuttle, trying not to show my fear in case it makes Theo panic. I must stay strong and get us out of here, get my master out of danger. I failed my last master; I can't fail this one, too.

"There's something in the distance," Theo says. "It looks like a door . . ."

"It is. It goes to Naraka."

"Naraka? Isn't that hell in Hindu mythology?"

"Yep." I keep an eye on the gathering míhóu as I talk, dread filling my senses at the sight of them so close to us. It's a struggle to keep my voice even. "Every form of the underworld, be it Diyu or Naraka or hell and so on, overlaps every other on different planes, a nice little mille-feuille of places for humans to be tortured. There are doorways that lead from one to the other. In fact, three of the kings of the underworld—Hades, Yanluo, and

Yama—often have an afternoon cuppa together. They sip gingerbread tea and eat the usual stuff, you know, scones studded with torn fingernails, little sandwiches with sliced cucumber and human skin, that sort of thing."

Theo winces. "Nice."

Then I hear it. Or rather, I hear him.

I stop in my tracks, frozen, everything forgotten—the míhóu, the Doorway, the danger we're both in—they all fizz away. There's just me and him. My true master.

*Kai, you're finally here.*

"Is that—is it really you?" I cry out.

"Who're you talking to?" Theo says.

*I've missed you so much, Kai.*

"Me too! Where are you? Come out," I plead, my body straight as an arrow. I am aching to fly, to pounce on Jamie and lick his face like a dog.

"Kai?" Theo says, but his voice is getting softer.

*Follow my voice.*

I can't not follow his voice. It's him, it's him! I glimpse a flash of black hair disappearing behind a tree.

"Wait!" I run faster—*quick!*—before I lose him. I need to beg him for forgiveness for failing him. For not being a strong enough companion to help him. I need to explain that I'm trying my best to get justice for him.

"Kai!" Theo's galloping after me. Every footstep of his is a crash that sends an excited chittering above us, and belatedly, I realize I've let the spell of illusion fall by the wayside. And I. Don't. Care.

Jamiejamiejamie—there he is!

I catch a silhouette of him before he vanishes inside a dark cave. Behind us, the cackling, screeching macaques close in. As soon as the darkness engulfs me, the snapping teeth and scrabbling claws coming after us suddenly stop. The macaques remain at the entrance of the cave, baring their teeth and shrieking.

"Kai?" Theo calls out softly, fear making his voice wobble.

I ignore him and advance deeper into the darkness. The cave is strangely warm, a feverish sort of warmth, dank and suffocating. My paws bump into broken sticks and several round objects, which skitter and roll away, clattering. I'm in a dark cave filled with . . .

Bones.

*Kai? Hurry, I need your help.*

I plunge forward, ignoring the quailing tremor in my belly. More and more bones cover the ground, until I'm no longer kicking them aside easily but climbing through them. And the smell! Rotting flesh and mildew and something really, really bad. Something evil. Dread nearly overcomes me. Oh, Jamie, please be okay.

I burst into a cavern of blinding light. Crystals line the ceiling, flickering in a dozen brilliant colors. In the middle of the cavern is a huge fire whose flames flicker from green to purple to yellow. And, next to the flames, is he.

My master. My true master.

"Jamie!" I half howl, half scream. I leap toward his open arms.

Jamie smiles. There are way too many teeth. Also, they're pointy.

The shock is practically a punch in the face. I twist in midair, my paws flailing, and manage to crash in a rather unceremonious pile on the floor, a few feet away from not-Jamie.

Not-Jamie's mouth twists into a sad frown. *Kai? Please come to me. I've missed you so much.*

Anger. So much of it filling my senses. It was a trick, and I fell for it hook, line, and sinker. How could I have been so stupid? "Um, well, it's been nice to see you again, but I've got this really urgent appointment with my uh, accountant." Where's Theo? Did I lose him in the tunnel? Is he okay?

Not-Jamie throws his head back and gives a throaty laugh, shattering the last of the illusion. When he faces me, he no longer looks human. What stares back is a naked skull.

"Baigujing!" Curses! I should've known it was her. The cave full of bones was a dead giveaway. Baigujing's name translates to White Bone Spirit, which is a nice way of saying she's a walking, talking skeleton. The sight of her makes my lips stretch thin into a snarl. I can't help it; every part of me is screaming to get away from her.

The skeleton grins.[34] *Hello, Kai. Long time no see.*

I take a moment to compose myself before replying. I can't show my fear. "You look good, for someone who's a thousand years old."

*I've got all these spares to use once something is damaged.* She plucks off her right arm and picks out another from a nearby pile. It clicks into place, and she wiggles it at me. *See? Good as new.*

"That's really quite unhygienic. Well anyway, it's good to see

---

34 Typical.

you, let's do this again soon, like in five thousand years or so? Toodles!"

*Not so fast, little fox.*

Dozens of bones jump up and surround me, each end joining another with horrible clacks until they turn into a cage.

"Um, heh-heh, your security system seems to have mistaken me for an intruder. If you'd just tell your little minion bones to part, I'll be out of your hair—oh you don't have hair. I'll be out of your skin—oh you don't have skin, either. I'll be out of your um, your clavicle? That doesn't sound right, does it—"

Baigujing clicks her fingers, and a handful of tiny bones snick around my muzzle and tighten. She grins as I struggle to open my mouth, my muffled snarls filling the cavern. *There, that's more like it.*

I charge into the side of the cage and bounce off harmlessly. Oh gods. Am I truly to die here, eaten by a skeleton demon?

Baigujing waves a hand lazily, and a huge wok appears, settling itself atop the green fire. A cleaver flies straight into her outstretched hand. She approaches slowly, stroking the blade to test its sharpness. *You've ventured into the dark side recently, haven't you, Kai? That was how I was able to sense you—I can hear the thoughts of every demon in the vicinity, you know. Hmm? You're not a demon? Well, not completely. But you're getting there. Let's see, I think I've got fresh ginger and scallions somewhere—*

"Stop right there!" a small voice squeaks.

Theo steps into the light, visibly trembling. He stands tall and clenches his hands into fists, but fear's roiling off him in palpable waves.

I thought I would be happy to see him, but now all I feel is anger. Anger toward myself. I led him right into Baigujing's lair, and now we're both going to get killed. Yet again, I have failed another master.

*What's this?* Baigujing glances at me for a second, then laughs. *Your new master? My goodness, human flesh. What a treat!*

Theo can't hear Baigujing's voice, but he's taken in enough of his surroundings—the cleaver, the boiling wok, me in a cage—to make an educated guess. "I—I order you to l-let my companion go!" He looks so scared it pains me.

Baigujing clicks her fingers again and transforms back into Jamie's form, dimples and all. "Hello, Didi. I've missed you so much. Come here to Gege. Don't be scared!"

The trapped-rabbit look melts from Theo's face, replaced by a familiar glare. My chest swells at the sight of it. We're both about to perish, but at least my master's going to go down fighting.

"How dare you take my brother's form?" He raises his hand.

Baigujing laughs, an eerie sound that makes my fur bristle. "My dear child, I've fought the Monkey God himself three times and outsmarted him every time. There's nothing you can do to me—"

"Not to you." Theo points his hand at me.

"Uh, hang on—" I say.

He says the words of the Path of the Pig Be Big.

Except he mispronounces the words. Of course.

# THEO
# 35

The bone muzzle clasped around Kai's snout breaks apart, and she lets out an unearthly roar.

"Nooo!" she screams. "You said the words wrong!"

"Which ones?"

"You said *angry* big do—arrrrgh!" The rest of Kai's reply devolves into another roar, and she suddenly bulges out in every direction. The bone cage shatters, and there, standing before me, is a huge black dog with two tails.

How did that happen? I had said the words to make Kai bigger, hoping she'd get big enough to break out of the cage, but I hadn't meant to change her into a dog.

"Kai?" I take a hesitant step toward her. Her enormous head swings to face me, jaws open, froth flying from her mouth, and I dive away just in time. Her teeth snap shut a hairbreadth away from my head with a loud crack. An ANGRY big dog. Oh no. "Kai, it's me! Stop it!"

But Kai's no longer interested in me. The cavern full of bones has caught her attention. She gives an excited yelp-growl and pounces into the nearest bone pile, gnawing and crunching and digging.

"Noooo! Leave my beautiful bones alone!" the demon shrieks.

I flinch at the sight of Jamie's face contorting into such a cruel expression. "This is all your fault, stupid boy!"

She raises the cleaver, but there's a whirl of black fur and Kai's suddenly on top of her, growling. Her massive jaws clamp down on one bony arm, snapping it off. The cleaver flies through the air and thunks into the ground a mere inch from my foot. This is it—our one chance to get out of here. I wrench it free and leap at Kai, grabbing hold of one of her tails. With one last look at the demon—I want, need, to see my brother's face again, even though I know it isn't him—I press the cleaver into my left arm and slice.

Pain burns through the entirety of my arm. My insides feel like they're being wrenched straight out of my body. But before I can even scream, I am yanked into the sky. The ceiling with its million glittering crystals rushes at me—oh my god, I'm about to splatter all over it—and then all goes dark, and I realize I'm in the actual mountain. My body has become immaterial. I tighten my grip on Kai, who's still struggling and snarling and trying to twist around so she can bite my hand. We whizz through the mountain and straight into the boiling sky. Up above the clouds, there's a rift—a gigantic, jagged scar in the very fabric of the air. We're sucked toward it, all of the hairs on my body standing straight as needles as we get close. Kai stops growling and gives a strangled cough. Then her form shimmers and stretches and warps and she changes back into a fox.

"Kai!" A laugh burbles out of me. I'm so relieved to have my companion back I could cry. "Hang tight!" I shout. "We're leaving this place!"

"Thanks for stating the obvious!" she yells, and I laugh again, because it's so good to have her back. Then there's no room for more words because we go into the rift and the air is sucked out of our lungs and we whirl this way and that like leaves. Through it all, the only thing I can grab hold of, the only thing that's real, is Kai.

I jerk awake with another gasp and immediately scramble to my feet, patting myself down from cheeks to legs. Okay, I'm all in one piece. But I'm also somewhere in the woods, and it's very nearly pitch dark.

"Kai?" I call out in a half whisper. Anxiety gnaws at me. Did she make it out? Oh gods, please don't let her be left behind, please—

The bushes behind me rustle, and with a melodramatic groan, Kai tumbles out.

"You made it, then," she says, slumping to the ground and licking her paws.

Relief floods my limbs. I rush to her and hug her.

"You'll mess up my fur," she says. Her voice is flippant, but her little paws wrap around my neck tightly.

It's unbelievable how good it is to see Kai again. Maybe she and I share a bond after all. I squeeze hard, inhaling the familiar scent of her.

After a while, I release her and look around. "Where are we?"

"In the woods. I don't think we're far from the facility. Ohhh, even my fur's aching!" she moans.

My eyes adjust to the dark, and I can see the lights of the Reapling building in the distance. Kai's right—we're not far away at all. I'm about to start walking toward the lights when realization crushes me like a boulder.

"Wait!" I gasp. "I failed my task. I was supposed to get a vial of river water from the spirit world, remember?" How could I have forgotten? I could punch a hole straight through a tree trunk, I really could. "I'll be kicked out for sure now."

Instead of waving off my concerns and telling me I'm stupid for whatever reason, Kai lowers her head and glances at me with the world's guiltiest look.

"What is it?"

She looks away, whining.

"Kai?"

"It was my fault!" she howls all of a sudden.

"How was it your fault? I got lost on the way to the spirit world because of my stupid pronunciation."

"While you were traveling to the spirit world, I was stuck in the Doorway, and I called out for you and you got sent toward me instead."

"Wait, but—I don't understand. Why were you in the Doorway in the first place?" I say.

Instead of answering, Kai lowers her head, her ears flattening, her bushy tails tucked between her legs. She whines and gnaws on her front paws.

"Kai? What's wrong? Are you okay?"

She refuses to meet my eye. "I don't want to say. I'm not proud of it."

"Kai, please, whatever it is, you can tell me." She looks like she's in so much anguish I want to pet her on the head.

"It doesn't matter, all right?" she cries. "All that matters is I called out for you and interrupted your journey to the spirit world. And then when you and I were trying to get to the spirit world, Baigujing sensed my thoughts and decided to trick me and I fell for it—"

My head spins. I can't even begin to make sense of what she's saying. "Hang on. Baigujing tricked you? I thought you ran off because you sensed a way out of the Doorway!"

"She took Jamie's form—you saw Jamie yourself—and his voice, and she called out to me to follow her, and—"

The tentative bond I felt with Kai earlier shatters. "And you fell for that?" My hands are trembling with rage. I tighten them into fists. "You're what, two hundred years old? And you fell for such a simple trick? I'm twelve, and I saw right through it!"

"I thought—I don't know what I was thinking," Kai mumbles. "I just heard Jamie's voice, and . . ."

"Never mind, it doesn't matter." But it does. I hate to admit it, even to myself, but it does matter, because the mention of Jamie is too painful to bear. To see that demon wearing his face . . .

A sob wrenches out of me. I shake my head, forcing the sobs back. "Never mind," I say again, louder this time. "But, Kai, I can't fail my task. We can't get kicked out of the program. We still need to find out who kidnapped Peng. Otherwise, he's going to come back and destroy the Bay Area."

Kai whines and turns in agitated circles, gnawing at the air. "I know."

The sight of her obvious anguish makes my chest tighten. "We need to fix this somehow. I need to—"

"No, you don't need to do anything," she says. "This was all my fault. I'll fix it." She looks me straight in the eye, her two tails standing up. "I vow to you, I will bring you a vial of river water no matter what. We will stay in this program until we bring justice for Jamie and Peng."

Before I can say anything more, she changes into a sparrow and flies away into the night sky. Within a few seconds, she's lost among the stars.

# KAI
# 36

This entire mess is my fault. I failed Jamie before, by not realizing he was in danger, by not saving him, and I'm not about to fail him again.

Theo's face, so much like Jamie's, flashes through my mind, granite cold and hard with anger and disappointment. I can't bear to see that expression again. I will do anything to get Theo his vial of river water.

"Anything!" I roar out loud, thumping my chest fiercely.

Unfortunately, since I'm currently a sparrow making its way across the sky, this means: 1. The "roar" comes out as an extremely cute and sweet chirp, and 2. my wings aren't flapping, and I plummet to the ground. It's a bit of a scare and somewhat distracting, but I manage to flutter my wings frantically enough to prevent myself turning into bird pancake.

How can I get a vial of river water?

I can't pop over to the spirit world and take some because we can't just pop back and forth between the human and spirit worlds at will. Dreams are an entirely different matter, because that's just the soul floating naturally to its home, and we can't really control it.

I mentally sift through places that might have the spirit world river water. The first and most obvious one is the California

Academy of Sciences at Golden Gate Park. The place is a treasure trove of all sorts of magical trinkets smuggled from Egyptian tombs, or stolen from black markets in Shenzhen, or London, and so on. There are talismans, ancient books of dark magic, centuries-old cursed mummies, all for gormless kids to come and gawk at during some school outing. No doubt they'd have all sorts of souvenirs from the spirit world there . . . locked under a reinforced glass case and protected by half a dozen of the strongest charms, most of which would pulverize me if I even grazed the case with the tip of a claw.

So. Let's mark the Academy of Sciences as a backup option. Hmm. Which leaves me with . . .

My mind remains stubbornly blank. Dejected, I alight on a tree at the outskirts of the Reapling facility and peck forlornly at my feathers.

A rustle catches my attention. It's a kid from the summer program. I don't know his name[35] but I recognize him as one of the Indian children. He's walking toward the buildings and clutching something in one of his hands. I jump to my feet, my muscles tingling, my feathers standing on needle points. This is it! This is plan B! Well, not this child specifically, because I don't need river water from his spirit world, but all I need to do is locate one of the Chinese children and borrow some of their river water.

I fly off the branch and begin a perimeter watch.

Within a few minutes, I'm rewarded by the sight of a boy heading in the same direction as the first child. Yes! A Chinese kid,

---

35 All you humans look alike to me. We spirits are so varied—we come in the forms of insects and fish and mammals, but you all come in one single form. Honestly, how do you tell one another apart?

stumbling a bit as he walks. I fly closer, excitement giving me renewed energy, but when I get close, I realize with a sinking feeling that it's Danny. Which means Xiaohua must be nearby.

But wait, why's little Mr. Look-at-Me-As-I-Fly-Everywhere-on-My-Dragon walking? He's clearly exhausted; every few steps or so, he lurches forward like he's about to fall flat on his face. If he's in that state and Xiaohua isn't giving him a piggyback—dragonback?—ride, then it must mean that Xiaohua has been temporarily dismissed.

Oho! This is perfect. It is meant to be that the very rude boy who's been terrorizing my master would be the one who helps him pass this task. I could swear it's the universe conspiring to help us balance out our karmas.[36]

I fly toward the floating playground and hide inside one of the colorful tree houses. When I'm sure I'm out of sight of any wandering Eye, I make a switch. A moment later, I emerge as Xiuling and smooth down my hair.

All right, it's showtime.

I take the first step into battle. My delicate ankle twists and I fall flat on my face. For the love of Guan Yin! The ridiculous footwear that female humans subject themselves to! I grab hold of my shoes and am about to break off the needle-thin heels in a fit when Danny spots me.

"Xiuling? Is that you?"

I struggle to my feet. It takes a huge amount of effort to keep Xiuling's trademark smile on my face as I limp toward Danny.

---

36 Remember, this is only happening because Danny is an odious person who deserves punishment and not at all because I am desperate to make up for my own mistakes.

"Are you okay?" Danny says.

"Don't be silly, of course I am!" I bark.

Danny's smile slips, and I correct my voice. "Yes I am, just a bit tired, is all. How are you? Did you just come back from the spirit world? Got your river water, have you?" Now that I'm so close to Danny, I can sense the river water on him, and its proximity is awakening something in me. A certain wildness. Hunger, laced with desperation. I need it, I need it, I need—

"Um—yeah, I do, actually. It was really tough," he mutters while he rummages in his pockets for the vial. "The shén and yāoguài there kept offering me gifts in exchange for—"

"Your liver? Yeah, we—I mean, they—like to do things like that."

Danny gives me a weird look. "No . . ."

"Your kidney? Well, there's a reason why you've got two of those little buggers, am I right?" I throw my head back and give a sharp laugh. "So, about the river water . . ." I shift my weight from one foot to the other, my hands with their long fingers twisting, knotting the entire time.

"Is everything okay? You seem slightly um, I don't know . . ."

I try a reassuring smile, but instead of being reassured, Danny shrinks back, his eyes wide with fear.

"Um—your teeth—"

I run my tongue across my teeth. Oops. They're all pointy canines. "Ah well. It was a good try, though, right?"

I grab Danny by the throat.

# KAI
# 37

The moment my fingers find their way around his neck, I feel a surge of demonic power overcoming my senses. I roar with delight. I feel SO powerful! It's intoxicating, like a shot of adrenaline straight to the center of my brain. I can't think clearly, but who needs to think clearly anyway? Thinking is overrated. A small voice at the back of my head warns me about Ox Head and Horse Face. This is going to bring me even closer to their clutches, but I can't even make myself care in this particular moment. Danny struggles futilely against my iron grip, his spindly human legs kicking wildly. He might as well be made of paper. I rip his pocket as easily as though it were made of tissue. There's a small tinkle as the vial drops to the ground, and I throw Danny aside and pounce on it.

As soon as he lands, he shouts out an incantation. A small star streaks across the night sky. It crashes down in front of me, and from the flames, Xiaohua steps out with a roar. At her full height, surrounded by flames, she's a terrible sight to behold.

Or at least she would be if I were my usual self. But hurting a human and stealing something of theirs has given a shot of power straight through my veins. In fact, it's given me so much demonic strength that I can't hold my current form. My false human skin rips at the seams as my essence bulges out.

"Demon!" Xiaohua thunders. "How dare you step foot in the human world! Return this very second to where you came from!"

"My gods, you're so tiresome." I focus my qì—there's so much of it!—and change into a long-armed demon monkey.

"Desist now, and on my honor, I will not destroy—"

See what I mean about dragons being tiresome? They're always droning on about honor this, honor that. While Xiaohua delivers her never-ending speech, I leap up to a floating tree house and start flinging poo at her. As expected, she flies up at me in a rage. I lead her in a merry chase through the tree house, out the windows, through the doors, until she's tied herself into a delightful knot around the little house. I stand on the roof, a mere foot away from her jaws, and laugh at her.

"Look, wormface! This is called intelligence. You might want to try it sometime." I'm about to fling more poo at Xiaohua when her whole body starts glowing red. "What are you doing? Stop that. That's arson, that is."

Not that she cares, the horrible vandal. I barely have time to leap aside before the entire tree house bursts into flames, singeing the soles of my feet. Midair, I make another switch and turn into a giant hawk. I chance a backward glance and lurch aside just in time to avoid a jet of fire so superheated, it's blue.

I can't outfly her, and I can't turn into a dragon to try to fight her because the dragon form is considered a celestial one, and thus inaccessible for the likes of me. Just as I'm about to despair, a small shape catches my attention. I shoot straight toward it, my claws out. Danny shrieks as I whisk him off the ground.

"Master!" Xiaohua cries. I note with a surprising rip of pleasure that the anger in her voice has been replaced by true, desperate fear. Who's got the upper claw now?

Another wave of raw power surges through my body. The more wicked deeds I do, the more power I have—I register all of this dimly. The knowledge is no match for the wonderful joy gushing throughout my entire being. I swoop up with a screech and laugh when Danny screams and begs me to put him back down.

Xiaohua streaks past me and stops, blocking my path. "Hand my master over, demon," she thunders.

I attempt to make a face, but hawks are limited to two expressions: hawkish and . . . that's it, actually. I puff out my chest and make the evilest laugh I can think of. "Mwahahaha—oh, oops, sorry about that." I tried to mime twirling an imaginary mustache like a proper villain and accidentally let go of one of Danny's arms.

"Careful!" Xiaohua screams while Danny dangles precariously, shouting nonstop.

"Sorry, I haven't had much practice holding humans hostage." I catch Danny's flailing arm once more. "Is that all right? Are you comfortable? Splendid."

Steam spurts out of Xiaohua's nostrils, and she utters a sky-cracking roar.

"Stop that," I say. "If you try to burn me, you're likely to burn your precious master as well."

"P-please, Xiaohua," Danny squeaks. "Listen to the demon!"

"See? He agrees. All right. Here's my proposal: I will take your master with me—will you let me finish?" Fire dragons, I tell you. Ask them to negotiate and all they do is burst into flames and roar. I wait until Xiaohua stops raging. "So, here's the plan: Danny and I will travel for a bit, and you, Xiaohua, are not to follow us. If you do, I will kill him, have no doubt about that." Another surge of delicious power. I'm almost overcome by a sudden need to stab my beak into Danny's neck, to feel the warm gush of his blood on my skin. I shake my head and blink a few times. "Um. Where was I?"

"You were talking about kidnapping my master," Xiaohua says.

"Must you say 'kidnap'? I'm only borrowing him, I don't want to keep him. Once I'm done, the two of you can go back to doing whatever it is you do. Sound good?"

"I cannot enter into agreements with a demon!" Xiaohua says.

"Stop with the slurs already. I'm not a demon."

"You literally are—"

"Shut up, both of you!" Danny says. "Xiaohua, you're dismissed." With some difficulty, he flicks his hand and mutters the incantation, and mid-sentence, Xiaohua's sucked into the Gray, the realm where dismissed companions go. "Can we please get to wherever you were planning on taking me? My arms are starting to hurt."

"You're hardly in a position to give any demands, you know." Still, there isn't much use hanging around, so I fly off into the woods with my prize in tow.[37]

When we're sufficiently far away from the facility to avoid any Eyes or people, I descend toward a small clearing and deposit Danny in an unceremonious heap.

---

[37] I may or may not have performed a couple of loop-the-loops while flying, as well as a series of sudden plunges. But after I got spattered in the face by Danny's vomit, I cunningly decided to fly straight.

"Why are you doing this?" he asks, once he's regained his balance.

"You humans and your never-ending questions." I wave my wing lazily at him, casting a small spell of obfuscation, and his face goes blank. "Well, this has been a nice little chat, but I can't stay." After checking I have the vial of river water on me, I wave goodbye to Danny (he doesn't wave back, the rude thing) and fly in search of my master.

Who knew that being naughty could feel so nice?

# THEO
# 38

I pace about the woods, shivering. Kai needs to come back soon. The longer I wait, the stronger my worry becomes, threatening to overwhelm me into full-blown panic. The memory of the demon wearing Jamie's face stabs into me, a red-hot knife. I miss my brother so much, it's a physical ache. I clap my hands over my face and groan out loud with all the different warring emotions bubbling inside me.

"Oh, that doesn't sound good—that sounds like indigestion, that does," a voice says. With an unfamiliar laugh, Kai emerges from behind a tree.

"Kai!" I rush over to her. Never have I been so relieved to see anyone. "Are you okay? Did you get it?"

Kai pecks at her feathers. She's in the form of a large hawk, and as I near her, a note of unease strikes deep in my gut. She seems different somehow. She's smiling, but it's not her usual self-satisfied smirk. It looks more like a shark's grin—unpredictable and . . . hungry. I pause in my tracks. "Kai? Everything okay?"

"Of course. I feel amazing. Look at me, I'm a hawk. And now—" She does a full-body flip, and when she lands back on her feet, she's a giant wolf, towering over me. "And now—" A tiger. A lynx. And finally, a python big enough to swallow a full-grown man. She slides toward me, her forked tongue slurping in and out, tasting the cold night air. "Do you know how exhausting I would've normally found those changes, especially done in such quick succession?"

She coils around my legs.

"The answer is: very. Actually, it would've been impossible. Shape-shifting's very energy-consuming." She winds herself around me until her face is at eye level, and then she starts to squeeze.

My sense of unease sharpens into fear. "Kai—"

"Surprise!" There's an explosion, and when I blink, the snake has turned into a bunch of confetti. And in front of me, on top of a layer of gold and silver confetti, is a small vial of water.

Relief overcomes me. Kai's just being her usual annoying self. "Is this it?" I stoop down and retrieve the vial, studying it. The water inside looks like normal, boring water.

The mess of confetti swirls up, clumps together, and turns into an origami fox. "No, that's just tap water."

"Kai—" I groan.

"Yes, of course that's it. You're no fun at all."

"Wow. I wasn't sure if you'd be able to get it." I stuff the vial in my pocket, hope thundering in my chest. "Let's go, I want to turn this in as soon as possible."

Kai nods and turns into an origami fish.

"Very funny," I say. "What's up with you? You seem more . . . annoying than usual."

"I'm just in a good mood, is all." With that, she switches into a proper goldfish and swims ahead of me.

"So how did you get the water?" I have to jog to keep up with her. I don't think I've ever seen her this energetic. Usually, she'd be flopped over some piece of furniture or other by now, moaning about how tiring the human world is. I should be glad that she's so bubbly, but something seems off, and I can't help but feel worried. I shouldn't have allowed her to attempt such a dangerous task all on her own. I should've gone with her, made sure she was safe.

"Trade secret," she says, and she won't look at me the rest of the way back.

I know something's wrong as soon as I step within the perimeter of the Reapling facility. A travel bubble swoops out of the night sky and stops in front of me. An imp, hovering above it, says, "Theodore Tan, please step inside the pod. It will take you to safety."

"Safety? What?"

The imp repeats its instructions. I glance at Kai, my eyebrows raised in a universal sign of *What the heck's going on?* She shrugs. We bundle into the bubble, and I look out the window as it ascends. Below us, the few employees who have remained at the facility this late at night are running around like panicked ants. They gesticulate wildly and send Eyes and companions out to fly around the compound. Guards are prowling the grounds in twos, all of them carrying rifles.

Kai snorts, pointing to the nearest pair of guards. "Look at those idiots with their idiotic guns."

"What's wrong with the guns?"

Kai sniffs. "Well, nothing, if you don't have anything against fighting dishonorably."

"How's it dishonorable?"

Another sniff. "Of course you wouldn't see it as dishonorable. But those evil things are filled with silver bullets. You know what silver does to noble spirits such as myself?"

I fidget. Silver is poisonous to all creatures who aren't from the human world. Doesn't matter if it's a friendly spirit or a hungry demon; silver would tear apart their souls. "But we only ever use them on demons," I say lamely.

"Right, like I'm going to trust that some trigger-happy guard isn't going to shoot before thinking. I'm going to keep out of sight." With that, she burrows deep into my jeans pocket and remains silent.

I continue watching the guards as they do a search around the facility. What are they searching for?

When we finally arrive at the cluster of cabins, Xiuling rushes up to me and practically yanks me into our cabin.

"Are you okay?"

"What's going on?" I flinch when she shines a light directly in my eyes.

"Sorry, that's a sun ray. We've got to make sure you haven't been possessed."

"Possessed?"

Xiuling ushers me into the living room, where the others are gathered. "You guys stay in here, understand?" She gives us a smile meant to be reassuring, but it ends up looking like a terrified grimace instead. "Things will be back under control soon!" With that, she leaves.

I walk toward the group of kids, who are huddled near Danny. He has a blanket wrapped around him and is clutching a mug of hot chocolate. Xiaohua is draped across his shoulders, hissing at anyone who comes too close.

"What's going on?" I say.

Namita rushes forward and gives me a tight hug. "Theo! I'm so glad you're okay." She lowers her voice into a stage whisper. "Danny was attacked by a demon."

"What?" I'm saying that a lot lately, but holy cow, a demon?

"He was on his way back to the compound after traveling back from . . . what do you guys call it? The spirit world?" Namita's eyes are wide with terrified excitement. "When a demon wearing Xiuling's form tried to trick him into giving it his vial of river water. It happened in the woods, so there were no Eyes around to see what was happening."

Ice trickles through my veins. I don't want to hear the rest of Namita's story.

"The demon turned into a giant hawk and took Danny even deeper into the woods and left him there, after taking his vial of river water."

I try to swallow, but it's like swallowing a bag of nails.

"Isn't that crazy?" Namita cries.

"I wonder why it was after the river water, though," someone else pipes up.

Danny looks up from his mug, his face pale. "Maybe the demon was summoned by someone in our program. Maybe someone failed their task and needed to steal a vial of river water."

My entire body turns to jelly. Can he smell the guilt steaming out of my every pore?

Someone laughs and says, "Yeah, right. Who'd summon a demon just for a stupid task? Plus, no kid's strong enough to summon a demon, especially one powerful enough to fight a fire dragon."

Everyone else nods and murmurs their agreement, and the room resumes its anxious buzzing.

"I need to go to the bathroom," I mumble, and scurry off into the farthest bathroom.

Once I've locked the door, I dig in my pocket and yank Kai out.

"Ouch, hey, be gentle!"

"Shut up!" I pinch her little goldfish body between my thumb and index finger and glare at her. "Kai, I have a very serious question to ask you, and you must be honest with me. Understand?" I take a deep breath. "Kai, did you steal the river water from Danny?"

No answer. She stares at me for a second, then she looks up at the ceiling and starts whistling.

"Kai...," I say in a dangerous tone.

"I am pleading the Fifth—"

"You don't have Fifth Amendment rights! All right, you're making me do this: Kai, I order you to tell me where you got this vial of river water."

Her little body trembles with the effort of not telling. Her scales turn a bright red, and steam puffs out of her ears. Then, right before she's about to explode, she blurts out, "TOOKITFROMDANNY."

With an enraged cry, I let go of her, and the two of us glare at each other, breathing hard. "How could you do that? You attacked him? Are you crazy?"

"He deserves it! He's been picking on you since the very first day, he stole Peng from you—I could argue that we wouldn't be in this whole mess if not for him constantly bullying you."

"This is unacceptable!" But even as I say that, a small voice at the back of my mind pipes up and says, *Well, actually, Kai has a point.*

"Look, we're even now, don't you see? Danny stole Peng from us, so we stole the river water from him. It cancels out. The karmic balance has been restored."

"That's not how—wait, no, that sounds so wrong." But is it? My mind is a mess, thoughts flying every which way. Part of me agrees with Kai. Danny did steal Peng from us, so it sort of serves him right that we stole the river water from him. But then I think of Danny's pale face and how vulnerable he looked, and I feel sick. Revenge doesn't feel anywhere near as good as I thought it would. In fact, it feels the opposite of good. It feels terrible, like I've got food poisoning.

I shake my head. "I'm going to have to fix this somehow. I can't have you around while they're doing a search for the culprit. It's too dangerous."

Kai's eyes widen. "Wait, you can't—"

I don't give her a chance to argue before raising my hands and saying the words for a temporary dismissal. Even as she's sucked into the void where companions go when they're temporarily dismissed, she still manages to raise her fin to perform what's no doubt a rude gesture.

# KAI
# 39

Dismissed! Me! Normally, I don't mind dismissals; in fact, I welcome them as a chance to rest after what is no doubt an exhausting stint with my masters. But to be dismissed in anger by a little whippet of a kid after I risked life and limb to fulfill his task! The audacity!

I flit about the Gray. There are other shén in the Gray, all of them slumped over and sleeping. Snores fill the air. The sight of them fills me with even more anger. The youngest shén here must be over a hundred years old, but instead of being venerated, we're here to serve at the whims of our human masters. Honestly, where's the justice in that?

The Gray, like the spirit world and every other plane of existence, is controlled by rules. Shén who have been dismissed here are bound to this place, and only a summoning is able to break the bonds and free us.

In a fit of anger, I barrel into the boundary of the Gray. Instead of bouncing off it, I depress the wall as if it were jelly. I raise a paw to poke it, and it shudders away from me, as though afraid. Realization dawns slowly. I am no longer a pure shén. I've done so much mischief, wreaked so much havoc, that I'm more than halfway to becoming a demon. I'm no longer bound by the tedious rules of shén!

The Gray is afraid of me. It doesn't like me being here. I don't have to stay here if I don't want to. And I don't.

I bounce around the slumbering shén, crowing and somersaulting over their forms, and as they sputter awake and try to catch me, I bend my knees and spring up like a gazelle with one last "Wheeee!"

I reach for the smokelike ceiling, which retreats from me. A hole opens up, and I plunge straight through it. "To the human world!" I shout.

If Theo thinks he can just get rid of me whenever he wants, he's got another think coming.

$$\qquad=\!\ast\!=\qquad$$

The children are still huddled in fear inside the cabins, which are surrounded by dozens of guards and Eyes. I suppose I should look at the security as a compliment. All that, just for little old me.

I'm disguised as a fly, tiny enough for the Eyes not to sense me unless I get too close. I zip around for a bit, looking for a gap in the security lines, and catch sight of something far more interesting than Theo.

Creighton Ward.

Oooh. I buzz a bit closer, careful to stay out of range of the Eyes' senses. Creighton Ward is barking at some poor guard. She salutes him, and he slinks off (does he ever walk like a normal human, I wonder). I take the chance to make a quick change.

Unlike Theo, Creighton Ward does not strike me as the type

to have head lice, so I change into something more suitable—a puff of Drakkar Noir, best perfume in the world. Normally, changing into gaseous form would be beyond my reach. But thanks to my newfound energy, the extra qì and focus that are required to hold such an unusual shape feel almost effortless. There's a moment of irritation as I realize Theo isn't around to see the kind of cunning shape-shifting that only fox spirits are capable of. Honestly, my species is so underrated, it's painful. I waft through the air as quickly as I can and settle round the back of his neck. I narrow my eyes.[38] There's a strange smell wafting off Director Ward's skin that I can't quite place. A familiar smell, not entirely unpleasant. A smell that reminds me of the spirit world, and even more familiar than that, a smell that reminds me of my own smell when I'm back in fox form. Maybe it's just the intense scent I'm giving out in my current form mingling with his natural musk. Hmm.

Director Ward gives no hint of noticing my presence, aside from a little sniff as he walks back to the magnificent main building. He strides all the way to the top floor, where his office is, and after a sip of ice-cold water, he straightens his jacket and calls out, "Send her in."

An Eye detaches itself from the ceiling and replies, "Yes, Master."

Wow. He's gotten the imp inside to call him master. How obnoxious. It's level Maximum Slime.

The office door slides open, and Xiuling walks in, looking harried.

---

38 No, I do not have physical eyes in this form. *Sigh*. We've been over this, Bertha. Just go with the story, all right?

"Clear the room," Director Ward says, and four Eyes emerge from various hiding spots and fly out of the office.

"Any updates?" Xiuling says once they're gone.

Instead of telling her off for being so rude, Director Ward merely shakes his head.

"That's good. I think that's good," Xiuling mutters, more to herself than anyone else. "The guards are confident the demon has left the premises, so now the pressing question is how it got in here in the first place." She grunts in disgust. "Why does the company spend millions of dollars on security if demons can just slip in and out?"

"Why, indeed?" Director Ward says.

Xiuling slumps into a chair. "You know the publicity [bleep] storm[39] this will cause if it ever gets out?"

Wow, she's really not holding anything back. Color me surprised. Director Ward doesn't strike me as the type of boss who'd be sympathetic to an unraveling employee.

"Do we know where the demon came from?"

Xiuling scowls. "It must have come from Golden Grass. They've been curious about Know Your Roots ever since we announced it, and it's more than likely that one of their overeager employees summoned a demon to spy on us."

"According to the victim, the demon specifically asked for his vial of spirit world river water," Director Ward says. "Why would Golden Grass bother doing that? They have pretty much all of the resources we do."

---

39 Just because I'm turning into a demon doesn't mean I'm about to lose my manners. Hmm? What was that? I was flinging poo two chapters ago? Hey, shut yer [bleep] [bleep] pumpkin [bleep].

Xiuling shakes her head. "I don't think the demon knew what it was supposed to look for. It strikes me as a very primitive creature, not very intelligent . . ."

Excuuuuse her?

Director Ward pauses and sniffs the air. "Do you smell that? Smells a bit sulfuric."

Oops. In my fit of rage, I must've leaked a bit of essence. I take a couple of deep breaths to calm myself down.

When they're both satisfied that they can't sense anything awry, they continue the conversation.

"Hmm. So some enthusiastic employee summoned a mediocre[40] demon who was too stupid[41] to know what it was looking for . . . well, fair enough, we've been highly secretive about the true nature of our project." Director Ward pinches the bridge of his nose. "But the demon got away, didn't it? It took the victim's water and flew off?"

"Yes," Xiuling says. "Which means it won't be long before Golden Grass realizes the whole program's designed to summon mythical creatures belonging to countries with lax summoning regulations."

My non-fur bristles at this. I'm mostly angry at myself for not realizing what they're doing sooner. Now that she's said it, it's so obvious. All that stuff about reconnecting kids with their ancestral culture was just a cover. How could I have missed it?

---

40 Gah!

41 Double gah!!

Her speech ends with a groan. "This whole thing's just been disaster after disaster."

"When you came up with the idea of extracting cirth from mythological creatures, we knew it wouldn't be easy. The logistics alone are a nightmare, and then there's the emotional burden of strip-mining your own cultural heritage for profit," Director Ward says. He doesn't take his eyes off Xiuling.

Xiuling snorts. "Trust me, there is no emotional burden on my part. When the Chinese government failed to punish the charlatan summoner who got my brother killed, any loyalty I had toward China died a quick death."

Director Ward purses his lips. "If you say so. I'm glad you have no reservations about the plan, but it doesn't cancel out the fact that we have a situation on our hands."

"It's all my fault, trusting that cursed intern. Jamie Tan." She spits out the name like it's a dirty word.

I freeze.

"You couldn't have known," Director Ward says kindly.

"I should've," Xiuling hisses. "This is the problem with using kids. They're so unpredictable! If we could only do the whole thing ourselves—"

"No use wishing for that," Director Ward says. "It's unfortunate, but these revolting kids are the only ones who haven't lost the ability to tap into their qì."

"It's costing so much to transport them back and forth from the spirit world to the human world," Xiuling moans. "A staggering amount of cirth!"

Director Ward shrugs. "Yes, there's a reason why human travel between the two realms is beyond the reach of most people."

"If only we could leave those kids in the spirit realm," Xiuling mutters.

They both laugh, but Director Ward's laugh is cut short as he scratches at the back of his neck, frowning.

"I don't know. I feel as though there's something here with us." He scratches his neck again. "Can't quite put my finger on it."

I'm rapidly increasing in temperature. Practically boiling, really. Through the haze of rage, I manage to unwrap myself from Ward's neck before I scald him and raise any more alarms. I need to calm down.

Calm down! As though such a thing were possible when faced with Jamie's killers. His murderers. Theo was right. Jamie was *murdered*. The word pierces through my very core.

I'm in the midst of pondering how I can kill these two monsters in the most painful way possible when Xiuling says, "We need to move on to the last part of the program now, before everyone finds out."

Director Ward nods, which seems to bolster Xiuling's confidence.

She stands up and starts pacing again, her voice rising with excitement. "We've got everything ready. The kids will be summoning Niu Mo Wang. Jamie Tan may have been rash enough to release Peng, but even he wouldn't have been foolish enough to release a demon king." All thoughts of revenge suddenly grind to a halt. Niu Mo Wang is the Bull Demon King. He's one of the most powerful demons in Diyu. Reapling must've invented some contraption that makes it possible to suck the qì out of mythical creatures and convert it into cirth. A creature like Niu Mo Wang would provide them with an almost infinite amount of cirth. If I could steal into the lab, I'd be able to free Niu Mo Wang from that fate. And maybe I could even use the machine to siphon off a little bit of his qì to me.

"Good," Director Ward says, flashing a quick smile, his teeth shiny and somehow predatory. I can't help shuddering at the sight. "What about Saanvi's group?"

Xiuling waves a flippant hand. "I don't think she'd be happy about being told to rush the Indian group. We'll do ours first, and they can do theirs afterward."

"Sounds good. Listen, you know I hate to ask, but after all this is done, could you perhaps . . ."

"You need a cleanse?" Xiuling says.

Director Ward nods.

"Of course," Xiuling says, but I detect the slightest hint of reluctance in her voice.

I glom onto the back of Xiuling's neck as she leaves. Once she's outside Director Ward's office, Xiuling sniffs and mutters, "Revolting. Why does he wear that disgusting perfume?"

Once we're through security, I fly up into the clouds in a rage, nearly tearing myself apart. I should tell Theo what I've discovered.

I should.

But if Theo finds out, he'd . . . well, I don't know what he would do, which is the problem. He'd probably go all flappy and ruin everything somehow. No, I can't risk telling him. I need to make sure that Jamie's death is avenged, and to do that, I need all the power I can get. My lack of power contributed to Jamie's death. The memory of it, of how helpless I was, sears my skin. All those times I failed Jamie because I wasn't strong enough to help him when he needed it most. The way I wasn't even able to shape-shift into the simplest of items for him. I was a disappointment to Jamie, but I don't have to remain one.

Now I have a demon king at my disposal. If I could get just a little bit of Niu Mo Wang's power, I could do anything. I won't be at anyone's mercy, not even Ox Head and Horse Face's. No matter what, I must get to Niu Mo Wang before anyone else does.

# THEO
# 40

When I wake up the next morning, the first thing I remember is last night's incident. I close my eyes with a small groan. When I turn my head, I see the shape of Danny's silhouette across the room, breathing softly as he sleeps. My stomach churns. He's a bully, and he did steal Peng from me, but I'm no better than him now. By letting Kai steal his river water and letting her hurt him in the process, and then not owning up to it, I've stooped to Danny's level. Lower, actually.

I wish I could be the type of person to own up to my mistakes, to bravely take responsibility and tell everyone that the demon who attacked last night was, in fact, my companion. Jamie is—was—that type of person. He wouldn't have even hesitated before coming forward to take all the blame.

I'm about to curl into a tight ball and shut out the rest of the world when an Eye flies into our room. The imp inside says, "Good morning, Theodore Tan and Danny Chang! Please assemble at the auditorium for an important announcement."

We blink blearily as the Eye flies out of the room.

I glance at Danny, and the guilt inside me is so strong that I'm compelled to say, "How're you feeling?"

Danny looks pale and listless, hardly at all like his usual self.

Who would've thought I could ever miss the old self-important Danny?

"I feel . . . terrible, actually. Feverish and . . ." Danny winces.

Oh gods. Despite everything that's happened between us, I can't stand seeing him suffering like this. I reach over to give Danny a pat on the shoulder, but he flinches like I've just poked him with a red-hot iron. Immediately Xiaohua flies from the bed and wraps herself around Danny, as gently as though he were a newly hatched chick.

"I'm sorry! Did I hurt you?" I say.

Danny's loose pajama top slips down one shoulder, and Xiaohua and I both gasp out loud. His shoulder is covered in claw-shaped bruises, dark red, purple, and black.

"Master, your shoulder!" Xiaohua cries.

Danny looks taken aback. "It didn't hurt too badly last night, but it feels so much worse now."

Bile boils its way up my throat. I caused this.

As we make our way out of the cabin, every twitch that Danny makes is a twist of the knife in my guts. We file into the auditorium, where Xiuling awaits us. The grip around my chest tightens when I see her expression—her brow's furrowed, and she looks like she's aged about ten years overnight. Once we're all seated, she speaks in a low tone.

"I'm afraid we were unable to catch the demon from last night. We can't afford to risk having it attack any of you. You're like my little brothers and sisters." She smiles sadly. "So we're going to have to cut the program short and send you home."

The other kids look just as dismayed as I feel.

"But the security team is all on the lookout for the demon," one of the girls says, as her companion, a golden monkey, climbs fluidly up to her shoulder, his tail twisting round her arm. "Surely it'll be okay for us to stay? Please let us stay."

Xiuling sighs. "Well, there is one way. It'll also help Danny, but it's so risky, the company would never go for it. This means it's just our secret, okay? You guys promise?"

We all say yes.

She takes a deep breath. "Wellll . . . I know this sounds crazy, but we could try summoning a xièzhì."

Everything inside me comes to a halt for a second. My heart stops thumping, my blood stops flowing. A xièzhì, one of the most revered celestial beings there is.

Apparently, everyone else is just as astounded, because they're all staring openmouthed at Xiuling. We're just a bunch of kids. How could we possibly summon such a powerful entity?

"A xièzhì would be able to help us capture the demon and take it back to Diyu, where it belongs. I believe that once the demon has been exorcised from the human world, its effects on Danny will also dissipate."

"But how would we summon a xièzhì?" someone says.

"We have the ability to open a pathway to Tiantang, where most celestials live. All we need is—well, you guys. Specifically, we need your qì, and the longing inside all of you for your ancestral heritage, to complete the connection."

My mind isn't merely spinning, it's flying and whizzing in every direction at once. This feels so wrong. Especially since I know how Peng was kidnapped. Is this part of their scheme? So the whole company really is in on it? On the other hand, Xiuling is right. A xièzhì, a celestial symbol of truth and justice, would be able to take away the curse that's been placed on Danny. And if we did the summoning rites, I could tell Peng which ones Reapling used, and maybe we'd be able to figure out how to dismiss him to the spirit world.

"I'll do it," the girl with the golden monkey says. "I'll do whatever it takes to summon a xièzhì."

"Me too," says another kid.

"Me too."

I swallow my misgivings. Whatever suspicions I have, I can't get in the way of something that might cleanse Danny of the demonic curse that my companion put on him and help Peng get back home. I add my voice to the rest of the class, and soon, everyone's hand is up, even Danny's, though his is trembling.

Xiuling nods grimly. "You're all brave kids. I'm so proud to be your group leader."

# THEO
# 41

The travel bubbles drop us off in the middle of the woods. Gigantic redwoods tower over us on all sides, blocking out the sunlight. There's a hushed sensation, like the world is holding its breath. It feels like we've stepped into a land of sleeping giants.

Xiuling goes straight to one of the redwoods and mutters a spell. The outline of a door in the tree appears, fizzing with gold sparks. It yawns open, and Xiuling beckons us to follow after her.

Once I step through the tree door, it's as though I'm in an entirely different plane. We're still in the woods, but at the same time, all the trees, the grass, and the animals are immaterial. They exist only as shimmering outlines, and a large white building is built straight through them. There are altars, hundreds of burning incense sticks, and statues of Chinese deities placed right in the middle of tree trunks that flicker in and out of sight. It's like one of those drawings where if you look one way, you see a young woman, and if you look a different way, you see an old woman.

People wearing long gray robes walk about. With a start, I realize they're weavers. I've never, ever seen a weaver in real life before. Weaving is so difficult and dangerous that very few people want to do it. The few who do tend to lead very secluded (and short) lives. But here, the weavers are walking around normally, moving through the shimmering trees without blinking.

There's security everywhere: Eyes floating in groups like giant bees and guards prowling about on silent feet, carrying a multitude of weapons. I avert my eyes. They look like they could sniff out guilt.

"This is a very special place," Xiuling says. "It exists between the human and spirit planes, acting as a bridge to make summoning large, powerful beings possible."

A bridge that makes summoning powerful beings possible . . . A sour taste fills my mouth, and Peng's jumbled memories come rushing back. I need to focus. This is my chance to figure out exactly what rites were used, so I can help dismiss Peng back to his home.

In the center of the room, sticking up through the invisible floor, is the tallest redwood I've ever seen. It surely can't be a normal redwood tree; it's at least three times as tall as the next tallest redwood in the forest.

"This is the oldest redwood tree in the country," Xiuling says. "Come on over and stand around the tree. Everyone has their vial of river water from the spirit world?"

We all nod and take out our vials, except for Danny. Xiuling conjures an empty vial and goes around siphoning off a bit of water from every kid until it's full, and then she hands the newly filled vial to Danny.

"Drinking the river water will allow our spirits access to Tiantang. Everybody ready?"

This is it. My hand tightens around the vial. *This feels wrong,* a little voice inside me says. I tune it out. I have no choice. After all the trouble I've caused, I need to do whatever it takes to help Peng and Danny.

"One."

But if the xièzhì sniffs out the root of Danny's curse, it will link it to Kai and banish her back to the spirit world, breaking my bond with her.

"Two."

The thought of having my bond with Kai broken is surprisingly painful. I very nearly change my mind because of it, but no. I can't. I must go through with this, and I'll figure out another way of preserving my bond with her. Perhaps with her temporarily dismissed, the xièzhì won't be able to get to her. It'll all be okay. It has to be.

"Three."

I lift the vial to my mouth and drink.

—❋—

The floor disappears. There's a split second of weightlessness, and then I plummet straight down. I shriek as I fall, my arms pinwheeling, trying to grab hold of something, anything. I catch flashes of the others falling as well, mouths open in terrified screams, eyes wild, hands grasping at empty air.

I'm falling through earth, through gnarled tree roots and moist soil and surprised badgers. Then, to my horror, I slow down.

What if the effects of the river water stop now, and I exist on the human plane once more? I would be entombed immediately, too deep within the earth for anyone to hear my shouts.

Suddenly, within the profound darkness, miles deep within the earth, I see a light. The light grows and grows, flickering yellow and red. It's a fire. A large one. I flap my arms and legs, trying to maneuver myself closer to the flame, and to my surprise, it works.

The flame, as it turns out, is the caldera of a bubbling volcano, and on top of it is a giant cauldron filled with oil. Inside the cauldron are human souls, shimmering red as they scream and thrash around. Yāoguài stand on the lip of the cauldron, carrying tridents that they use to stab at the souls that try to scramble out.

"Th-this isn't Tiantang," someone says.

"No. It's Diyu." Xiuling's voice comes from nowhere and everywhere.

We all look around, but she's nowhere to be found.

"Don't waste time trying to look for me or a way out," her voice says. "I'm back in the human world. I'm sorry, kids, but change of plans: Your task is to summon a different sort of celestial being."

"What sort?" I say, an ugly feeling uncurling in my stomach.

"A demon from one of the great circles of hell. An ancient one."

"Why?" I cry. My voice is echoed by the others.

"You don't have time for whys. I've cast a spell of protection on all of you—it's why the Fire of Damnation hasn't melted your souls yet—but it won't last long."

She's right; even as I stand here, my skin has started prick-ling and my hair's starting to curl from the unbearable heat of the fire.

It hits me then.

"It's you," I say.

Gods, I was so dense. I knew *someone* at Reapling had done horrible things, unspeakable ones—Peng—and Jamie—but I assumed it had been some mysterious person high up in the company. Creighton Ward, maybe. Not Xiuling.

I underestimated her. "You once told me and Kai that the com-pany has found ways of 'extracting' cirth, and then you corrected yourself and said the company's 'creating' it. But you were telling the truth the first time. You kidnapped Peng to extract his cirth. How could you? You're exploiting your own heritage."

"My heritage?" Xiuling laughs, an unpleasant sound. "I have long severed ties with the Chinese culture. Isn't that what you've been trying to do your whole life?"

Shame churns my stomach. She's right. I've spent so much time and energy trying to separate myself from all things Chinese. Is this what would become of me if I were to continue going down that same road?

"Do as I say and I'll bring you back to the human world," Xiul-ing says.

She won't. She *won't*.

"I don't believe—" I say.

"This is hopeless!" another boy cries. He's rubbing at his arms fiercely, his eyes bright with unshed tears. "We're starting to burn down here. We don't have time."

Shouts of agreement meet his words. "My skin's turning red!"

"Get us out of here, please!"

"I'm telling you," Xiuling says with exaggerated patience, "there is no way out unless you do what I say."

There's a moment heavy with desperate, expectant silence, and as the pain grows, there is a defeated collective murmur of assent.

Everyone is agreeing to do it. Everyone except for Danny, who's hugged himself into the tightest, smallest ball possible. I go to him, everything inside me crying with guilt, and put an arm around his shaking shoulders.

"I'm so sorry, Danny," I say.

"P-please," he whispers.

Please? I lean a little closer. "What is it?"

He looks at me, terror written all over his face. "I can feel them. The demons. They sense us. They're coming. We need to get out of here. Can you not feel them? Listen."

I catch something at the very edge of my hearing—a soft breath, a laugh, the heavy swish of leathery wings. A promise of something terrible rushing at us out of the pulsing dark. He's right; we need to get out of here.

"Don't forget," Xiuling says, "the strength of your magic rests in longing. In passion. I'm sure all of you are itching to kill me right now. Take that rage and channel it into the spell. Ready?"

She gives us the spell, and there it is. I have it. I can take it to Peng, I can fulfill my dead brother's last wish and free Peng. But even as I think that, the other kids raise their hands and cry out the incantation, all of them shouting it with so much desperation that I feel their words reverberate through me. "No—" I say, but it's too late.

From deep, deep in the bowels of hell, there's a bone-ripping bellow. The volcano shudders, the bubbling oil rippling. The yāoguài scream and jump away from the cauldron, tearing at one another with their sharp little teeth and claws.

"What's happening?" someone says.

I watch as the yāoguài scurry away, shrieking, leaving the souls to boil in the cauldron. "They're running away," I say.

The ground trembles as something trudges up, up, coming ever closer.

Shadows flicker. Snorts thunder across the cavern, and a musky scent fills the air—something beastly and wild. The scent of a predator. It reaches deep into my brain, activating the earliest nightmares known to primordial man—a dream of teeth and blood.

The air sizzles, clouds of sulfur fizzing from the cauldron. There's a breath of silence, and then as one, the souls inside the cauldron start screaming, clawing at one another to scramble out. The cauldron bursts apart with a thunderous crack, boiling oil exploding, masses of souls torn to shreds. Pieces of the cauldron, each one bigger than I am, whizz through us.

In the middle of the fire, a large silhouette slouches. Slowly, with the weight of mountains, it straightens up. Shadows snake out of it, slithering and snapping at the air around it, covering it from view. I catch a glimpse of a great snout, a bull ring. Then it lifts its head and roars.

There's a flash of golden light, and suddenly we are falling up, sucked out of the great cavern, flying back through the earth. I chance a peek below. The dark, slithering mass of the demon is right behind me. There's a flash of red eyes, a shadow snaking up to coil round my ankle. I kick at the air, screaming. The ancient demon is right at my heels. And it's hungry.

# KAI
# 42

It's warm and moist on Xiuling's scalp, and fast becoming warmer and moister, and not because of yours truly. I'm innocently disguised as a small tick, although now I'm starting to wonder if I should've chosen to become sweat. Now that I'm overflowing with demonic qì, I need to remember that shifting to more abstract forms like sweat is no longer a problem. Oh well, hindsight and all that. I cling to her hair with all my might as she rushes toward the middle of the room, barking orders. There are about ten uniformed Reapling employees stationed in the room, and everybody's nervous. You can smell the fear roiling off them. How did I never notice how delicious fear smells? I want to eat all their faces.

Five guards are positioned around a large portal, their arms raised.

We don't have to wait long. Less than a minute after we take our positions, the first child arrives, screaming and flying toward the ceiling. The guards aim their hands at the child and zap, and the child stops flying. He also stops screaming. His body goes limp, his head slumping forward, and the guards levitate him toward a prepared travel bubble. The bubble floats away, presumably to a sick bay.

"Don't miss even a single child," Xiuling says. "You need to make sure their minds are completely wiped."

One by one, the children arrive, and one by one, they're all hit with spells of obfuscation,[42] followed by a spell of sleep. They will wake up with no memory of having been to Muir Woods, no memory of having done the greatest summoning of the century. When Theo finally arrives, he's zapped as well, but he doesn't get bubbled away like the other kids. Instead, Xiuling nods at one of the guards, and she levitates Theo's unconscious form into a corner of the room. I feel a pang of something as I watch Theo sleeping soundly, his normally scowling face slack. I start to scuttle toward him, but a huge roar shakes the portal, and my essence shudders. I freeze.

The demon king the children have summoned is nearing the portal. Everyone in the room stiffens. Hands are raised, eyes locked on the portal, lips licked with nervousness. The very edges of my qì curl up as the beast nears. I gulp audibly; if Xiuling weren't so distracted by the arrival of the demon, she would hear me.

Finally, it arrives.

It enters at full charge, bellowing loud enough to rattle the clear glass beneath the humans' feet. Golden light appears in cracks along the invisible floor. Darkness spills out from the demonic mass in every direction, filling the room with whispering shadows.

"Now!" Xiuling shouts, and all of the guards release their

---

42 Xiuling doesn't seem concerned with what casting spells of obfuscation on so many subjects will do to her karma. I suppose when you decide to go over to the dark side, it's best to go all the way.

pent-up magic at the creature. Bolts of blue and gold light spear into the darkness, smashing it apart.

There are screams, the shadows retreat, the darkness shrinking before me until a clear outline shows. I can finally see the creature, right before steel wires reinforced with pure silver and imbued with all sorts of holy spells appear and spiral around it, twisting and tightening until it resembles a giant ball of twine.

When Niu Mo Wang is bound by so many spells that I can barely see him, Xiuling smooths her hair back and clears her throat before casting the Route to Connectivity Through Affinity. Her eyes focus on something in the far distance, and she says, "Director Ward, it's done. Yes, sir."

She turns to the remaining employees. "I need some privacy." Without question, they file out.

Once she's alone, Xiuling strides over to Theo and crouches down. She sighs. "I never wanted things to come to this." Raising a hand, she summons another travel bubble. "Goodbye, kid." With a wave of Xiuling's hand, Theo's sleeping form is lifted into the bubble, and it floats away. Then she calls Creighton Ward again. "He's through."

I should leave now. I should find some way of getting to Theo and waking him before Creighton Ward gets to him. But even as I think that, a much bigger part of me, its voice deep and irresistible, says, *No, you'll be better able to help him once you get Niu Mo Wang's power. What use are you now? So weak and powerless.*

*But Theo—*

*Theo doesn't care about you. Look how he's rejected you. He dismissed you. He doesn't want you.*

With a quick flash, I hop off Xiuling's head. Midair, I make a switch, turning into a tiny fruit fly, and land on the giant, shuddering ball shape that is Niu Mo Wang. Even though he's bound by dozens of spells, there's still so much intense power radiating out of him that my essence quivers. This is the only way I can make things right. The only way I can bring justice for everyone who has been wronged by this awful company.

I grit my teeth[43] and hold on tight as Xiuling casts a spell of levitation on Niu Mo Wang. Here we go. A chute opens up in the middle of the floor. Uh, hang on—

There's no time for me to react as Niu Mo Wang is dropped into the hole and plunges down, deep into the darkness of the earth. Without hesitation, I jump in after him.

---

43 What's that you say, Bertha? Fruit flies don't have teeth? Good point. Very observant. I don't actually know what fruit flies have. Do you?

# KAI
# 43

Niu Mo Wang's fall doesn't end in a splat, as I feared, but instead, with him levitating a foot off a dungeon floor.

A dungeon. That's literally where we have ended up. Worse than that, it's also a lab, an operating room where mythical beings are taken apart, piece by excruciating piece. The room's awful. Horrible. There are manacles and scalpels, and everything's imbued with enchantments so they not only slice through flesh and bone, but the very essence of each creature. The floors are pockmarked with sewer holes, no doubt to let the blood drain after each grotesque procedure.

My essence curdles at the thought of Reapling employees ripping and slicing into shén, yāoguài, deities, and other mythical creatures, all so they can extract qì to power their little cirth pendants.

There's a handful of assistants, all of them busily casting various spells in preparation for Niu Mo Wang's arrival. In the middle of the room is a vast, cylindrical tube, its width the length of a truck. Xiuling, following behind Niu Mo Wang, carefully levitates him into the tube. I detach from Niu Mo Wang and fly away in the nick of time, just before the tube closes with a final click. As soon as it closes, tubes float up and attach themselves to it through prepared holes on the side. Needles spring up and stab into Niu Mo Wang's hide. There's a muffled roar, and the giant ball twitches, but the bonds around him remain strong. My breath catches, horror overwhelming my senses. There are so many tubes attached to him, so many needles boring through his hide and sucking away at his qì, he mustn't have long to live.

An assistant scurries over. "The amount of qì he generates . . . it's amazing."

Xiuling smiles. "If we keep him well-fed and sedated, we should be able to draw qì from him to create cirth for at least three months."

"Yes," the assistant says. "The second enclosure's nearly ready for its occupant . . ."

They walk over to a different part of the room, where sure enough, another giant tube awaits. Weavers are working on imbuing it with layers upon layers of magic. I want to savage each and every one of these people. They've only just caught one mythical being, and already they're planning the next kidnapping.

I fly around the room carefully, doing my best to avoid detection. The ceiling's buzzing with Eyes, surely one of them will sense me. But when I chance a peek, they're all riveted on Niu Mo Wang. Ah. Niu Mo Wang's incredible essence is pulling every magical element toward it.

I land on one of the awful tubes attached to Niu Mo Wang and rub my two front legs together. How in the blazes do I unlock the cylinder, not to mention break the numerous bindings trapping Niu Mo Wang? The spells are too strong for the likes of me. Curses, am I to be thwarted once more because I don't have enough power to make a difference?

Sighing, I look down at the tube I'm on. Like the other tubes, this one is sucking out liquid that shimmers with a multitude of colors. No doubt they lead to some factory, where the qì is diluted and then poured into millions of cirth pendants. An idea hits me. One that would kill two birds with one stone. Or rather, a lot of humans with one strike. Cue the evil laugh!

I look around, checking to make sure no one has spotted me. Coast clear. I close my eyes and change into a needle and syringe, complete with little wings on the side to propel me forward.

With one last deep breath, I stab into the tube and plunge myself into Niu Mo Wang's essence.

# THEO
# 44

Freezing cold water splashes my face, wrenching me from a troubled sleep. I jolt awake gasping and find myself lying on damp grass. I'm in a clearing surrounded by tall redwoods. I must be somewhere in Muir Woods.

"Believe it or not," a voice says, "there have been times when I woke up just as roughly as that." Creighton Ward steps out of the shadows and appears right in front of me, so close that the back of my neck prickles.

I scramble to my feet. "Where are we? Why am I here?" I back away from him and startle when I bump into something granite-hard. I swing round. Somehow, he's materialized behind me. Dread squeezes my chest. He's toying with me, the same way a cat plays with a mouse right before it kills it.

"You're here because you've outlived your usefulness."

"You can't kill us all! You'll never get away with it."

Director Ward scoffs. "We're not monsters. We've wiped the other children's memories clean of the last twenty-four hours. They'll go home with nothing but memories of a summer well spent."

"So why not do the same with me?" I cry.

"Because I thought—correctly—that your grief and longing for your brother would lend you the strength you need to summon a large creature. Summoning Niu Mo Wang wouldn't have been possible without you.

"Unfortunately, this longing that makes you so useful to us also makes you inconvenient. You'll always long for your brother, and that yearning will fray and worry at the edges of whatever spell we cast on you. Over time, the spell will come apart, and you'll remember the true events. The easy way out just isn't an option for you."

I raise my hand, draw on my qì, and try casting the only halfway-aggressive spell I know—Pushcart's Lend Me a Push spell. He raises his hand, almost lazily, and the spell is neutralized and dies as a puff of air.

"My dear, stupid child, when will you understand that whatever spell you've learned at school, I know its counter?"

An Eye flies into the clearing. Thank gods, I'm saved! I wave frantically at it. "Help! I'm about to be killed!"

The Eye opens, but the Imp averts his gaze and stares behind me, directly at Creighton. "Sir, there is an urgent connection to be made."

The Eye is loyal to him, I realize with a sinking feeling. Never mind that, this is my chance! But before I can take a single step, Creighton waves his hand, and my feet are yanked out from under me.

"Stop moving."

I'm caught in an unforgiving grip.

"What's happened?" he says, holding the Eye to his ear. From where I'm held, I can't hear what the imp says, but Creighton's face changes from impassive to cold anger. "He's free? Who did this?" Suddenly his calm veneer cracks. He bares his teeth and gives a cry of rage. "Call the tactical team. Hunt them both down right now! I'll be over immediately."

He rakes a hand through his snow-white hair, shaking his head. "The demon you summoned has been let free by some fox spirit."

Kai!

Smiling's the last thing I want to do, but I force my mouth into a grin. I have no idea what Kai's up to, or how she even got back to the human world after I'd dismissed her, but Director Ward doesn't know that. "The fox spirit's my companion."

He releases a string of curses. His hand shoots out, and pain stabs at me from every direction. I can't even shout; my lungs feel like they're being crushed.

His footsteps crunch through the underbrush toward me. "I can't decide who's more contemptible, you or your wretched brother."

I writhe desperately, trying to escape the pain. My mind blasts through all of the almanac's spells and seizes one. Summoning the last of my strength, I twist to face Director Ward and point at him. Teeth gritted, I start the incantation. His smile widens, and he leans back like he's enjoying the show. I finish the spell in a scream.

Though I mangle the pronunciation, the warped ancient magic rips through the air and hits him right in the chest. There's a bright, sharp flash, and the pain suddenly releases its unforgiving grip. I slump to the ground. Jamie would've been proud.

Director Ward is still standing and smiling, but he looks different somehow. It's his teeth. They're no longer normal human teeth, but sharp canines, long and so horribly pointed they stab at his lips, bloodying them. He looks like something straight out of a nightmare.

He notices my look of horror and puts a hand to his mouth, touching his teeth gingerly. "Oh dear," he murmurs. "My form. And you've gotten blood on my shirt. You putrid child, this is an original Zegna."

I gape at him. "Your—form?"

He waves a hand over his head, and his face melts like candle wax. I blink, and before me stands a fox spirit.

He has the same vivid orange fur that Kai does, but that's where the similarities end. He's much bigger than Kai, and instead of two tails, this fox spirit has six. I shiver at the sight of the tails—the more tails a fox spirit has, the older and more powerful it is.

"Close your mouth," the fox spirit says in Director Ward's voice.

"But how—"

"I'm Xiuling's companion." He moves like water and slinks close to me, leaving Director Ward's clothes behind him in a puddle.

"That's impossible," I croak. "She said she doesn't have a companion, because of what happened to her brother—"

"So gullible," the Creighton-fox says, laughing softly. He's huge, about three times Kai's size. He can easily fit my throat in his jaws. "Just like Creighton Ward when I replaced him." He winces when he says this, as though something is physically hurting him.

A rotten taste sours the back of my mouth. "What do you mean, 'replaced'?"

The Creighton-fox gives me this look, like *C'mon, you know what I mean.*

"Does the whole company know?"

He laughs. "As if!"

"But I don't—but—how come none of the security has detected you?" I cry.

The Creighton-fox grins, showing a mouth full of needle-sharp teeth. "We've had to do a few adjustments to the Eyes, make sure that they're—shall we say—blind to the auras of fox spirits."

That would explain why none of them has detected Kai. Little did he know that by doing this, they would inadvertently help me gain a path into the program.

"Why are you telling me this?" I croak.

The Creighton-fox sighs and sits on his rump, licking his front paw. "Do you not know anything about fox spirits? We love to share our stories, child."

I think of Kai and her near-constant babbling. They do love to talk about their accomplishments.

"Can you blame us? We come up with the most brilliant ideas, and yet we're rarely given credit. I have been the trusted companion of emperors. Under my guidance, entire dynasties have been razed to the ground! The blood of my enemies can fill an ocean."

"If you've done so many bad things, how are you not a demon—oh." Memory dawns, sharp and cold. Kai telling me how Xiuling mentioned a "purification ritual."

"Your master cleansed your soul after each misdeed," I whisper.

The Creighton-fox doesn't say a word, but an eyebrow lifts in a wry arch. "Go on," he says.

I try to remember what little I know about purification rituals. "They're very costly, aren't they? And it requires . . ." Horror sinks in. "Qì. Your master's qì. They mentioned it in Chinese class. A lot of it, enough to shorten the human's lifespan. And it doesn't even really work. It only slows down the process of turning into a demon."

There's no doubt about it, the Creighton-fox is pleased that I know so much about him. He's practically grinning, and only now do I realize that he's so huge not because he's an old fox spirit, but because he's halfway to turning fully demonic. There are little rips in his fur where his form can't contain his corrupted soul.

"Why would she do that? Why would she give up so much to purify you?"

"You don't know?" the Creighton-fox says, twitching his head to one side. "My dear imbecilic child, if your companion turns into a full demon, then you, as its master, will be doomed to Diyu when you die."

My breath catches in a painful rush. I had no idea of the consequences of letting Kai turn bad. And now I recall how strange her behavior has been, how she kept trying to explain to me the importance of not doing bad things, but I didn't take her seriously. Has she turned into a full demon? Is it too late to save her?

I have to get out of here. I must get to Kai before it's too late. I rack my brains for a way out. But how? I look desperately at the Creighton-fox.

If he's turning demonic, he'll have traits of a demon—he'll be brazen, wild, unpredictable, even to himself. All he needs is a little push to distract him.

I go full-on Skinner-on-steroids, bullying the new kid when he thinks no one's watching.

"You don't know humans very well, do you? Unlike you, we don't live for hundreds of years. We've only got a short time here—a hundred years, tops." I sneer at him for good measure.

He's breathing hard, and the gaze he levels at me is pure hatred.

"The more demonic you turn, the more of a drag you are to Xiuling. If I were her, I would banish you for good."

"Ridiculous—" he says, but I barrel over him.

"It makes sense now, why Xiuling's always complaining to us about how a 'bad companion is worse than no companion.' I used to think she was talking about my companion, but now I know. She was talking about you!" I exclaim, adding the loudest, most insufferable laugh to the end of the sentence.

My laughter is cut short when the Creighton-fox leaps at me. I crash to the ground with a loud "Oof!" My breath rushes out of me, and all that goes through my head is: Teeth! Teeth! Teeth!

The Creighton-fox releases a sound that's somewhere between a howl and a shriek, rattling my bones. "After all the sacrifices I have made for my master! I was the one who came up with the plan. All of it! When Hassan Taslim died and left the company in shambles, who thought of summoning ancient creatures for cirth? That was me, all me!"

As he roars, I slip my trembling hand into my pocket and grip Peng's feather tight in my fist. I try to train all my focus on it, try to calm myself down enough, despite the sharp teeth a hair-breadth away from my throat. I think of the words for a spell of fire.

"It was our chance to finally climb the ranks. Do you know how hard it is for Xiuling—a woman, a person of color—to be taken seriously—"

I say the incantation under my breath and feel the warmth sizzling out of my palm. Is the feather burning? I can't tell. The heat grows, becoming unbearable, and the Creighton-fox finally notices that something's off. He stops talking mid-sentence and sniffs the air.

"Smells like something's burning." He stares at me for a second. "Are you trying to burn me?" Laughing, he casts a water spell and drenches my whole body, putting out the small fire in my pocket. "I think I've had enough of this." He opens his jaws, but just then, a massive shadow blankets us, as though day has suddenly turned to dusk. My heart leaps with hope.

The spell has worked, and now Peng is here to claim his vengeance.

# THEO

# 45

I blink, and suddenly the clouds aren't clouds, but the tip of a gargantuan wing, so large I can't see its entire span. Fear overwhelms hope. Peng is going to crush all of us.

Right before the monstrous bird flattens everything, there's a shift, like time has suddenly been jostled a bit, and the giant bird abruptly shrinks. One moment, Peng's as big as the sky, and the next, he's the size of an elephant. The ground shudders at his weight. His voice skips my ears and thunders straight through my head.

*For your sake, I hope you have fulfilled your end of the bargain.*

The Creighton-fox leaps up, snarling.

*What is this?*

I scramble up and shout, "He's one of the ones responsible for kidnapping you!"

Peng moves his gargantuan head slowly, and even I quail in fear at the sheer size of that unforgiving beak flashing in the sunlight. The Creighton-fox takes a step back.

"You can't possibly take the word of this child over mine," he says.

Peng casts a slow, thoughtful gaze at the Creighton-fox. *You are more demon than spirit. Your evil deeds hang over your aura like toxic fumes. Guilt is written on every inch of you.*

The Creighton-fox cringes, rising up on his haunches. "No, wait, I can explain—"

But Peng is done with explanations. With one swift stab of his beak, he captures the Creighton-fox. I gasp and cover my eyes, and when I open them again, there are no traces of the Creighton-fox. My breath releases in a whoosh. I feel sick. I know it's what the Creighton-fox deserved, but seeing him eaten up in less time than it takes me to blink leaves me shaken.

*He wasn't the one who summoned me,* Peng says. *Unfortunate. I shall have to destroy this place after all.*

"No!" I cry. "I'm not completely sure who did the summoning—I think it might have been a whole bunch of kids who were tricked into doing the summoning—but I know which rites they used. We can reverse them and send you back to the spirit world."

Peng turns his head and I find myself staring into one impossibly huge eye. *You are telling the truth.*

"Yes."

*Tell me those rites, then.*

My insides are writhing with fear, but I force myself to say, "Um, but before that, I need a favor from you. Please? In exchange for helping to release you from the human world?"

Peng regards me for a while. *Very well. You may have one favor.*

He blinks slowly as I tell him about Niu Mo Wang.

*I cannot be involved with beings from Diyu. This is so from the beginning of time.*

My stomach plummets to my feet. "Okay, but can you help me get to my companion, please? I think with her help, I may be able to stop Niu Mo Wang."

*Unlikely, but yes, I will take you to your companion so the two of you may perish in your foolhardy quest. Now, do you know where your companion is?*

Despair washes over me, but then I recall what Kai told me about making a mind link with Peng, and I try it with Kai now. I reach for my memories of Jamie and then focus everything on Kai, and within the swirling darkness of my mind, I catch sight of her. I make the link, and finally accept what I've been fighting this whole time. Kai's my companion. And I open my heart to her.

Completely.

Sorrow surges into my heart, sharp and agonizing, and I catch it. A shred of sound. A canine yelp, frightened and angry and hurting.

Kai!

My eyes spring open. "I know exactly where she is."

# KAI
# 46

Power! There's so much of it surging through my veins like iced lightning, like sizzling lava, like electric wind. Is this what it's like to be a proper deity? To be a *god*?

I could totally get used to it.

I have no idea how much of Niu Mo Wang's qì I've absorbed into my own being. I am filled with dazzling light, and everything I touch splinters, smashing into tiny bits. The walls of the room, so thick and firm and dense, shred like paper with the slightest caress of my claws. I touch Niu Mo Wang's enclosure with the same gentleness and watch with wonder as the glass, reinforced with hundreds of layers of protective magic, splits apart like tissue.

Niu Mo Wang roars, tears off the remaining tubes, and explodes from the broken case. He shoves me aside and barrels through the room, mowing down anyone stupid enough to stand in his way. Screams fill the room, and with every human he swallows, Niu Mo Wang's demonic aura grows. Dark tentacles of shadows latch on to him, shrouding him under protective layers of writhing darkness. The air around him shimmers, the molecules bending and warping at the proximity to such unearthly power. Sickly heat radiates from him, filling the room with the wild musk of sweating, snorting bull.

With another thunderous roar, Niu Mo Wang charges straight at me. Right before I am trampled under a ton of angry bull, one of the shadow tentacles shoots out and bashes me aside. I catch a flash of him as he storms through the wall of the facility, barreling through the dense earth and leaving me behind with a handful of Reapling guards.

I get back to my feet, swaying slightly, and am immediately blasted by some version of a fireball spell. Under normal circumstances, the spell would deal quite a bit of damage. But in my current empowered state, it only makes me angry. All I've done is politely release a mad demon from captivity, and now for some reason these humans are attacking me. It hurts my feelings, to be quite honest.[44]

I fly away but realize with a start that my lower body's no longer there; it's just a pile of smoke trailing behind me. I make myself stop, and for a second, I rematerialize in fox form, but then I blink and vaporize again, just in time to avoid getting smashed by another aggressive spell from the guards. Why can't I hold on to my physical form?

Realization dawns. I can't hold on to my physical form because I'm between two states: spirit and demon. I'm so close to crossing over and turning into a demon for good. Just one step away. I just need to do one more misdeed to seal the deal. What should I do? What destruction can I wreak? I cast my gaze about the room, laughing at the way the guards quail.

With a sound like the very earth grinding and crunching to a

---

44 It might seem like a mere human and their pesky, endless feelings wouldn't bother a superior being like me, but I am sensitive and deep.

halt, the ceiling's ripped off, revealing a spot of blue sky above a seemingly endless tunnel. A shadow flies overhead, blotting out the light.

"Kai!" a voice shouts. An annoying voice. One I remember, vaguely.

I look up, and a guard takes her chance to attack. She doesn't waste her time with aggressive spells; she takes out a small knife from her pocket and plunges it into my side.

Pain! So much of it! It burns through my entire being. The knife is poisonous—imbued with a dozen blessings, no doubt. I swipe at the guard and send her flying like a rag doll into the wall. She's knocked unconscious, though she isn't dead, for I don't receive the surge of power that taking her life would have given me.

"Kai!" The annoying voice slices through the haze. I can't bear it. It's a serrated blade, and I can't deal with that *and* the burning in my side. I launch myself up, through the massive hole, aiming myself at the sky.

A giant bird awaits me, with a tiny speck on its back. The speck waves. I'm close enough now to see that it's a human boy. How my side burns! I scream as I explode out of the hole in a cloud of black smoke.

"Kai!" the boy cries, again.

*Shut up!* I rage at him. *Stop saying that word. I don't know what Kai is.*

Even in my frenzied state, I know enough not to leap at the bird. Its aura is blinding, and my essence, already in pain from the stab wound, cries out and begs at my consciousness not to get any closer. I skirt around the bird, hissing and spitting at it.

"Kai, don't do this! This isn't you!" the boy says.

If only I could eat him. He's so close, and yet so unattainable. If I could somehow get to him—

But before I can lunge at him, the boy stands on the bird's back and runs toward me. At the very tip of the bird's wing, the boy launches himself at me, his arms outstretched.

I can't believe this. It's like a mouse launching itself straight into a cat's open mouth. I catch him, cackling, and bend my amorphous shadow head forward to consume him.

He doesn't scream or try to wriggle away. Instead, he lifts his face and looks directly at me, into my soul. I squeeze harder, and the boy yelps, but he doesn't try to hit me or wriggle out of my grasp. Instead, even as he pants in pain, he smiles at me.

"Kai, it's me. It's Theo. I'm so happy to see you again. I'm sorry, Kai. This is all my fault. All of it."

*Theo.*

Rage pounds through my essence. *Theo. He who didn't want me. He who used me. He who dismissed me.*

As though he hears my very thoughts, Theo's mouth trembles and his eyes shine with tears. "I—I did all those things, yes. I let my anger blind me. But if you forgive me, I will be the best companion to you."

*Lies! You never wanted me—you said so, on many different occasions. You only wanted to use me for your own needs.*

"I did. I was selfish, I—"

*Enough!* More so than demons, humans lie. They spin pretty webs with their lovely words to ensnare and consume. I focus and start to absorb the boy's qì. His life force bleeds into me, and as it does so, I start to change. But not the change I was expecting.

Instead of the surge of demonic power I should be getting from eating his qì, warmth envelops me. I look down at him, and beyond all reason, he's smiling.

*Why?* The thought comes out as a quiet murmur.

*Because you're my friend. My best friend.* He closes his eyes, still smiling.

I break the connection. Everything goes impossibly bright, and I shatter.

# THEO
# 47

It doesn't feel like dying. Floating away into Kai's memories, surrounded by images of Jamie. It's warm and comforting. I close my eyes.

Instead of darkness, there's a flash of blinding light, and my body becomes heavy once more. I plummet like a rock and almost splatter on the ground, but something swoops down at the very last second and catches me.

I land gently on the grass and open my eyes.

Kai grins, morphing from a large bird back into fox form. "You look like a bag of tra—"

I grab her face and turn it this way and that.

"Ow, hey, careful, that's pure fox fur you're manhandling. You know how much Louis Vuitton would pay for fur this gorgeous?"

"It's you!" I throw my arms around her neck and hug her tight, burying my face in her fur. "You're back. You're okay. I can't believe it. How?"

Kai turns away, hiding what looks suspiciously like tears in her eyes. "I don't know, probably has to do with you sacrificing your life for me or something equally trite. The question is how you're still alive."

*Ahem.*

We both look up at Peng's ginormous form.

*The boy is still alive because his sacrifice drove the demonic energy out of the fox spirit.* Peng turns his head toward me. *I wouldn't be surprised if your lifespan has been shortened a little.*

"Oh." I look down at my hands again and notice they're quite a bit paler than before.

"Hey, Theo?" Kai says.

"Yeah?"

She scratches the back of one ear, glancing at me bashfully. "Um, I'm sorry I tried to kill you."

"I'm sorry I made you go down that path."

She shrugs. "Eh, it was somewhat entertaining while it lasted. I can't complain."

We smile at each other.

*I hate to break up this touching moment of camaraderie, but I can see a trail of destruction heading straight toward a bustling city. I am not opposed to sitting here and enjoying the show, of course, but I thought you might have an opinion about that.*

I startle. In the struggle with Kai, I completely forgot about Niu Mo Wang. "Why aren't the Reapling guards going after him?"

"I think Reapling's priority is to cover its tracks," Kai says.

"We've got to stop Niu Mo Wang," I say. "But first, can we make a stop to pick up Namita? We need all the help we can get."

"Onward! Giddyup!" Kai crows.

*Tell the fox spirit I will eat her if she's not careful.*

"Peng says—"

"Yeah, yeah, I heard." She climbs to my shoulders and wraps her warm body around my neck as Peng flies the two of us across the darkening sky.

# KAI

# 48

We intercept Namita and the other kids as they're running away from the secret facility in Muir Woods. As I expected, most of the children are keen to escape and go back home, but Namita seems, strangely enough, happy to see us.[45]

"Theo! Oh my gods, are you two okay?" she shouts, running toward us the moment Peng lands on the ground.

"Yes. Look, I don't have time to explain, but we need to go to the Golden Gate Bridge now," Theo says. "The bull demon king we summoned is about to destroy it and we need to stop him."

Namita gapes at him. "You summoned a bull demon king?"

"We didn't have a choice," someone says. We turn to see Danny walking toward us.

Theo gasps. "Danny, your memory—they didn't erase it?"

Danny frowns and shrugs. "I don't know what they did. Maybe the fact that I had been cursed by a demon muddled their memory-erasing spell?" When he notices me, he flinches. "It's you. You were the one who attacked me. I can tell because . . . I don't know, but I can just tell."

I wince as Xiaohua unwraps herself from Danny's shoulders and towers over me.

_____

45 I worry about this girl, I really do.

"Is this true? Were you the one that attacked my master?"

"Uh, I mean, if you want to get all technical about it . . ." My tails are down between my legs. "Um, sort of? I'm sorry for, you know, marking you with my demonic essence and all that hullabaloo."

Xiaohua's mouth opens, but Theo steps between us, shielding me from a fiery end. "It was my fault," he says. "I kept giving Kai impossible tasks, pushing her to do bad deed after bad deed until she almost turned fully demonic. I'm very sorry, Danny, Xiaohua. I swear I will make it up to you somehow, later, but for now, we really need to stop Niu Mo Wang."

Xiaohua and Danny look at each other, and for a second, I wonder if they're going to go back to their odious selves and insist on causing trouble for us. People don't change. Especially not horrible ones like Danny and his snooty dragon. I prepare myself for an attack, but then Danny says, "Actually, I owe you an apology, too. But later. Now, let's go stop this bull demon."

"Master, are you sure? It's going to be dangerous," Xiaohua says.

Danny nods. "I know what it's like to be marked by a demon, and I don't want it to happen to anyone else."

Well, well. Sometimes, humans surprise me after all.[46]

---

46 Not often, but sometimes, you humans do come through.

# THEO
# 49

A path filled with scorched earth and burned tree stumps covered with ichor goes straight through Muir Woods. Niu Mo Wang's almost at the Golden Gate Bridge. It's rush hour, and the bridge is twinkling with lights from various cars and buses, filled with people like my family, who can't afford flying vehicles.

Peng lands far enough away from the bridge so we're not in immediate danger, but we're close enough to hear the honks of the cars and feel tremors in the earth as Niu Mo Wang descends upon the bridge. We all scramble off Peng's back, and Peng shrinks down quickly to avoid detection. Together, we take a few hesitant steps toward the bridge.

"This is bad," Danny moans. "This is so bad."

I nod soundlessly, feeling nauseated. What monstrous thing have we summoned?

People scramble out of their cars, clambering over one another in a mad dash to get away from Niu Mo Wang.

"Watch out!" Xiaohua says, wrapping herself around us and knocking us to the ground as cop cars zoom out of the sky and land near the bridge. Cops spill out in protective gear. They fly through the air, yanking people out of the way and aiming their guns, wands, and other magical weapons at the thrashing, giant mass. I'm terrified for them—Niu Mo Wang's almost the size of a skyscraper, and even the cops, with their magicproof vests, look so tiny and helpless.

Someone shouts an order, and magic blasts through the air from all directions. There's an unearthly shriek as the various attacks reach their target, but just as I feel the bright edges of hope, two thick tentacles shoot out of the mass and swipe at the cops. They go flying like toys. My heart stops. But then little parachutes open up from their backs and the cops float safely down. They're unharmed, but they also can't seem to stop Niu Mo Wang.

The remaining cops lob more fireballs and lightning bolts and unload silver bullets at Niu Mo Wang, but all of the attacks appear to only make him angry. He lowers his head and starts pawing at the ground.

"He's going to charge," Kai says, right before Niu Mo Wang rushes at the barricade of cop cars. The cars are flung about like Lego blocks, the cops scurrying to avoid the flying detritus. "Called it."

"We need to stop him," I croak.

"Why isn't any of their magic working?" Danny says, shrinking back so he's behind Xiaohua.

Namita suddenly jumps up. "Of course! I get it now. It's an ancient Chinese creature and they're using modern Western magic! Danny, you need to cast a Chinese spell on him."

Danny sputters and stumbles back. "I can't—I'm sorry."

"My master is still recovering from the damage the fox demon wreaked on him," Xiaohua snaps.

Namita and Danny look expectantly at me.

There's no time to second-guess myself. I mentally scramble through the almanac's spells again. The Path of Pig Be Big, nope. A Lamentation for Chicken Ovulation, definitely not. A Balm to Calm and Cool an Angry Bull . . . yes. Yes!

I raise my hand and shout out the Calm Angry Bull spell, but the moment it gets close to Niu Mo Wang, one of the dark shadows around him bats it away, like it's just an irritating fly. Who am I kidding? Here I am, a twelve-year-old kid, about to take on a demon god. I don't have the power—

"Yes, you do," Kai says.

"You can read my thoughts?"

"One of the side effects of fully accepting your companionship is a mind link," she says. "What do you mean 'I hope they don't smell my fart'? That's very unbecoming."

"I wasn't thinking that! And you're wrong. I don't have enough power."

"Maybe alone, you don't," Namita says. "But I have an idea." She claps her hands and mutters something. Within a second, her right hand swells up until it's the size of a small car. "Cast that Connectivity Through Affinity spell on me, Theo. The one that Kai told you about in class, remember? Use me as a conduit for your spell. Magnifying my hand may have a magnifying effect on your spell."

"This is crazy. It won't work!" But even as I say that, a thought is swirling in my head: Why won't it? I've never heard of such a thing, but that doesn't mean it definitely won't work. There's a first time for everything, right?

"You must try," Kai says, losing her impish grin. "And you

won't be doing this on your own." For once, there are no traces of humor on her face as she holds out her paw.

I take it.

*Close your eyes.* Her voice is in my head, or was that my own thought? I could've sworn I closed my eyes right as she instructed me to. I let my instincts move me. Despite the fact that my eyes are closed, I can sense that I'm pointing my palms at Namita's enlarged hand. I focus all my energy on it. I no longer know where my mind stops and Kai's begins. Our minds join into one big river, rich and rushing with thoughts. Somehow, we reach for the same thought together. We reach for Jamie.

This time, instead of emerging with our shared sorrow, Kai and I lock onto our happiest memories of him. Tears course down my face as I take out my best memories of Jamie and allow Kai to see them. Jamie and I salvaging a wooden plank from a nearby dumpster, standing on it, and then casting a spell on it to see if it would work as a flying skateboard. It shot up like a rocket and I broke my arm when I fell, and then Jamie tried Scrabble-son's Grow Scab on Skinned Knees spell on my arm, only it went wrong, but even though the pain in my arm was awful, I remember knowing that everything would turn out okay, because Jamie was there.

And I get to see Kai's memories, too, and they're so full of love my heart could crack open. I see flashes of her rolling on the floor like a dog, wagging her tails while Jamie rubs her belly. I sense her embarrassment, her shame at behaving in such a dog-like manner, and yet she can't contain her affection. She, who has had nothing but contempt for humans, had opened up her soul completely to Jamie. And now she's done the same with me.

We laugh and sob at each other's memories, and then we take our joy and love for Jamie and tease it into shape, piling it in our hands until it's heavy, so heavy, and absolutely buzzing with electric power, and then we direct it at Namita.

"I think it's working, guys," Namita cries. "I can feel your energy coursing through my arm!"

*You need to say the incantation now*, Kai says.

My thoughts reach her instantaneously. I can't hold them back or temper them or hide anything from her. *I'm scared. I know I'm going to get it wrong.*

*Why?*

I throw memory after memory at her, of kids laughing, their voices turned all nasal as they imitated my strange speech. The disgusted looks whenever I opened my lunch box. The names they called me, the hateful words and cruel smiles.

Kai accepts it all, even though I know it hurts her, each memory a jagged piece of glass piercing her. And then I'm spent, an empty husk, and for the first time, I feel free. Free to be myself.

I open my mouth and allow myself to speak the way I used to know, before other people took that ability from me. I speak in the tongues of Mama and Baba. Of Jamie. Of Nainai. Of my ancestors. For the first time, I feel all my family history coursing through my entire being, a river of aunties and uncles and great-great-great-grandparents from our village, all of them with open arms, smiling proudly at me. Tears run down my face. I have denied them for so long. But no more. I understand now that they will always be a part of me.

The words flow flawlessly from my mouth, carrying with them our combined powers, and the magic streams, strong and bright, becoming amplified through Namita's giant hand. It multiplies in strength, growing to the size of a tree trunk, and spears straight into Niu Mo Wang. The thick blanket of tentacles shriek as they are penetrated by the blazing light and lunge at us. Caught as we are in the middle of our spell, we're sitting ducks, but a sudden, angry red streak flies between us and the tentacles.

"Demon! You shall not hurt that which is innocent!" Xiaohua roars. She claws and rips into the tentacles, tearing them into pieces. Danny, his pale face set in a grim expression, lobs various spells at the remaining tentacles.

Namita, Kai, and I focus all our strength and will the beam of magic forward, boring through Niu Mo Wang's side and into his heart.

The demon king's mad thoughts spill into ours. His pain, his rage—*where am I why am I here I can't breathe the stink of this city the humans I must kill them kill them all*—threaten to overwhelm me. I falter, my feet scraping back in the dirt.

Then there's the gentlest of nudges, and I move forward. Peng winks at me. He's a lot smaller than his real size, probably to avoid attracting any attention from the nearby cops. *Keep going, child.*

I pour all our happiness and love into Niu Mo Wang's consciousness. Jamie's unwavering courage, Ma's naggy concern, Nainai's loving patience, and last of all, my everlasting family history. My ancestors' forgiveness. I sense a change in the swirling mess of pain. I let his anger plunge into the cool river of my mind. Behind me, I feel my ancestors opening their arms and clustering around him. Together, we embrace his presence, feeling him cease his thrashing and begin to float, gently, to the surface.

*You are safe*, we tell him, over and over again. *You are safe. We won't let them hurt you. Come home, come home.*

Tears prick my eyes, because I realize that my ancestors are saying these words to me as much as they're saying them to Niu Mo Wang. I sense them all around me, smiling gently, but when I look behind, all I can see is a blur of shimmering blue.

Niu Mo Wang closes his eyes.

What remains of the shadow tentacles disintegrates, turning into dust, leaving Niu Mo Wang exposed and vulnerable. I yell out the reversal of the Pig Be Big spell, and Niu Mo Wang disappears from sight. We catch a glimpse of the tiny bull, the size of a hamster, scurrying through the wreckage.

"Quick, take him!" I say to Kai.

The cops are standing still, looking confused at the sudden lack of giant bull. Kai switches into a raven, flies about thirty feet to tiny Niu Mo Wang, and grabs him gently but firmly in her claws. Nobody notices Kai among the burning rubble, and she flies back to perch on Peng. Peng lifts me and Namita up and plops us down next to Kai while Danny clambers onto Xiaohua's back.

"Did you see them?" I say to Kai.

"Who?"

I hesitate. It sounds crazy, even to my own ears. "My ancestors."

*They've always been there.*

"Come again?"

Peng gives me a long look. *Child, I see every being on every plane. They've always been with you, urging you on throughout this foolhardy quest. I'm pleased that you have finally opened your heart to your ancestral heritage. I do wish they wouldn't step on my tail, though. They are quite literally ruffling my feathers.*

I look into what seems like empty air and give a hesitant smile. "Um. Thank you for your help."

*They say you are most welcome. Now, it is time to make ourselves scarce.*

I smile at my friends. "Let's go home."

# THEO
# EPILOGUE

I hide outside the classroom and peep at the boy standing at the front of the room. He looks exactly like me, down to the tiny freckle underneath his left eye. But unlike the real me, this version is obviously enjoying being the center of everybody's attention. He raises his arms with a flourish, a smirk on his face, but before he can say anything, there's a snort from Skinner.

"Are you gonna channel your inner qì?" he calls out.

Time for my entrance.

I step inside the room and have the satisfaction of seeing Skinner's stupid face go slack with surprise. Everybody else stares with open shock.

I wink at Skinner and say, "Yep, I am." And then I snap my fingers, and everyone gasps as Kai melts from Theo-form into her original fox form.

"When we turn twelve, as part of my culture, I'm allowed to have a companion," I say, and the words "my culture" come out with so much pride and joy. For the first time, I am so proud of my cultural heritage. I no longer want to hide it. I want everyone to know that I'm not just Chinese or American, I'm both, and it's nothing to be ashamed of. In fact, I can't wait to learn as much as I can about my heritage. "This is Kai. She's a fox spirit. Her specialty is shape-shifting."

Right on cue, Kai turns into a bright green hummingbird and zips around the room, amid cries and gasps.

"Kai's over two hundred years old, so she's learned a lot of different forms. But we're working on a few new ones of our own."

Kai shifts into a small jaguar and lands on the floor noiselessly. Everyone around her scrambles away, and Mrs. Reeves raises her hands, but just as she's about to hit her with an aggressive spell, Kai changes into a chubby little panda cub.

"Don't worry," I shout over the nervous laughter, "she can't harm any humans. Well, unless it's in self-defense. But I can't see why she'd ever need to do that." I grin at Skinner, who's looking pale.

Kai makes one final jump, changing midair into a scarf, but her head and tails stick out of the ends of the scarf. She wraps herself around my neck and gives the class a toothy smile.

Silence falls, as thick as jelly. Then Joan Rapaport shouts, "That was awesome!" and the room erupts into a cheer.

We did it! I can't believe I shared something this personal with my class.

Kai can't keep herself as an inanimate object for long, especially not when there's a whole group of adoring kids, and with a small pop, she changes into a hamster with wings and flies around the room, blowing raspberries and taking bows.

Mrs. Reeves pulls me aside. "Um, that was . . . impressive."

"Thanks," I say.

"The school doesn't allow students to bring dangerous pets, though."

My smile freezes on my face.

Mrs. Reeves hesitates for a second. "However, since you say she's not dangerous . . ." She gives a meaningful pause before winking at me and walking away. I stay there for some time, grinning. I'm going to have a lot of fun with Skinner and Co.

$$\sim \!\! \ast \!\! \sim$$

"Hey, look at this," I say later that afternoon.

Kai's curled up on my pillow. One pointy ear twitches and an eye cracks open, but she doesn't move.

"Wake up, you'll want to hear this."

"What is it? Did you dig out a record-breaking giant booger?"

I sigh. "Look." I gesture at today's newspaper. The headline screams REAPLING CORP. UNDER INVESTIGATION FOR GOLDEN GATE BRIDGE MONSTER. Below that, the subtitle reads *Police uncover evidence of Reapling Corp.'s involvement in illegal summonings and are actively searching for Interim Director Creighton Ward.*

Kai bounds toward me noiselessly, agile as a cat, and reads the rest of the article. "'The company was exploiting children in a dangerous experiment to summon ancient creatures in order to salvage their depleted cirth supply . . .' Hmm, no mention of Xiuling."

"I wish we knew what happened to her. I wish—" I don't know what I wish for, really. I guess a chance to confront Xiuling the way I faced her companion. "At least we got the summer program shut down."

"Jamie would be proud," Kai says. "You managed to figure out the specific ritual they used to summon Peng, and you dismissed him back to the spirit world. That was what Jamie wanted."

I smile and touch my fingertips gently to a framed picture of Jamie. "Yeah. Wouldn't have been able to do it without everyone's help, though." In the end, it had taken me and Danny, with the help of Xiaohua and Kai, plus Namita enlarging her hand again, to release Peng back to where he came from. I can only hope he's now soaring happily, freely, in the spirit world.

There's a frantic rattle from under my bed, and a voice squeaks, "Release me immediately, foul human!"

I crouch and pull out a small cage. Inside is tiny Niu Mo Wang. As soon as he sees me, he charges into the side of the cage and bounces off.

"Please, please calm down," I say. "We're trying to find a way to return you to Diyu. It's turning out to be more difficult than I thought . . ."

"Then let me out of here, at least!"

"No can do, chief," Kai says. She's enjoying this a little bit too much. "We don't trust you to not go on another killing rampage. Humans don't appreciate it when you try to destroy their city. It's sort of one of their pet peeves."

I set the cage down with a sigh. I hate keeping him caged up like this. I thought that I actually turned a demon king into something peaceful and kind. Peng knew better. Before he left, he warned me to keep Niu Mo Wang securely caged. I waited until I saw the shadows creeping back, and when one of them wrapped itself around Niu Mo Wang's tiny form, I pushed him into a cage with much regret. It's been weeks since our fight at the Golden Gate Bridge, and I'm no closer to finding a way of returning Niu Mo Wang to the underworld.

"Stop that," I say to Kai, who's making faces at Niu Mo Wang and laughing when the little bull charges into the side of the cage. "I'm sorry. Trust me, I'm doing the best I can—"

"Enough of your excuses! When I regain my powers, the first thing I'll do will be to flay your soul—" He pauses, his attention caught on something. Jamie's picture. His little bull eyes narrow, and then his muscled shoulders shudder. He's laughing.

"What is it?" I say.

"That boy . . . he is of relation to you?"

"He's my brother."

Niu Mo Wang gives me a sly grin. A predator's grin. "Oh, this is perfect. I think I won't kill the two of you after all. No, I think I shall take you both prisoner and make you watch as I petition King Qin'guang, the judge of Diyu, to condemn your brother's soul for eternity."

I lean forward, my whole body on fire. "You don't have access to his soul. It's in Tiantang."

Niu Mo Wang throws his head back and laughs. "Is that what you think? That your brother is in heaven?"

"You're lying." Kai bares her teeth at Niu Mo Wang, a guttural growl rumbling out of her. "I'll eat you alive, demon."

"I do not lie," Niu Mo Wang roars. "I'm a king of Diyu. I've never had need to lie, unlike you, fox spirit!" He turns back to face me. "Your brother's soul is caught in between heaven and hell this very moment."

"But why?" I cry. "He was the best person. He was kind, and—"

"The accident," Kai says in a hollow voice, a horrified expression flooding her features. "I should've known. I assumed they'd done something to his car, maybe sabotaged the brakes, but they didn't, did they?"

Niu Mo Wang grins. "Indeed, they did not. They sent a spirit to capture his soul and take it to Diyu. But it caused quite the confusion. He wasn't supposed to be in Diyu, since he was so good, as you said, so the other kings and I couldn't reach an agreement over what to do with him. We left him in the waiting room. But now, I will claim him as my own. I will—"

I choke at the idea of Jamie's soul being stolen like that. No wonder there weren't any signs of sabotage, that everyone thought Jamie had just fallen asleep. I can just see it now. Once his soul was snatched out, his body would've slumped over the wheel, just as though he'd nodded off. The car would've careened off the road, and—

I squeeze my eyes shut, shuddering at the thought.

I can't focus on the car crash right now. What's more important is that Jamie's soul is trapped between Tiantang and Diyu.

"I will create new torture devices just for him, and you will watch as I—"

I focus my qì and cast Libba Ryan's Make Life Easier on Librarians spell. There's a flash of light, and though Niu Mo Wang's mouth keeps moving, no sound comes out of the cage. For a few moments, the room's silent, save for the sounds of my ragged breath. Then I stand up and grab my backpack.

"What're you doing?" Kai says.

"We're going to find a way to save Jamie." I shove the cage inside my bag and pack up everything I think might come in handy—my notebook, energy bars, a jacket.

"Wait, what are you going to tell your parents?"

I groan out loud. "I can't just stay here, knowing he's trapped somewhere."

"I know, I'm not saying we shouldn't go." Kai leaps up and retrieves my notebook from the backpack. She flips the pages open and locates the spells that I copied down from the almanac.

"'Who Is Playing the Erhu,'" I read out. "Is that a spell to make the erhu play itself? What's that got to do with anything?"

"It works on a violin."

"How would you know—wait." I stare at Kai, who looks back at me innocently. "You're kidding. He loved practicing his violin. He played all the time . . ." Realization dawns. ". . . in his room. Behind a locked door. No. Way."

"You two are more alike than you think," Kai says.

"I can't believe he did that!" I reach underneath my bed and take out my violin case. It's covered with a thick layer of dust. I take out the violin, prop it up on my chair, and say the incantation, half expecting it to go wrong. The bow flies up, rests across the strings, and begins to play a sonata. The exact one that used to come out of Jamie's room every evening.

Laughing through my tears, I scrawl out a quick letter to Mama and Baba, explaining where I've gone. They're going to go absolutely insane, but maybe some part of them will understand. One can only hope.

I stuff two more things into my bag—the almanac and Jamie's journal.

"You do realize the journey will be very dangerous," Kai says.

"I have you with me. I'll be okay. And Namita will probably want to come along as well. Maybe Danny, too."

Kai bounds up with a smile and wraps herself around my neck, warming me through to the bone. I hadn't even realized I was cold. With the strains of my violin fading into the cool night air, I climb out of the window and head off with my companion.

# THE END

# ACKNOWLEDGMENTS

It would be impossible to write acknowledgments for this book without first telling you about its history.

*Theo Tan and the Fox Spirit* had one of the most difficult journeys in my publishing career, a twisty roller coaster full of downs and more downs that made me quit writing for almost a year. When I wrote it, I could tell that it was something special. I immediately fell in love with Kai's dry British humor, a reminder of the books that I grew up reading, and I had so much fun building the magical world that Theo and Kai lived in. I felt very strongly that this was a good book. All of my writing friends who read it fell in love, yet when my former agent submitted it to publishers, it was repeatedly rejected. *Theo Tan* was my seventh book, and I decided that after so many years and so many failed manuscripts, it was time to quit writing.

This was where my loving, patient writing friends came in. My Menagerie friends, my chosen family, my people. Toria Hegedus reached down to the wreckage that I was at the time and lifted me up, reading *Theo Tan* and giving me an in-depth, line-by-line critique. S. L. Huang must have read it at least three times, and continued to be patient with each draft. Rob Livermore, who has such a wonderful eye for middle grade fiction, encouraged me endlessly, convincing me to keep trying with this manuscript. Elaine Aliment, our den mother, assured me that *Theo Tan* was worth working on. Maddox Hahn read the first draft and blew me away with how insightful her critique was. Emma Maree as always was a sweetheart and so fiercely loyal. Lani Frank, who really should have her own imprint, gave brilliant feedback. Tilly Latimer, I have lost count of how many of my terrible manuscripts you have read, and yet you are still unfailingly supportive. Without these Menagerie folks, *Theo Tan* wouldn't have been published. I would've given up and walked away, maybe from writing altogether.

I am also so grateful to my friend Nicole Lesperance, who is somehow able to predict which of my books have that special something. She was one of the early readers who told me there's something special about *Theo Tan*, and I'm so glad and so proud to call her a friend. To my mind soulmate, Taylor, who took a huge chunk of her time to read *Theo Tan* and provide line-by-line feedback. And to Shannon Morgan, who has such a great eye for middle grade fiction. So many of you took the time and effort to read the manuscript and to hold my hand when I cried over every rejection.

It's incredible that after such an exhausting journey, *Theo Tan* ended up selling, at auction, to a dream house. This book found the perfect home with Holly West, my editor at Feiwel and Friends. Holly's notes were mind-blowing and took the story to a whole other level.

This was made possible by my wonderful, magical agent, Katelyn Detweiler of Jill Grinberg Literary Management. Katelyn is a godsend. I honestly don't know what I would do without her. There would definitely be a lot more flailing without Katelyn.

On the personal side, thank you to my husband, Michael Hart, for being an actual bona fide genius. Thank you for supporting me for so many years, even though there was nothing but failure for the longest time. You never wavered, and without your confidence, I would've given up after the first book failed to find a publisher.

I can't wait for my babies, Emmeline and Rosalie, to be old enough to read this book. I hope this brings them excitement and joy, and I hope that it brings you, dear reader, some magic. Thank you so much for picking up a copy of *Theo Tan and the Fox Spirit*, and I hope you've enjoyed your stay at Reapling.